SHADOW of ME

BOOKS BY PAUL OLSEN
SHADOW OF ME
COUNTRY OF OLD MEN
THE VIRGIN OF SAN GIL

SHADOW of ME

A NOVEL BY PAUL OLSEN

HOLT, RINEHART AND WINSTON
NEW YORK   CHICAGO   SAN FRANCISCO

Copyright © 1968 by Paul Olsen

Published simultaneously in Canada by Holt, Rinehart
and Winston of Canada, Limited.

Library of Congress Catalog Card Number: 68-10054

First Edition

The quotation from *The Persecution and
Assassination of Jean-Paul Marat As
Performed by the Inmates of the Asylum of
Charenton Under the Direction of The Marquis
de Sade* by Peter Weiss, copyright
© 1965 by John Calder Ltd., is reprinted
by permission of Atheneum Publishers.

Designer: Ronald Farber

8655607

Printed in the United States of America

To my mother and father

Marat
these cells of the inner self
are worse than the deepest stone dungeon
and as long as they are locked
all your revolution remains
only a prison mutiny
to be put down
by corrupted fellow-prisoners

—PETER WEISS
The Persecution and Assassination of Jean-Paul Marat
As Performed by the Inmates of the Asylum of Charenton
Under the Direction of The Marquis de Sade

SHADOW of ME

ONE

1

"No."

He stared, squinted, then shook his head and said again, the sound like a small sharp blow, "No."

The body lay on the dissecting table, sheathed from feet to groin, the trunk incised, flapped, grouted.

"No, no," he said wearily, almost mumbling, looking up at her pale, pleasant face gone vaguely translucent like green-toned marble. A scalpel hung from her fingers. "Are you trying to cut him in half, Miss Ramsey?" And when she did not answer: "*Are* you?"

"No."

He took the knife from her, bent over the body, made a few quick passes with his hands; then, like a conjurer, produced from the depth of flesh something bulbous and spongy and held it out in his palm. She recoiled from it with twitching shoulders, turning her profile toward him.

"Did you know where it was? Perhaps your plan was just to whittle away until you found it?"

"I knew."

"Splendid." He replaced the organ and wedged the handle of the knife back between her fingers. "Academic question: Why do I bother?" He went to the sink, washed his hands, then changed coats. "Remain, Miss Ramsey. Work all night again if you have to—though God knows what good it will do."

He left, descended in the elevator, and emerged into a cold May street, cold enough to produce a wisp of steam on his breath. Lighting a cigarette, he shook his head at the memory of her, a tableau of fear, the scalpel as limp as the fingers which held it. She was a good student generally, but the dissecting room immobilized her; she often stayed evenings, quite willingly, but the extra sessions seemed to have no good effect.

When he arrived mornings at the lab he saw that she had not even begun her work. Did she sit alone with a body, hour after hour, wringing her hands? Crying? Perhaps she masturbated. It was absurd. Corpses weren't bad company at all; silent, not a single regurgitated inanity or complaint. But sitting with them (nail-chewing?) was a bit out of order. He had thought of flunking her; but although he criticized and patronized her, somehow he didn't care a damn for her aversion, not even professionally. A breach of professorial ethics; he reminded himself to slap his hand someday and *tsk-tsk* at a mirror.

He walked. At the emergency door his path was blocked by an ambulance being unloaded by two attendants. They drew out a stretcher humped with sheets at the rounded peak of which was a dark stain spreading like a curious amoeba. As they manipulated the stretcher a hand sprung from the sheets, taut, shivering, then limp; a Negro's hand, the wrist mottled darker than the skin.

One of the attendants said, "*Mira*, mon. Put him back in."

The other tucked the hand under the blanket, saying, "Yeah, yeah, already. Like they say, baby, gonna be a long hot summer if they're rolling in in May."

2

Watching, his brain ground to a halt, assaulted by the cliché; he quickly diagnosed the sheets as death by knife or bullet wound, stomach. Prognosis: good with miracle. He angled away, walked on, then went into the main entrance through revolving doors, through the vaulted-beamed lobby, pausing to squash his cigarette.

He entered the cafeteria, plucked a tray from a stack and silver from a bin, then ordered indifferently, poking a finger at steamwells of food. They smelled strongly, fogging up at him in frontal attacks of hot air, but he could rarely distinguish their taste once they were on a plate, so he did not care what he chose. He paid and sat alone at a small table, but before he began to eat three doctors in white laboratory coats came toward him; in the midst of a hope that they would not join him it occurred to him that they never did. Passing, they nodded uniformly and quickly, like Prussian soldiers. He nodded back, then turned to his food and prodded his fork at a sheet of roast beef.

One of the doctors had looked at him with a slightly lingering gaze, reminding him of the week or two some years ago when he had felt acutely paranoid. Sitting one day at the same table he found himself the focus of deliberate stares; once he looked up into at least twenty pairs of eyes. His discomfort grew until the salesgirl in the lobby magazine shop pointed to a portrait of his father, the somewhat dull brass plate: ADAM GREGORY, SR. SURGEON. BENEFACTOR. The imperious head was drawn back above a massive swell of academic robes, the right eyebrow arched as if eternally shocked by someone's effrontery and presumption. Examining the portrait, he decided that the resemblance had solidified since the sudden onset of his own graying; and after the decision he was no longer bothered by the stares. Whether they ceased once his identity and relationship to the portrait had been clarified by the hospital grapevine, or whether he paid no attention once he had checked the likeness, he didn't know. He simply was no longer bothered.

Now the doctors began to talk and laugh, completely un-Prussian now, and he gazed abstractedly at them, suddenly realizing that he had no appetite; he might as well have gone home. But he returned to the beef and chewed a mouthful before wondering

3

if he had washed his hands. He sniffed them, caught the scent of soap, and began to eat again. As usual, he tasted nothing.

❧ 2

He followed the curving turn of Haven Avenue toward 170th Street, approaching the dormitory building where he could visualize Miss Ramsey locked and bolted inside her room after a devastating session with her corpse; weeping, gnashing teeth, beating her pillow with tight, livid fists. His thoughts were too much with her; paternal feelings of a man of sixty for a girl of twenty-three? He could almost feel the twist of his cynical grin; and to refute all possibility of universal harmony and warmth, he shot a malignant glance at the spring treetops clustered along Riverside Drive, briefly visible over a low stone wall. The dormitories cut the view and he walked on.

Near his corner Vasiliev hove into sight, a blob of white under his arm, his perpetual monarchist-Russian newspaper, never folded, always bunched into the size of a medicine ball. Impossible to avoid him now, his reedy gauntness set defiantly on the sidewalk as if ready to beat back Lenin's hordes. He thrust out his arm and prodded the air with a multi-ringed forefinger, beginning to incant, his Adam's apple like a metronome.

" 'For, behold, the day cometh, that shall burn as an oven; and all the proud, yea, and all that do wickedly, shall be stubble: and the day that cometh shall burn them up, saith the Lord of hosts, that it shall leave them neither root nor branch.' "

Belligerently, he folded his arms across his chest, waiting, as he always waited, for rebuttal, debate.

"Well?" he said. "Well, Dr. Adam Gregory?" Cracking out the name like a caricature of the angel of doom on Judgment Day.

"I can't help you, Vasiliev," Adam said, hearing as he turned his corner:

" 'Is it fit to say to a king, Thou art wicked? and to princes, Ye are ungodly?' "

"Why not," Adam mumbled, opening the front door. Ammonia

4

reek attacked him as he entered the lobby; breathing choppily, he winked at the optical tricks of the close-set white-and-black tiles undulating on the floor. Nearer the elevator ammonia faded to roasting meat, then a pocket of cabbage, finally a fog of garlic.

In the far corner of the elevator, leaning on a pushbroom, Ford, the superintendent, said, "Evening, Doctor." His teeth smiled explosively; Adam almost looked away.

"Spring's here all right. Bit cool though."

"It seems that way."

The smile hung frozen, an identity proclaiming itself, a blaze of gold-capped white against the brownish-black skin, something powerfully intact between the frayed bow tie and the gray hair flecked with departing black. Adam found himself almost morbidly suspicious of the smile, perhaps because Ford's son accused it of masking other feelings. Perhaps it was simply that all smiles were suspect, and Ford's an unbearably accurate parody, an essence.

"Is Walter upstairs, Mr. Ford?"

"Sure is. He been at it for on to an hour." As the elevator trembled up and stood still at Adam's floor, Ford said, "You're a real gentleman, Dr. Gregory. I know Walter ain't much for thanks, but I'd like to tell you just the same."

"Mr. Ford, I have more work than I can handle and Walter has the talent to ease the load." Almost reflexively, he added, "Do you understand that? That Walter has talent?"

"If you say so, Doctor. Thank you."

"Goodnight, Mr. Ford."

He entered his apartment.

"Adam?"

"Me."

He hung his raincoat in the closet, then went to the studio he had converted from his second bedroom. Walter was hunched over the drawing board, his hawklike profile, clean and sharp, perplexingly unlike his father's almost squashed features. He was working with a fine brush, his eyes too close to the board, his teeth clamped on the tip of his tongue.

"Halt," Adam said. From an envelope he slid out an advance

issue of a slick medical magazine, flipping the pages until he found a colored plate of the cranial nerve nuclei. "Look." He jabbed a finger at the block letters in the lower right corner: w. FORD. "Congratulations."

"Well, well," Walter mumbled.

"They'll give you independent work." He handed Walter a business card. "Call him."

"I'll just do that." He stared at the illustration for some time, then shook his head. "It isn't exactly what I wanted. The surface of the brain stem is too smooth."

"Walter, listen to what I say." His eyes flicked. Adam said, "What is it, ingrained? Do you really believe I can't teach you anything or do you just have to look that way?"

"Sorry."

"All right." He touched the plate. "You *want* the smoothness. You can't clutter these things with realistic backgrounds because the whole concept here is unrealistic to begin with. It's always like that with the nervous system. You studied brains in the lab—can't you see it's a visual concept, an illusion you have to get across? That's where your ventricle work went sour. You buried the illusion in the convolutions. You never saw red or blue or green nerves, did you? No. But you need the color—like a map-maker. The plate is fine as it is; I've never seen the nuclei schematized so well."

"A regular pulmonary Picasso, aren't you?"

"Listen to me about *this* work. I don't tell you about your abstracts." Glancing at the illustration on the drawing board: "Your muscle groups are poor. You need another trip to the lab."

"It bothers me, Adam."

"Liar."

"Not the bodies. Just going. I feel like a thief in the night. Like I'm *not* supposed to be there."

"Tell them Gregory sent you. Then kick them out."

"Is there anybody in that whole hospital you don't have contempt for?"

"I haven't looked lately. —Listen to me. I'm exploiting you. I

6

pay you peanuts to stuff my pockets. I'm reinstituting slavery—otherwise I wouldn't let you within two feet of the lab."

Walter laughed; yet the sound was tinctured with edginess.

"It's *my* lab, Walter. Whoever enters it accounts to *me*. You've accounted." Still looking at the drawing board: "The muscles aren't just poor, they stink. I'll show you something Tuesday night." He paused, then suddenly, "I don't think you can get work direct from other journals. You need an M.D. This one,"—tapping the magazine—"is a little less trade conscious."

"Why'd you say that? I mean now—just like that, in the middle of nowhere?"

"Because I just now saw the limits. Because you won't be happy making money through me this way, not for long."

"You can't know that."

"You're a man, a very sensitive one. You've brooded for the twenty years I've known you."

"You're right. Three times."

"Besides which, you won't be satisfied doing this kind of work. Not the way you can paint."

"I asked *you* for work, Adam. Maybe you should leave it up to me."

Adam turned to the window, training his eyes on the dusky sky; he was annoyed by the growing power of the fluorescent behind him.

"You should be somewhere in Paris," he said, "studying painting."

"I can't stand formal classes any more. You know that."

"I'm not talking about a classroom. I was once sitting, having a coffee near the Seine. It was about this time of day, except the sun was still strong. There was a breeze blowing through a willow and the sun suddenly lit the branches at the same time. The sun and the wind in the tree. I knew what impressionism meant. I saw it leave a canvas and come alive. You should be watching that."

"What is it you really want to say to me?"

Turning from the window, he stared at Walter, then said, "Maybe I mean that you can stay here and work, but when you want out—go. Before you feel you're taking charity." A strange paradox, because he wanted to say: *Go to Paris. I'll give you the money.*

"I don't feel I'm taking charity."

"I assumed you might. I could be wrong."

"I exploit *you*, Doctor. While I *really* paint. Just like any other work that keeps my face full. Just so I can have my own place downtown. Just for that."

"It's not from my pocket. It's found money. I can't handle the work. Besides, I don't do it for the money. I'm a rich man."

"All right, so it's a draw. No winner."

"No winner."

"When's the next A train to Paris?"

"Keep on with the muscles."

Adam sat, lighted a cigarette, and swiveled his chair toward the window, watching dusk deepen, the darkness a parallel to the mood he had felt beneath his memory of the willow on the Seine. He wondered if it were still there, undestroyed by the war or the burden of hopes placed upon it blighting its leaves, branches drooping over the stone wall of a quay touching the water like the hands of lovers trailing in the wake of a boat. But that was thirty years ago, a desperate time for him to have been in Paris; desperate for everyone, he had felt. He had meant to go to the Spanish war, but had gone instead to the Louvre, to Versailles, Montmartre, to struggle with coins in the Métro. In the beginning he could not understand what had happened to him, why he had left his father apoplectic with rage, defeated his plan to bestow upon his son the title of Third Surgeon of the Lineage, smashed on the cause of Spanish Loyalism. No sense, any of it. He disliked his father, but felt no profound malice toward him; when he left, he offered no political dialectic, no humanitarian polemic; he had simply bent the full force of his mind on Spain, almost as if it had been done for him.

The energy evaporated in less than two weeks; in Le Havre he knew that whatever had buttressed the dream had collapsed, and Spain, because or in spite of its physical nearness, was as distant an idea as the thought of his father in a mood of gentleness. It had been frighteningly strange, what he had done, a man who was

8

essentially bored by people, who once wondered where his passions lurked and concealed themselves, who finally believed that he was born with no passion at all. Ultimately, by inference, he decided that he must be a coward; the fact was not disturbing; he was troubled only because he relied on inference, because, like his passion, his cowardice was invisible; he could not see it, was unaware of it, never trembling, never shaken by fear. And so he was driven to deeper thoughts, plumbing nothing, retrieving nothing, except the one reiterated feeling: He needn't have terminated his residence in surgery, needn't have rebuffed his father. He could simply have vacationed in Paris. And he knew that what had happened to him was a disappointment over some premeditated plan that had gone awry; but the plan was a mystery.

Wearing old corduroy trousers he sat very often on the wall above the quay, watching the tree, resolving each day to cross the Pyrénées, until it was too late to cross them, then slowly turning his thoughts to an approach by sea. But it was too late for everything; he could no longer see the barest relationship between his ennui and the countless facts he had absorbed: the meaning of the war, its economic and political implications. The reading about it had bored him to begin with.

He had raised his arm, fist clenched in the Loyalist salute, and saw only what seemed ineffectual anger, then slowly uncurled his fingers and flattened them into the Fascist *ave*. And it no longer mattered who won. And when the arm fell, neutral and numb, he was disaffected, removed, sitting like a stone in the quay wall, lapped at by the water like the tree. Except that a painter, a Monet, could not have captured the fleeting moment, the brief light of his mood; it required a Cézanne, creator of monumental forms, to understand that before him sat an immutable subject who would not transform, not waver in light, who would stand forever, set and carved, the neutral arm eternally chained to the body.

Carved that way, he would not die; nor try to die like the foolish girl who plunged into the Seine from a spot on the wall not ten feet from him; he, unseen in his inviolability, as she removed her coat, rolled it into a pillow, and placed it gently on the wall, as

9

if to let another head take up the dream she had not the desire or ability to continue. Abstractedly, he watched her leap, her skirt ballooning above her head, in a moment seeing her fished out by a pair of lovers who had been hidden somewhere below in the shadows of the quay. He stared at the pillowed coat, then with a movement of his foot nudged it from the wall; it plopped on the stones without unfolding.

So she did not die; but his father did, and he returned home to Massachusetts and placed the body next to his mother, next to his grandparents, next to the whole line whose last heir was to be his strange self. When the ornate casket disappeared into its rectangular slot, his thoughts focused on the raising of his arm—the clenched fist, the flattened palm. But he could not say his farewells in either way. He merely perceived the earth turned into the hole; he might have been a medical student observing an operation, the setting of a simple fracture. Then he turned and went off and studied pathology and medical illustration, and eventually developed two original variations on established methods of dissection.

It was dark beyond the window; he shuddered slightly, gazing down at the floor where he had unconsciously mashed the cigarette stub beneath his heel, feeling uncomfortably spotlighted by the savage glare of the fluorescent light. He looked at Walter and said dully, "You didn't eat."

"I promised to have supper with the old man."

"Come up for coffee after."

The doorbell rang, followed by a brisk squeal of hinges and the exaggerated, imperative rapping of a cane against the floor. From the hall a loud voice filled with the self-amusement of a planned entrance, "It's Arnold Goldman—collecting for orphanages, nunneries, rare diseases, the UJA, and other assorted miseries."

🦋 3

"Lucille, this is some chicken," Walter said. "I never had it so good."

She smiled, but he wasn't sure if it was a reaction to his praise or simply to the attention. He waved the remnant of a wing and said, "Just great."

She smiled again, but her face was flat, as if someone had scrubbed the glow from her eyes. The dead look made him uncomfortable.

"How'd you make it?" he asked.

"Onna stove. Ova dere." She pointed with a limp, tremulous arm; she might have been indicating the stove, sink, steampipe—anything in the far corner of the room. Then she rose, took a plate, and, balancing it carefully, went to the sink. She seemed slightly undersized; once he had thought, was convinced that she would grow out of bounds, vertically and horizontally, and swell out of the house. But, remarkably, one day she had decided to stay as she was and grew no more.

"Where'd she learn how?" he said to his father.

"Well, I helped some, Walter."

"Oh." Disappointed, he knew now that his father had cooked the chicken alone. "It's still very good," he said.

"She thinks she done it, Walter."

"I guess she would if you told her she did."

"Now there."

"Now there *what?*"

"It don't matter, long as she thinks she done it."

That was probably true, he conceded. Anyway, it didn't matter. He scratched at his lower lip with the bone of the chicken wing, blinking, almost wooing himself back to the reality of his sister's limitations. Cook a chicken? She could not even tie her shoelaces without disintegrating, fumbling with the same gross, thick-fingered awkwardness at seventeen as she had at seven.

He watched her. She was wearing old blue tennis shoes without the frustrating laces; the tops of her white socks, their elastic dead, bunched breathless concertinas about her ankles. He wondered why all idiots had to look this way: dressed like caricatures, like an object kept as an afterthought, a broken toy retrieved from the garbage because some child could not part with it. He said, "She could dress a little more human. Next money I get, you buy her something nice. And get rid of those funky sneakers."

"Don't do no good," his father said, resigned. "She gets everything all tore up."

"She doesn't have to. I mean not be so helpless all the time." He began to talk of special schools, then abruptly ceased in mid-sentence, realizing that he had approached the subject countless times without effect. His father attended to him, but did not listen. Ever. So he stopped before he felt absurd.

"She carried the plate away," Ford said. " 'Bout the best I seen her do yet."

He watched her run water over the plate without using soap, letting the chicken bones fall into the sink. She had been standing with her back to them, contemplating the dish, the tap, as if she needed an eternity of time for her cogs to snap into gear so that she could execute the simple maneuver of rinsing a plate. A mispunched IBM card, Walter thought.

"I got to wash it over," Ford said. "Can't learn her to use soap." Ford stared at her, eyes sharp, a long vertical crease dissecting his brow like the wake of an awl in soft leather.

Walter wondered if the old man were not really waiting for the visitation of a miracle—all her broken cogs suddenly energized by a new cluster of nerves. She would wash all the dishes in the world, tie all the laces, even sing scat like Ella Fitzgerald.

She dropped the plate: made of plastic, it was immune from her; it bounced on an edge and rolled a short distance away.

Walter turned, his mouth open to speak, but his father was looking at him with a vaguely chastising expression, enjoining him to be silent. He recalled the time when he had blamed white men for Lucille's condition—feeling foolish while he had said it, yet needing to say it anyway—and his father had muttered: *Ain't no white man ever made her like that. God done it.* The

12

same expression now: invoking a higher power to salve his futility.

He was thinking this and so was confused for a moment when his father suddenly said, "Ain't no chance of you coming back, Walter?"

"I can't."

"I could use a man's help around here."

"I don't want to be a janitor." He hadn't meant to sound cruel; he had only meant to imply some higher ambition that he knew his father found almost impossible to accept or understand, that the ambition was less focused than what he wanted to avoid: janitors, elevator operators, busboys. Or perhaps he *had* meant to be cruel, because a father should want more for his son.

"No," Ford said.

"Why can't you keep a porter?"

"Oh, they come and go, Walter. You get up one morning and they off some place. Never see them again."

He understood by the abrupt clamp of his father's teeth on his lower lip that the old man was pondering some mystery; finally the lip freeing itself from the teeth, moving: "I guess no colored man'll work for no other colored man. I guess that's it." He gaped, disbelieving, then relaxed his features.

Walter said, "There's a fancy nigger chick I know hired herself an Irish cleaning woman. She bought a painting from me. The chick, not the cleaning woman."

Ford shook his head.

Walter wondered why he had invented the story, unpremeditated; it had just materialized as if it had lived hidden away in his mind. "I'm putting you on," he said; but his father was still shaking his head. Apparently the lie fitted perfectly into his unfolding theory of universal imbalance.

Lucille brought the plate to the table, her eyes distressed and wet, her free hand scratching the institution-like gingham above her breasts. Walter noticed that where her face was broad and soft like his father's, his own was fine and sharp like the photograph of his vanished mother. He could not discover the slimmest thread of physical identification with her, yet there was suddenly something in his throat, expanding like a soft mass.

13

His father said, "Walter? You want some tea?"

He looked at both of them; they were facing each other, but their eyes were trained somewhere on opposite walls.

"No," he said. Suddenly he had to leave.

❦ 4

When Walter returned to Adam's apartment Adam and Arnold Goldman were hunched over a chessboard playing an end game. By the time he had poured himself a cup of coffee and sat down to watch, Arnold was sliding a rook across the board, then peered up at Adam, and said, "Mate, wouldn't you say?"

"I would," Adam answered after a surveying pause.

"Woof. Thank God." Turning to Walter: "It was back somewhere in ice-cold weather the last time I beat him."

"That long?" Adam said.

"Walter, you play him."

"Play the winner," Adam said, scraped back his chair, and rose.

Walter sat in the vacated chair, awaited by Arnold's outstretched clenched hands; he tapped the left, finding the white pawn.

"*Nach*," Arnold moaned, "always uphill—my whole life."

"Bluffer. Trying to get me to feel sorry for you?"

"Are you accusing me of psychological warfare?"

"Heavens no."

They began to set up the pieces. Adam lighted a cigarette and sat on the couch, then after a moment turned slightly on his hip; finally he raised his legs and leaned his head on a pile of pillows. For a time he watched the opening exchanges, pawn against pawn, a knight brought out, the varnished black and white pieces glinting in the light. Arnold placed a forefinger on the head of a bishop— the arc of the wrist, the tentative tension of the finger reminding Adam of Michelangelo's *Hand of God*; then he saw the alligator watchband which nearly destroyed the illusion, which circled and smothered a wad of dampish steel-wool hair. His eyes followed the length of the arm up to the shoulder to the striking massive head crowned by the hair of an Einstein or Ben-Gurion, though slightly thinner at the temples and not as magisterially white. The eyebrows were still dark, wildly tufted, turned up impishly at the ends, hovering protectively above steady eyes. Steady and calm now; they must have bulged during the heart attack in pain and disbelief, perhaps more in disbelief.

Listen, Adam, I was sick. I was bending by the sink and then I was on the floor like somebody pushed me from behind. From behind! Where I couldn't see! And kicked me in the chest, a football game on my heart—twenty-two men. So I said, 'Saperstein, what is it? A coronary?' No, not for Arnold Goldman a thing you could understand—because he studied the Kabbalah he should get something nobody understands, not even himself. A good joke. Nach, I got it on a piece of paper; he writes like a pisher *in* cheder. *Says I will get a myocardial infarction if I don't look out. Look out? Where? Behind me? And listen, I can't eat salt. No salt! Vey iz mir. All these years I poisoned my heart with salt? No salt. Vey, vey.*

He was going to die, Adam observed from the couch, thinking it as if he were a psychoanalytic patient associating to some peripheral figure in his life. He would bet, if takers could be found, that Arnold ate salt, that he still found stairs less capricious than escalators, that his brisk early morning walks were constitutional, that he would find some peace march in New York or Washington or—it didn't matter. He probably should not be here now so late.

Staring at the ceiling, Adam aimed a last swirl of smoke upward, groped blindly with his hand toward the coffee table, found his cup, and edged the cigarette over the rim. He was not sure of the exact year, somewhere in the late forties when flu had hit the staff and he was doing some temporary half-interested clinic work. Sitting for a break on a bench, he watched the peculiarly dapper man make what looked uncannily like ward rounds, strutting through the lobby, pausing at the cashiers' booths, buttonholing interns and residents, until a young man in whites pointed—toward him. He sat, seeing the dapper man come at him, his posture edged with the awkwardness of one stranger approaching another stranger with some business in mind. The man came toward him, dressed, in screaming contrast to the clinic patients, in a soft luxuriant gray suit, marching hat in hand, silver-headed ebony cane minimally supporting the slight stiffness of his right leg. Prosthetic, Adam observed; at the knee.

"My name," the man said, "is Arnold Goldman," producing a business card which hung between them as if on invisible wires, until Adam finally took it, glanced at it, catching the word *jeweler.* "You are Dr. Adam Gregory?"

"Yes."

"May I sit?"

Adam shrugged.

Arnold sat heavily beside him, confirming Adam's observation as the shin of the right leg cracked resoundingly against the side of the bench.

"This is not easy," Arnold said, "because I need to indulge myself with questions at your expense. And you could say no, or wonder what kind of dummy comes to see you."

"I have five minutes."

"My younger brother Beryl—Bernard—who is now dead was wounded in the war. You might have helped him in Hawaii."

"His name was?"

Arnold looked at him quizzically, then said, "Bernard Goldman. Corporal."

"I didn't know him."

"He was wounded in the islands and sent back to Hawaii. He died in Hawaii." He removed a fraying sheet of paper from his breast pocket, unfolded it, then wedged a pair of rimless spectacles on the bridge of his nose. "He writes here that a Captain Adam Gregory of the Medical Corps—here: '. . . operated on me last week and gave me no pain, stopped the pain that these days has been so much a part of my life.' Then he becomes poetic; he was a poet."

It was true, Adam thought, at least that he had been in Hawaii. For a time he had been pressed into surgical service, mostly extracting bullets and shrapnel, the crack of Arnold's leg against the

16

bench suddenly reminding him of the clanks of blunted and jagged metal tossed into steel basins.

"I can't remember," he said. "There were so many, hundreds."

"Well. So. There's no sense looking any more. See, I checked in the physicians' desk guide, whatever it's called, and I first found you this year. You were in the neighborhood—I live on Central Park West—I couldn't believe it. So easy." He returned the letter to his pocket. "Too easy."

"How did you know I was here at the clinic?"

"A freak. The first place I came. Also too easy."

"I'm sorry I can't help you."

"So I just wanted to thank Dr. Adam Gregory for stopping my brother's pain."

"Just that?"

"There has to be a catch?" His nostrils flared and crimsoned at the wings; his eyes reflected a gleam of impatience, if not of outright anger.

"No."

"Wait," Arnold said, placid again. "Did you have a front tooth missing?" He tapped an incisor with his fingernail.

That, too, was correct—bad root-canal work, an extraction, later a porcelain cap.

"Yes," he said, and, as Arnold nodded, added, "Mr. Goldman, the evidence indicates that I'm the man. I'm afraid I just don't remember."

"A miracle if you did. But . . . I had hopes. In this world you never know."

"Hopes?"

"Maybe you exchanged a word—something he said you could remember. Maybe he gave you a poem. He gave poems to people he liked."

"I couldn't have been that close to him."

"No," saying it so emphatically that it seemed a character indictment. "Anyway, so you didn't know him. You should have; he was gentle. —I would still like to thank you. I feel a debt. I always feel a debt."

"It was my duty."

17

"Still . . . can I offer you dinner in my home?"

Was he serious? Adam found himself completely unable to answer, strangely lost. Finally he said, "Mr. Goldman, did he—your brother—die because the operation was unsuccessful?"

"No, no. It was later—pneumonia."

Adam was oddly relieved.

"Thursday at seven?" Arnold said.

"Thursday at seven," Adam repeated without inflection; and although he could not say yes, he could also not say no. But his repetition was an agreement; somehow he wanted his consent drawn from him; he wanted no responsibility for it.

"Address on the card. Where it says *home*."

Adam fumbled with the card. Arnold extended his hand and Adam took it, feeling the hard prod of a signet ring, an eerie sensation that he, not Arnold, was wearing it.

"I'm glad you accepted," Arnold said. "Thank you for your help." He nodded sharply, rose, and walked stiffly away, relying on the cane until his steps became more co-ordinated and secure. At the door he flourished his hat to his head, drew a deep breath, and strode out.

Adam sat, hunched forward, the hand holding the card drooping between his knees. What was the mystery? How had this man entered—with amazing ease—into his life? He shook his head; he spent hours, days, each an eternity, appraising and judging others —predictably rejecting them, avoiding engagement with them. Yet this man in not five minutes, hardly even time for a stereotyped opinion, had drawn him in. So quickly. Astounded, feeling that some ineluctable blade of fate had fallen. Why did this seem so inexplicable, unbelievable? A dapper jeweler with a wooden leg and a dead brother. Something had impinged on his order, had jolted his self-perception.

And then he knew; the mystery was laid bare; in five minutes' time he had come to like Arnold Goldman. Impossible, but there it was, the source of his amazement, the feeling of submission to fate. He liked him.

"Mate," Arnold called, "wouldn't you say?"

"Fox," Walter said accusingly.

During the second pot of coffee Arnold's mood darkened. Adam sensed its sourness, but said nothing, watching Arnold's teeth rake his lower lip, his eyes peering down into his empty cup, somehow like a customer in a gypsy tearoom discovering unpleasantness in a peculiar configuration of leaves. Then his eyes flicked up at Walter; he said, "I wish I had your youth." As if to illustrate the contrast, his jowls sagged, his face profoundly old.

"It's not so hot."

"For you, maybe not. For me, everything." Then, "It amazes me, stupefies me. You people never seem to enjoy your youth."

"You mean us darkies?"

"I mean everybody, dummy—and stop cutting me off."

"You enjoy yours?"

"How would I know? While you're living it, nothing. You look back, where was it?" He scrubbed his jaw with the back of his hand. "Feeling sorry for myself, that's what I'm doing. But I tell you, I wouldn't waste my youth if I had it again."

"You hung me again," Walter said, "through the back door this time."

"With less pressure. It must bother you."

"I can't sleep; it keeps me up."

"I'm sorry, but it eats at me. I never could understand your reasons."

Adam leaned back on the couch, vaguely annoyed at the prospect of another lecture directed at Walter's aloofness.

"You see," Arnold pressed on, "if I was young I would really be militant—especially if it was so close to me. A pogrom came, I'd be in business."

"I don't feel it, Arnold."

"You *have* to feel it."

"I don't have to feel anything."

"*Feh.*" He clattered his cup against the saucer. "So don't feel. What do I care?"

"Why do you get so mad about it?"

"Because I don't understand. Because I say to myself, is he afraid? No, he's not. So what is it? Could you tell me just once? Because if my heart attacks me again I won't be around—and how can I die without knowing?"

Walter laughed.

To Adam, Arnold said, "I'm serious and he laughs."

"You're right," Walter said, "I'm not afraid. I just don't feel it the way they feel it—SNCC, CORE, those people."

"Elaborate. Give a dying man a break."

"Knock off that dying bit, will you? It's annoying."

"Hah! A feeling. Adam, look, he's annoyed. Annoyed at *me*, but he can't get miffed at the Ku Klux Klan."

"It's impossible to have a quiet night with you any more," Walter said. "It honest-to-God is getting impossible."

"I don't want quiet nights any more. If I could put on the Beatles and dance, I'd put on the Beatles and dance. Give me a sign, I'll picket."

Walter glared, then said, "I can't lay down in the streets, Arnold. I can't lay down and let my face get cracked open or pull a limp-fish routine on the cops. Anybody ever touched me, I'd try to kill him—plain and simple. And I don't want to get killed back. Anyway, it's all as useless as hell."

"So join the Muslims, take up ju-jitsu. At least that's something."

"Look, I just haven't got it in me. So please, Arnold, forget it. Lay off me."

"Why isn't it in you?"

"Man, I *just don't know*. It isn't there. Like it's not my problem. But don't ask me why, because I don't know. Christ, Arnold!"

Arnold snorted and looked supplicatingly at Adam who merely pursed his lips; then said, "It's his business."

After a long pause Arnold sighed and said, "Well, we're even. I don't really know why I push you so hard. I suppose," looking steadily at Walter, "it's hard for me to believe a Negro doesn't feel he has to act. God knows, lots of Jews don't—never did. They plant trees in Israel now. Israel sells guns to Germany. Feh."

"No feeling?" Adam said.

"Well, sure. Sure. I get a crazy feeling when I see the flag. But live there? Never. But I get a feeling. So, Walter—am I so mistaken when I think *you* could have a feeling?"

"No, no mistake."

"And I can understand that you can't lay on the sidewalk. That much I can see. —A funny world. Action is no action, a fight is not fighting." Then, deliberately melodramatic, stretching out his arms: "Life has worn me out—a mystery, the knowledge of which has been denied me." He smiled. "I'm serious. Lately I feel I'm an affliction on my friends. I'm confusing myself." He glanced at his watch. "Late. I should go home before the subways run when they feel like."

"Take a cab," Adam said.

"Maybe."

Arnold rose, struggled into his coat, squared his hat, and waved his cane. Adam walked with him to the elevator and waited silently. Suddenly, jarringly, Vasiliev opened his door, both hands clutching a bag of garbage, eying them suspiciously, then bellowed, " 'And, behold, there came a great wind from the wilderness, and smote the four corners of the house, and it fell upon the young men, and they are dead; and I only am escaped alone to tell thee.' "

Arnold, livid with a rage that Adam had never before seen in him, shouted, "Dummy! *Schmuck!* It is also written: 'Be of good courage, . . . and let the Lord do that which is good in his sight.' " Then, menacing with his cane: "Stick your head back in your hole before I cave it in."

Vasiliev retreated and slammed his door.

"Doom," Arnold muttered, "always doom." The elevator arrived; he placed a hand on Adam's sleeve. "I'm sorry for picking on Walter. For Vasiliev, too. I'm tired tonight; I have no patience." He smiled. "Tonight I couldn't be content unless the whole world changed." He pressed Adam's arm and stepped into the elevator, Adam watching the door slide shut, the face vanishing behind the chicken-wired glass panel. He went back to the apartment and poured out a tepid cup of coffee.

Walter said, "I had a hard time keeping cool. What's with him?"

"He's going to die." He stared into the coffee, seeing his dark reflection gaze back at him; then he looked up at Walter. "Arnold's going to die."

TWO

Disgruntled, Arnold sat by the window in the early afternoon
sun, a section of the Sunday *Times* on his lap, squinting at the
print dancing in the glare. Instead of shifting the paper, he let it
slide to the floor, then tightened the collar of his slightly thread-
bare, anachronistically ornate smoking jacket, Turkish motifs
woven into the wine-colored cloth. He stared off toward the park,
the trees greening steadily in the Spring air. He liked what he saw;
soon the cold would creep from his bones (why was this May so
frigid?), his walks would be more pleasant. Sniffing, he nurtured
the impossible thought that he might attract some fragrance from
the trees, catching instead an aroma of nearly done roast beef.
Remembering that soon he would have to eat, sitting opposite

23

Esther, her expression concerned and vaguely perplexed (it read: *Is there some special way I should act? Am I acting properly at all?*), flanked by David and Joseph, his sons, and Joseph who would mope and inflict himself—as Arnold felt he himself had been doing for the past few weeks. Dinner, he reflected, did not promise pleasure; threats of pain mumbled in his heart.

His thoughts wandered: across the park, away from New York, settling somewhere on the Chicago lakefront where, with distant omniscience, he could see his daughter Miriam (why me, an atheist, did I surround myself with a wife and children named from the Bible? Answer, Mr. Freud), Miriam emerging from some Catholic church with her husband and twin daughters, the girls dressed in pink and white and gleaming patent-leather pumps, clothing that only gentiles could blend into a particular kind of shiny, scrubbed mirage. And of course straw-colored hair (how the hell. . . ?). He had his differences with Miriam; but if she were here there would at least be life at the table. Even—yes, even—with Joseph only two feet away.

And so later he sat ensconced in mild pessimism, and it was all precisely as he knew it would be, except that for gratuitous torture Joseph had not come with his wife; was it a sign, Arnold wondered, that he might attack some family business that he did not want shown to a "stranger"? Well, he had no desire to sit all day and parry thrusts; yet deflecting Joseph's aim would give him a case of apoplexy, and God only knew the result. Slyly he watched Joseph's talking mouth, commanding, finally getting full attention; then Arnold stole his hand toward the salt shaker, cradling it like a desirable woman in the loving crook of his finger, inching it toward him. And just as he was about to make love to it, he treated it as he treated Esther; he pulled too hard in his eagerness and clanked it against the rim of his plate.

"Arnold!" Esther shouted.

"What? What, what?" He raised the shaker for a quick sprinkle.

"Salt! No salt!"

"*Nach*, I forgot. I always forget."

"Stop acting like a child," Joseph said.

A frontal assault, he thought; she gets at me through my guilt, and he gets at me through my bum heart—so he looks humane instead of mean. Her, I forgive.

"Don't talk to your father like that," Esther said.

"Give him hell," David yelped, smiling.

"Both of you," Arnold said, "stop defending me."

In a wide arc he returned the salt shaker to the table, deftly showering a few grains onto his plate. Then he noticed Joseph's surly face, his surly fingers pushing his almost full plate away as if it contained medium-rare disgust. The same maneuver when he was a child, Arnold recalled; refuse to eat when rebuffed.

"Why don't you eat?" Arnold said. "Should we get another set of dishes? You didn't bring Muriel; I said to myself, 'He's up to something.' But there's less here than meets the eye. —Esther, our son of the striped coat is about to tell us that if we don't keep a kosher house he won't eat here any more."

David roared. Esther seemed remotely hurt, and Joseph glared.

Arnold said, "So nobody defend me. I can do for myself."

He bent over his food, immediately repentant and angry with himself, trying to control an admission that he did not like Joseph in any way; it troubled him; it was unnatural. Perhaps he had made Joseph the way he was. He ate slowly and intently, feeling quarantined, doubly sorry now because he had frozen the table. In a few moments he glanced furtively at Joseph, who was too paunchy for thirty-one, already balding with the speed of a molting bird, soft exaggerated features inherited from God-knew-what ancestor. Unlike David, who was perhaps a trifle too pretty for a man, but at twenty-one he still might mature; his face needed one or two aggravation lines. Finding no problem in David, he returned to Joseph and saw what seemed to him a fathomless reservoir of perplexity tempered with a rage his perplexity had probably caused, the reaction to a puzzling frustration. Perhaps the damaged capillaries webbing his own cheeks was a burst of anger, not some trouble with blood flow. The jaw muscles munched, a vein throbbed in his temple.

Maybe he didn't really dislike him; maybe he loved him. He didn't know; it was all upside-down like a Chagall cow. He could love certain strangers with more ease than this son; yet he felt that the blame was entirely his own. Giving to Joseph was always difficult (Didn't he refuse even food as a child?); was he angry because Joseph could not take? Or give? Or because he rarely, if ever, laughed? Or because he had returned to orthodoxy and made it known that eating in his father's house was a self-violation? (Anticipating Joseph's request that he become religious, Arnold had said: "Children keep kosher for the old people; my son is not my father; hence my last word." Except that Joseph had asked nothing; two upside-down cows.)

He saw Joseph's face sag, his eyes trained somewhat dumbly on the wall, unhappiness iridescing from his features like a dubious halo. And suddenly he felt a pressure in his throat and wanted to touch Joseph's arm; but Joseph blinked roughly, returned to his food, and broke the spell. Arnold thought: he doesn't want to be here, and since this is my house the fault must be mine. But neither had Miriam wanted to be here; and perhaps David's attachment to the house was excessive. Yet he didn't want to be in Joseph's house either, and by his reasoning, that fact must be Joseph's fault. No, the cows were all right-side up; it was the world that was cockeyed.

He shook his head and washed his dialectic down with a half glass of water. Then he said, "I think I dampened our dinner. I'm sorry."

Esther smiled and made table noises; she somehow equated the clattering of dishes with harmony, if not outright joy. David was noncommittal, but Joseph said, "I was out of line."

"I started it. I shouldn't have pussyfooted with the salt, like a baby."

"I had no right."

"It doesn't matter."

"I'm sorry."

"All right—accepted."

"I wanted a quiet afternoon."

"All right."

"I had a fight with Muriel."

"*Mazel tov.*"

"That's why I came alone. Not for *any other reason.*"

26

"Who said any other reason?"

"You."

"A bad joke."

"You thought worse."

Arnold stared at him, squinted one eye, then said, "You know something, Joseph mine? You're right. Completely correct. What I really thought was, you came to kill me."

"Arnold!" Esther screamed.

"Joseph, what's the matter with you?" Arnold's question immediately convoluted and became rhetorical, and he was truly startled when Joseph answered.

"You just don't like me, that's what's the matter. You don't like my life. You make snide remarks about *your* lawyer just because *I'm* a lawyer. I'm nothing to you."

"*Feh.*"

"Miriam marries a *goy*, turns Catholic, that's fine. My brother gets suspended from school for a week because he knows how to run a university better than the administration, that's even better. I keep a kosher house, I'm some kind of freak. But I tell you, behind it all you must have a lot more against me."

Arnold prepared to counter, but Esther, her voice alarmed, said, "Joseph, Joseph—please. He isn't well. Please. God forbid anything should happen. And you, Arnold, don't bring anything on yourself."

"He's jealous," David said.

"Shut up!" Joseph bellowed.

"Wait," Arnold said, "Wait. Joseph, you're right about some things, maybe more than just some. I don't know. It could be that I'm not a good father." But his calm was only momentary and he left the table, afraid his fury would mount to a corrosive explosion. Having lost control of it, not fully aware of why this rage should be in him, he retreated from its irritant and sat again by the window, gazing into the park, comforted slightly that conversation began to build again in the dining room.

He was excluded from their talk, and they probably felt easier now—as Walter must have been relieved to see him go a few nights ago. What was he doing, pushing Walter so unmercifully?

Why had he screamed at Vasiliev, whose reality had ceased with the death of the Romanovs? Could it really be that for all his years he had hated everyone? And now, like old men in state homes, was he expelling his hate through the privileged voice of a rusty heart? He was briefly fond of Joseph because he had snapped back, unwilling to give the heart much quarter. Anyway, how could anyone respect anything that was doing such a bad job?

No, he didn't hate everyone; just mad at the son-of-a-bitch who was fooling with his heart, who had kicked him sprawling to the floor. He wanted to kick back, but everyone was getting in the way.

Still, he wanted to fight with Joseph; as he burned to understand why Walter stood aloof from other Negroes, he burned to understand Joseph's rigidity, his intent quest for meaning in the ancestry of Israel; why his son had come to oppose him with such desperation, his voice—if you knew how to hear it—saturated with tears. It was as if Arnold threatened to tear down the world and Joseph had been pressed into service as guardian of the temple.

They had quarreled interminably; one battle began when Joseph had incessantly harped on the stupidity of a Negro maid who had displeased Muriel.

Finally Arnold had shouted, "You make me sick. What I truly hate is a Jew who forgets what happened to the Jews in the world, who is insane enough to carry on like Hitler himself, but only with his maids and his *shabbas goyim*. You should die of shame. You should remember how a Jew once needed a hand to hold, to keep him from dying. A hand he didn't get. So what's orthodoxy to you? Superiority?"

What sort of point had he made? Because Joseph had stared at him, appraising a strange whirling planet that made no sense in the universe; then immediately negated his existence, saying, "You know something? There are two acceptable positions for an old Jew. *Acceptable*, you hear? He can be a strictly kosher product or he can be like you, an atheist, a Red, a Marxist, a revolutionary, an anarchist. The only trouble is, it's phony."

"I'm a phony?"

"All the way."

And after a quick stare, Arnold seized a wastebasket, emptied the rubbish on the floor, and placed the basket on his head. It fell almost to the tip of his nose, and he said, "When I talk to you, what I need is a helmet."

But Joseph's words had hurt, profoundly, agonizingly, like the beheading of his life; and worse, he suddenly wondered if it were true—now, his eyes fixed on the trees. He lived the best he knew how, but maybe that, too, was phony. Remembering again, he was certain that he had counterattacked Joseph, barked out some reply, but Joseph's words echoed and resonated within him as if they had just been said. Was it true or was it simply Joseph? And why care now, after so many battles? Did he want something from Joseph? His love? Now?

For the first time in years he did not feel like leaving the house; the fading sun shadowed the trees, streaming gold-umber along the paths, the time of day he liked best for walking. Yet he was too weary. And there was no sense going to Adam's either, pretending that he was not tired, that his legs were rubber instead of lead encased in lead, bolted to the floor. He called Esther.

"Will anything be left for supper? I want to ask Adam."

"Plenty. You're not going out?"

"No. Too lazy."

She kissed his forehead, then said, "The weather *is* too chilly."

"I'll call." And when he lifted the receiver he saw Joseph, hat in hand, standing in the doorway, looking at him, then quickly waving. Arnold waved back and said, "Love to Muriel. Kiss and make up."

As Joseph left, he knew that he did not want to see anyone; he dialed Adam, saying when he answered, "Listen, do you mind if I skip it tonight? I'm not up to much. I'm not myself today."

❧ 2

Adam cradled the phone, holding his hand on it for a time, reluctant to break the contact. Yet he wasn't sorry that Arnold had called; he, too, was not up to much. Thinking that Arnold was behaving as though he knew what lay before him; almost as if he had monitored Adam's call to Saperstein, had heard the rather removed voice confirm that the heart could not fend off the next barrage; purely a question of when it would happen. There was also malignant high blood pressure to contend with, to make medication almost impossible; Saperstein had not included this in his talk with Arnold. But he knew it, Adam believed, knew everything was malignant, because he had lived with a kind of naïve joy that, slightly inhibited, pointed to the end. Like the threshold of a nerve; it fired on impulse or it did not fire at all; there was no middle ground.

Perhaps fifteen years before, in a boat at Cape Cod, the two of them alone, fishing, Arnold had said, "Does it ever occur to you that if fishes knew they could get killed when they bit the hook, we wouldn't be here in this boat? And does it ever occur to you that a fish can live a whole life, and die of whatever it is they die of, and be blessed with the ignorance that he escaped from Arnold Goldman or Adam Gregory or the Bumble Bee company?"

"Blessed?"

"Because they're like people. If they knew their whole life was a fight to escape, to avoid the hook, they would hide; they wouldn't swim around. Just like people. Like me, honest to God," knuckling his artificial leg. "If I knew that was going to happen, sheared off like a piece of velvet, would I go in the streets?"

They re-baited, Arnold helping Adam who had never fished before, who felt terribly incompetent and vaguely ludicrous wearing Arnold's red flannel shirt and spare baseball cap with a long pointed peak. Dropping his line again, he gazed off at the concave shore of North Truro, at the misty tower in Provincetown. His eyes smarted in the haze, and he pushed the peak of the cap farther down on his forehead.

"You don't ask me how it happened," Arnold said.

"No."

"You're not curious?"

"Certainly I'm curious."

It was difficult then, difficult even in the years following, not to

30

feel nervously defensive, pinned like a chess piece when Arnold was direct. He knew that he over-reacted, that he was asked to bare no dreadful secret; yet his arrival at some level of comfort was long in coming, slow and painful, and he was constantly impatient with himself.

"How then?" he managed.

"I was living in Brooklyn at the time. I fell in front of a trolley car. Crossing the street, running like an idiot to beat the traffic— which, believe me, was nothing much then. But me? I had to run and get my foot twisted in a track."

Adam winced. Arnold went on.

"One of those *cheder* boys coming back from a rote session with Moses—the ones you see with the *paes*, the gray face trimmed in green, like death warmed over even on the nicest day in summer. The ones who ride the subways day and night to get to all their schools; so many subways, the idea must be, that they have no time to get in trouble. Anyway, a really, truly, gray one pulled me away in time to keep me from the dead. I don't know what shocked me more, the leg or that pasty hungry face looking at me. He was so afraid, I'll never forget it. When I got out of the hospital I found him again and put him through a few of his schools." He laughed. "I'm blowing my horn in case you didn't notice. 'Listen,' I said, 'you want to emerge from the subways and get some light, or you want the air down there?' He took the subways."

The man paid his debts, Adam reflected, just as he had been sought out because he might have (no, obviously *had*, why deny it?) helped the poet, Bernard.

"What became of him?"

"A rabbi in Freeport, Long Island. Conservative. He writes me a letter every year, insists on paying me back. He gets very tortured about it sometimes. I could ease his mind by accepting, but that wasn't the reason I gave in the first place. 'Yankel,' I wrote last time—on a Christmas card to make it stick—'Yankel, you saved my life. Objectively, it maybe wasn't much; but from my position, from where I stand, the act achieves a certain importance. Therefore you owe me nothing.' Then I went a little bit into how I, as a businessman, never enter a bum deal. Still he goes on."

"Tell him to give money to a charity, some fund."

"I'm afraid what he'd give it to. He's conservative in religion, orthodox in life." After a mulling silence Arnold said, "After the crutches, the fake leg gave me some trouble, but once I could walk on it I was in business. It was always walking with me; if I can walk, everything is all right. The worst time was the Spanish war. I couldn't do anything about it; people I knew were going . . ."

A topic Adam wanted to avoid; he braced himself, but Arnold did not go on. His trailing voice, the crane of his neck toward the surface of the bay made Adam feel somewhat like the fish turning down the option of a hook. They both knew that information was wanted, that Arnold's mention of the war had been an almost imperceptible breeze that promised a wind, perhaps even a storm. He avoided, escaped, refused the hook, would not elaborate. And such was the tension, the strain of his silence that Arnold never asked again—at least not directly.

The hours in the boat may or may not have set a tone for his woeful feeling of superfluousness; but the feeling ebbed away with excruciating slowness during the two weeks at the Cape, until at the end, when he could fish like an adequate novice, had bought his own cap, had treated them all to a monstrous shore dinner, he was less like a poor relative—laboring to overcome that feeling which, he knew, was not created by them. Perhaps, too, much of his unease sprung from his amazement about Esther, finding her, as he had at their first meeting, ten years younger than Arnold and incredibly beautiful, the kind of woman he could somehow not associate with wives or mothers but only with lovers. Her beauty was dark and sensuous; long hair which, unpinned and freed at the beach, poured in a torrent to her waist. Part of his surprise, he realized, was that he had thought of a man with an artificial limb in the context of a specific kind of woman: a nurse, a fat clucking mother hen. She was none of that; and more, he learned later that she had chosen Arnold after his accident, when she was seventeen, and had immediately produced an heir. ("A good match, her father had thought; I was on the threshold of my fortune.")

A beautiful woman, perplexed by her beauty and oblivious to its uses—which somehow kept her seventeen. And watching her then, Adam saw that he had been both wrong and right; because with imperceptible smoothness she could transform herself into not only a mother but its quintessence: hurrying, bustling, coddling David's crab-lacerated foot, fighting Miriam's need to underdress on chilly nights, chasing Joseph's truculent expression with a kiss. And Arnold—she gazed at him adoringly whenever he spoke. Adam guessed that much of Arnold's manhood resided in her ability to need him as a man, not simply *her* man.

But it was when she stood or sat alone or swam by herself that Adam did not want her to serve his lunch or make his bed, when he felt a complete intruder. He contemplated her with perhaps too much intensity, and his watchfulness disturbed him; of course, it was a vacation and he had not much to do except sit and fish and look—perhaps he should not have come, a whim strangely satisfied—yet occasionally he might have looked elsewhere, away from her. But if he did, it would seem too consistently aloof, too cold, too much of himself. Out of his gnawing embarrassment he said to her one day, "I'm not a warm person. I'm not comfortable with people—at least not at first. I hope you don't think I'm a bad guest."

"It's good to have you; never mind. I'm happy you're Arnold's friend."

He wanted to talk about her, but she was so much Arnold's wife, he the odd guest, that he could only say, "I'm pleased to be his friend. Thank you both for inviting me."

Once, in a less awkward moment, she said, watching David do battle with another crab, "Just like my husband. Hard to keep up with, always getting into things. Sometimes I worry."

What she worried about he did not know, but he strongly suspected that she feared losing him; because, abandoning traditions and convention and moral comfort, she had joined him in his world, which she saw as freighted with mysteries, unsettling forces which could at any moment catch her off guard, mysteries with which she could not cope. All this was in her face during Arnold's political arguments, his criticism of modern art, his disenchantment and rage at Israel. She watched him intently, almost poised, as if hoping to capture him for herself in a single moment between oscillations. She seemed worried that he might swap her for one of his ideas.

Her scrutiny of him was particularly intense when, on an evening sitting before the glowing remains of a barbeque, he told them of Russia, an incident that occurred when he was ten years old, a sweeper in a jeweler's shop where, if the revolution had not exploded, he would have been fully apprenticed.

"You want to hear common sense from a child? This man I worked for, Levin, who became rich through two pogroms and three private beatings—one eye, yet!—wanted a revolution. Don't ask why. He stood to lose money. Maybe the beatings, the eye. Anyway, I didn't know this; I didn't know anything, a child. Until one day two *polizei*, two big Cossacks, came through the door and began to search. Against the wall in back was a gigantic cabinet— you don't see them any more—maybe eight, nine feet high. They didn't think to stand on a chair to see on top, so they lifted me up and said, 'What's there?' Papers, pamphlets, books, but I don't say anything just, 'This,' and throw down an old silver mold. They let me jump down, and one says to Levin, 'Jew, you're lucky. You're lucky, *Jideck.' Jideck*—over and over like a curse, an accusation.

"So they knocked a few things around and left. After Levin was sure they were far away he grabbed me and kissed me and his face was soaked with tears, and he kept saying, 'How did you know? How did you know? How did you know?' I tried to tell him I didn't know anything, but he wouldn't listen. 'Genius,' he said. And I still don't know why I said nothing up on the cabinet. Maybe I didn't like the Cossacks, I don't know.

"Only later, when my father's family ran away, my mother's family ran away, and poor Levin got lost in the revolution did I know what he was and what I really did. It impressed me a rich man could want a revolution. Maybe even less than a year after I was up on the cabinet the Czar's government fell apart and rotted. Sometimes I think of it and wonder maybe there's a moral: Governments that fall apart always think young people are stupid,

34

little puppies. Maybe down deep they know what to do—like I did."

He fell silent, staring at the coals, and Esther said, "Arnold." Simply that, as if calmly calling him down from the cabinet, gently, so that he might not fall and hurt himself or stay there forever.

And Adam saw that she was not only worried that he might abandon her to an idea but that he might, at forty-seven, artificial leg and all, embark on a binge of frightening, irrevocable action.

"What?" he asked her.

"You—were such a young boy."

Moving away from the phone Adam stretched out on the couch; his position, lying there, his memory of Arnold's Russian story, made him think of Oblomov in his perpetual dressing gown, supine on his sofa, using his pillows to soften the blows of the visiting world. At ten he was a serious little boy and climbed no cabinets; now, at sixty, the only palpable change was a sagging body and gray hair; and he still could not climb.

Perhaps, through a friendship to which Adam felt that he contributed nothing, he attempted to seize a portion of life. Because Arnold had climbed a cabinet, he found it hard to die; and because he had climbed nothing, Adam found it hard to live.

Suddenly he heard Vasiliev screaming at the children who played in the courtyard below. Wearily, he shut the window.

❋ 3

On the borderline of sleep and waking Arnold sat in the semi-gloom, blinking whenever his gritty eyes threatened to close, feeling that he must turn on a light, yet too tired for the effort. He was barely aware of the huge body that filled the chair opposite him; then heard the heavy, labored breathing, the slight gargle of the clearing throat, the voice, "Arnold?"

"Who? Irving?"

"Me. You're not asleep?"

"I'm talking."

"It's late."

"So?"

"I was in the neighborhood."

"You live two blocks away."

"I thought I would come up because there's something I wanted to talk to you about anyway and I thought maybe now, if he's not asleep; why wait? You're not sleeping."

"Talk."

"I can't begin."

"So go home."

"You're a sick man?"

"Are you asking?"

"I'm asking."

"Maybe. I might be."

"I still can't begin."

"Irving, I'm tired."

"I'll begin. —You have a plot?"

"A plot?"

"In Beth David."

"You can't be asking, because you know I don't."

"The family circle sent me."

"So?"

"So they have to know."

"What?"

"If you want a space with the family. You should have taken one years ago."

"Years ago tomorrow always came."

"I don't want to bother you."

"Then don't bother me. Go home."

"There's a space since Morris was buried in Miami. Do you want it?"

"Go home, Irving."

"Where will you rest, Arnold?"

"I'm not dead."

"Nissel's grandson is seven. He has a space already."

"I'm sorry he's so sick so young. Send my sympathy."

36

"You don't want to be with the family? With our father and mother?"

"I don't like the dead. Not even my parents."

"You can't deny it."

"Watch me try."

"You're an impractical man, Arnold."

"Go home."

"What should I tell them?"

"Make something up. Say I flew away."

"Arnold?"

"Say I'm getting cremated. The whole family is afraid of fire."

"Arnold?"

"Say . . ."

"Arnold?"

"Get the plot. Go. Get it. What's the difference?"

"I can give you the costs."

"Bill me. Now let me alone, Irving my brother."

"Good night."

"For who?"

Watching the bulk extrude itself from the chair, move ponderously to the door and vanish, Arnold rose and went to the bedroom where Esther was smoothing the sheets.

Seeing him, she said, "It's almost eleven. I was coming to get you."

"Tell me, was my brother here?"

"Who else was here? He didn't talk to you? He left?"

"He left. He talked also. Too much. I'll lock the door."

"No, I'll do it. Get into bed."

He removed his artificial leg and, under the blanket, closed his eyes; he heard her return, the rustling of her robe, felt the sinking of the bed. As she clicked off the lamp the glow on his lids darkened and he reached out and touched her arm. His chest ticked; his breathing limped for a moment; and an odd warmth prickled his body—almost the same warmth that was once a signal to pull her to him. Almost, because he would rather think of it that way. Removing his hand, he turned on his side; and after a long time, enjoying the peaceful intake of her breath, he fell asleep.

THREE

1

Early Tuesday evening, Walter glanced uneasily down the corridor, ran his thumb over the teeth of his key, then slid it into the lock. It wouldn't turn to the left; slightly puzzled, he twisted to the right and pushed; the door didn't give, and he realized that he had locked it. Someone was obviously in the lab and his first impulse was to tiptoe away; but then a muffled female voice shouted, "*Hey!*" Only the cleaning woman, he thought; he unlocked the door and entered, almost put off by the antiseptic, sweetish odor.

A girl, standing behind a sheeted body, seemed uncertain whether to come fully into the light or retreat into the shadows obscuring the far corner of the room. Her shoulders were thrust back, but the rest of her body angled in a kind of rigid tentative posture, a sprung jack-in-the-box.

She was wearing a white lab coat; a medical student, he thought, hoped. And since Adam had not mentioned her, she might not belong here either. He said, "What are you doing here?"

She did not answer immediately, but her posture changed; she leaned forward as if, released from the box, she was now ready for flight. Then, attempting to settle herself, her eyes fixed on his, she placed a hand on the table, touched a shrouded foot, and snapped away like a child contacting a hot stove.

"What are *you* doing here?" she said, totally without conviction.

"Come on, now—what's going on?" He affected Adam's imperious tone; not only was it a successful imitation, it worked wonders.

She faltered, paused, finally clasping her hands in front of her, rocking slightly on her heels, her expression reminding him of a nineteenth-century calendar print—a little girl caught at the cookie jar.

"I have permission to make up some work. I'm in Dr. Gregory's group."

His own anxiety, infinitely better concealed, ebbed, and he regrouped by appraising her: short and thin, with a bird's nest of touseled tomboy's hair falling randomly on her forehead.

"Well, don't let me stop you," he said, turned from her, and went to another table. He snapped on a lamp, furled back the sheet, and saw that Adam had exposed the muscle groups. Quickly he saw where his illustration had been off in placement and points of flexion—and the old, persistent mistake: his attempt to capture a sinewy feeling of mass and texture when in fact there was none. Know thy audience, he thought.

Sitting on a high stool, looking down at the body, he opened his pad and began to sketch. He had been at it for almost a half-hour—it was coming easily—when he felt her next to him.

"What on earth are you doing?" she asked.

"What are your speculations?"

"I mean I see what you're doing . . ."

"I do medical illustrations."

"Oh. You work with Gregory too."

"You got it."

"I've never seen you here before."

"I've never seen *you* here before."

"I don't usually come on Tuesdays."

"I always come on Tuesdays." He found her consistently child-like, and because his desire to tease her was great, he deliberately resisted. "I'm Walter Ford."

"Barbara Ramsey." She extended her hand directly and brusquely, almost a caricature of a woman attempting to be appropriate in a profession dominated by men.

He took it, wanting satirically to pump it energetically; instead he squeezed it gently, then released it.

"Are you a physician?" she asked.

"God forbid. I paint."

She peered at his pad; then, with a far less neutral expression, at the body. She said: "That's terrific."

He signed the sketch with a flourish, tore the page from the pad, and handed it to her.

"Yours," he said.

"Don't you need it?"

"Yes. But it makes a better gift that way."

"But . . ."

He solemnly tapped a forefinger against his temple, indicating a vast reservoir of memory.

"Thanks." She looked at the sketch again, her lips pressed together, finally saying, "It's very nice of you."

"You don't put anybody on, do you?"

"What do you mean?"

"I was teasing you."

"I know. But thanks for the drawing anyway."

She returned to her table and he watched her for a moment as she selected a scalpel and looked down at a section of already opened leg she had just uncovered. Now she seemed even more like a child, all structure and parental guidelines removed, faced with the impending, threatening unknown. He sketched again, filling several sheets, then finally looked back at her. Sitting now, she was staring through the window, a small space between the sill and nearly fully drawn blinds. Her hands were clasped on her lap almost prayerfully; her face was pensive, downcast, miserable.

He said, "Barbara? What's a nice girl like you doing in a place like this?"

She turned her head slowly and he saw that she had been quietly crying. Her eyes were sore. "I was glad you came," she said. "I thought it would be easier with someone in the room. But it isn't. It just isn't at all." Her voice tripped, but she quickly controlled it.

"I don't follow."

"If you really want to know," she said, burying her tears in angry frustration, "it kills me to touch these awful damn bodies. I sit here alone, night after night, and I know I'll never make up my work. I'm going to flunk."

He looked at the body he had been sketching, adjusted his perception to take in the whole man, not simply his detached parts, and he could sympathize with her.

"Maybe," she said, "a woman really doesn't belong in med school."

"Has nothing to do with being a man or a woman." He left his stool and went to her table, tapping her shoulder to make her look up at him. "Now look. What I'm going to say might seem crazy at first. But just listen. Would you know what I meant if I said an artist can do this work better than a medical student?"

"No, I don't think so."

"Okay, now—if I have one natural gift as a painter it's that I can pretty much see what I'm looking at with a naïve eye—not all the time, nobody can—but at times seeing something as if you never saw it before, as if you don't know what it is. Picasso, Braque—that's how they do it when they really swing. Ever see paintings that look like bottles, fruit, guitars? Except that you never saw them that way before?"

She nodded.

"Okay. Now part of what they get in paintings like that is an attempt to look at something as if they have no idea what it is—until it becomes only a form, a mass of color. And that's what you paint, that pure impression, through eyes that don't impose

42

what you know about an object on your attempt to paint the light and form. You dig this?"

"I think so."

"If you can just turn off your knowledge of what things are supposed to be or do—like what," pointing to a scalpel, "is that long thin thing that gives back the light in a shiny kind of way? Well, what it is, is a long thin thing that shines. If you can see it that way then you don't throw in a line or a shadow, which are probably not even there, to make it look like a knife. I don't see any difference in cutting up a body. Try to look at the bones, the muscles, the nerves as some kind of massed form; the flesh as some blob of pigmentation. —What are you after in this body?"

"The sciatic nerve."

He reached down and, with a middle finger, pulled up a thick gray strand; it came up like a broken piano wire. He said, "Like nothing you ever saw. Not a nerve, not a piece of twine, not anything. Just something long, thick, and tough."

"I can't." She looked away.

"It takes practice."

"There's no time for practice."

"Then it's a bad profession. Maybe that's why a doctor has a practice and not a job."

"You see? You can joke. I can't. The students joke all the time to make it all less tense."

"Why can't you?"

"Somehow it's not funny."

He prodded the body. "Why?"

"Oh, I think he might have had a wife and children—all that."

"You're a liar."

"I am not."

He swiped his hand against the thigh with a loud slapping report. "See? You can't hurt it; it can't hurt you. You can't kill it either, because it's dead."

"Oh, God," she moaned.

He went to the sink and scrubbed his hands, then took her elbow and helped her from the chair. "How about a cup of coffee?"

43

She began to look at the body, but he turned her away.

"Coffee," he repeated. "It has nothing to do with the fact that he might have drunk it."

She nodded and went to the sink to wash up.

In the restaurant on the corner of Broadway they sat in a booth close to the back; out of her lab coat she seemed much older. He wondered if she might have problems simply with being a student; perhaps, not fully aware of it, she might not want to be a physician at all, and localized her troubles and ambivalence in the dissecting room.

Spooning sugar into his coffee, he said, "Hello again."

She smiled tightly. "I might as well quit. It's just such a waste."

"What?"

"The whole thing. If they gave you a body the first time you ever thought of med school, lots of things might be different."

"You must have seen some operations."

"They don't bother me. It's just the dead bodies."

"I suppose you will have to find a way to put up with it."

"If I can. Or get a chance to. Walter, I don't know if I can make it."

"You sure it's just the lab?"

"What else could it be? I'm passing everything; sick people don't bother me. Except with this, I can't even do enough to flunk with a try."

Watching her circle the rim of her cup with a finger, the sudden, surprising swell of her breasts when she breathed, it occurred to him that what she might really need was a man; somebody with a shoulder for her head. He focused on her accent; not New York, not Midwestern.

"Where are you from?"

"Los Angeles."

"You're a long way from home."

"Amen."

"That sounds like you left on not particularly the best of terms."

44

"No, not really—not all around. Mostly my fault. My family doesn't know I don't like them."

"Quite a trick."

"Not if you know them. I could curse them upside-down and they still wouldn't get the point. It really goes back a long way. I was always away at school. I liked it that way."

"Now?"

"Not very much any more. I've never felt more alone. If I flunk out, back I go."

"Is it so bad out there in Dreamland?"

"God knows why, but yes. I can't reason it out. Oh, it's not as though I'd return in disgrace, except for Aunt Marie who's footing my bills. It's just that they kind of sit around—I don't know." She smiled. "I'm very mixed up."

"You've just described the human race."

"You're not mixed up."

"Watch your language."

"No, you're not. I could see it in the lab."

"Catch me one time in real life."

"That's what I'm doing now, no?"

He blinked at her, convinced that she would deny any weakness he revealed; perhaps that was her problem.

She said, "It must be great to paint."

"Self-expression, creativity, all that—right?"

"Yes."

"Would you do me a favor? Put me on just once."

"No."

"Well, God bless your stubbornness. Yes, I like to paint, but it brings no bread. So if I don't take care I'll upset a few balances. I'm already in a little trouble between painting and illustrating; I fell into it because I didn't think it would affect my work, but it does, and I have to straighten it out. I could work in Macy's to support myself, but I'd rather not. In fact, I can't."

"You don't seem very bothered by it all."

"I suppose I'm not violent yet. Maybe the real frustration hasn't set in. I still have confidence in my blobs of paint."

"That's what I need, some confidence. I'm past frustration.

45

—Do you really think it will work, what you told me to do in the lab?"

"It might. Looking back at it, I think I might have been lecturing myself as well as you. You know, thinking out loud about things you don't want to lose. It might work, with time."

"Gregory isn't going to give me time. I feel it in my bones."

"Ask him."

"Plead, you mean. Do you have any idea what a medical student is compared to a professor? I remember one final exam when someone wanted to go to the john and he wasn't allowed."

"Well, Gregory lets you pee."

"Frankly, I'm afraid of him."

"He *is* a little formidable. But predictable."

"Besides, he's giving me this chance at night—without pleading. He *told* me. So in a way he's really being nice. Except I can't do anything about it."

"So there's nothing to ask."

"Nothing."

"Well, lady, we're at an impasse."

She finished her coffee and fished a dime out of a pocket; he refused it.

"I have to study for an exam tomorrow," she said helplessly, then stood. "Thanks for lending an ear. And for the drawing."

"I'll walk you. As a matter of fact I have to see the big man tonight. He lives right around the corner from you. You *do* live in the dorms?"

She nodded, then said, "So late? It's almost nine."

"He never sleeps."

"Don't tell on me."

And then he felt it, a slight questioning glance from the counterman; he looked down at the darkness of his hand which vaguely matched the color of her hair but not the forehead it framed. Thinking of the words he had wanted to say, dead now: *I won't tell on one condition. If I can pick you up tomorrow night at about. . . .*

"No," he said, "I won't tell on you."

2

"Walter, I got to see you." Ford sat on the step, almost hidden despite the glare of the two lantern-shaped lamps hung on each side of the lobby door. "The doctor said you was coming, so I waited out here." He added, apologetically, "I didn't want to bust in on you upstairs." He rose and faced Walter, but did not quite look at him, a habit which maddened Walter; the eyes pointed toward him yet trained somewhere on his ear or jaw or hair, always an indication that something difficult, almost impossible, was about to be said, the effect of which his father did not want to see.

"Can you make it later?"

"No, I don't see as it can wait."

Slightly annoyed, Walter capitulated. "Okay, what's up?"

Ford turned and Walter followed him through the service alley to the cellar apartment. Inside, Ford walked swiftly to Lucille's room, squinted into the darkness, then firmly closed the door. His face suddenly contorted with an agony he had obviously controlled on the street, and Walter quickly pushed a chair toward him. He sat, his eyes fixed on the twisted web of steampipes which crawled along the ceiling like warped beams, then switched to a calendar ornamented by a snowy mountain scene, one Alpine peak split by a thermometer. His lower lip trembled.

"Pa? What's the matter?"

"I . . ." Just that, taking a large blue handkerchief from a back pocket and pressing it to his eyes; he might be blowing them like a nose, Walter thought. "I took Lucille over to the clinic today. She been throwing up all the time." He stopped; it seemed that he knew no more, just some concrete fact which needed a context.

"Well, what's wrong with her?"

"Walter, she going to have a child."

His father had gone mad; tomorrow morning he would walk him across the street to Psychiatric Institute, admitted with the diagnosis of having invented the biggest sick joke of the century.

47

"You know what you're saying?"

"I know. I *know*."

Walter sat down, almost fell; he felt somewhere far off, in another world, regarding his father through the wrong end of a telescope. "She's pregnant," he said.

"Yes."

"I don't believe it. No, no. Somebody made a mistake, some dumb intern. Or you didn't hear right or something."

"Don't you tell me what I heard," he shouted, suddenly modulating his voice to a whispering softness. "No, don't tell me what I heard."

But Walter still wanted to consider it all a macabre joke, feeling his lips taut in a mirthless smile, denying what he knew was impossible to deny. And then the smile vanished, his face collapsed.

"My God," he said. "Jesus loving Christ." He leaned forward and plucked his father's sleeve. "How? In God's name, *how?*"

"I don't know."

"Well, it wasn't any angel."

"I don't know."

"How did it happen? Pa, don't tune out now. Please don't tune out on me."

"Walter, I don't know how it happened. She was throwing up, that's all. They gave her the tests."

"How long?"

"They figure somewheres around two months."

"Now you *got* to be joking! Two months? What about her periods? You didn't notice *anything?*"

Ford was silent, bent to the table, his fingers automatically tracing the checks on the plastic cover. No, he would not have known about her periods; even now, in the midst of this misery, he seemed embarrassed by the question, his face protesting his innocence of anything so uncomprehendingly female.

"I mean," Walter said, "you had a wife. I came from somewhere. You must know something about it."

"Walter, please leave off me. It's bad enough, ain't it?"

"It's going to get worse, you hear? The whole friggin' thing's just beginning."

48

"Oh, Walter." He looked across the table, nowhere. "Yes, that's what she told me. Told me, 'Daddy, why's it I ain't got no blood no more? Ain't I sick no more?'"

"How'd she get that idea, that she was sick?"

"Guess I must of told her. You can't explain to her." His strain was suddenly past endurance; he began to cry. "She going to have a child."

"Like hell she is."

For the first time Ford faced him directly, half tears, half ignorance. "Ain't nothing anybody can do."

"Oh, hell, *yes* there is. Don't tell me you never heard of it."

"We ain't doing away with the child."

"Yes we are."

"I said no."

"What then? Tell me. *She's* going to raise a kid? For Christ's sake, use your head. Don't we have troubles enough. We need *this*? Pa, it's a joke, a buck-and-wing routine—Luce with a kid. You have to be crazy to even think it."

Ford shook his head.

Walter said, "You *can't* want her to have it."

But Ford was no longer talking; he turned away.

"You want to choke on your misery, don't you?" Walter rose, stood for a moment, then lashed his fist at the chair, upending it, knocking it several feet away. "She is not going to have a baby."

"Nothing anybody can do."

"Then why did you even tell me?"

"I figured you'd want to know."

3

Fuzzily, through a mist of cigarette smoke, Adam watched him pacing the floor, flapping his arms like a strangely earthbound bird, screwing up his face either in utter disbelief or in a futile battle against knowledge. Lighting another cigarette from the stub of the last, Adam said, "Who did it, Walter?"

"The old man doesn't know—or isn't telling. Most likely he just

49

doesn't know. Anyway, what's the difference? White man, black man, a little in-between man yelling *mira mira*, a kangaroo—I mean," he said, finally coming to rest by the window and staring out, "we're all cosmopolitan here in this great city of Neuva York. Noo Yawk. This happens all the time. We are all created equal." Then less shrilly, "Like the man said, we're all bastards in America."

"What man?"

"An Italian writer. Went blah over one of our stars of the silver screen. The performance must have been bad because he killed himself."

"Who is it?"

"Man, you *are* all bound up in your mind, aren't you? You're more interested in some name than in this horror show."

"*You* brought it up. Why? Need another voice to say what you really want to?"

"Yeah. It gives a certain universality to—let's see now—to a feeling that might otherwise fall to the level of banal personal tragedy, hence no tragedy at all. It is the artistic heightening of this humdrum event . . . Man, life just does not copy art."

"You're a bore."

"As I was saying, this could only happen to a nigger. I mean it could *only* happen to a nigger."

"Thus lifting a banal personal tragedy to . . ."

"Yeah, you got it. Checks out right on the dime."

Adam smoked in silence.

Walter said, "What in the world son of a bitch could do such a thing? And what the hell did she think he was *doing*? Rape is rape; but this? It's the sickest—absolutely the sickest. See, I don't want to be hard, now I really don't, but farm boys, they bang a sheep or two before they graduate. Well, this guy never graduated, dig? He played farm boy with my sister."

Adam continued to smoke, observing the outrage which could still not emerge full-blown, which was blurred at the cutting edge like a blinding reflection of light, undirected, somehow without substance, and for special blunting, an outpouring of literary allusions and odd metaphor. In a way it was much like old Ford, vitiating his emotional force so as not to offend; blunted, the anger seemed to transform into disgust.

"How far gone is she, Walter?"

"The old man says two months."

"That's not good."

"Well now, we *know* that. What about a legal abortion? Is that on your mind?"

"On what basis?"

"Basis? She's an idiot."

"Not good enough."

"What do you need, a raving maniac?"

"Something like that, but not quite. The state allows it only if the mother's life is in danger. With a psychiatric patient, potential suicide is generally the argument. Every so often it's approved if the mother might produce a damaged child—if it's in the family history. But a damaged mother? It's doubtful."

"Oh come on, Adam, you know as well as I do that hospitals are loaded with women having this done—every day, around the clock."

"Not loaded."

"If I had the money . . ."

"You don't—not saying you could do it even then."

"All right, so she's underage. What about that?"

"No."

"Look, it's ridiculous. My father can't bring up a child."

"He brought you up. Besides, would he give consent even if it were legal?"

"No."

"Then we're wasting words altogether."

"Can you talk to him?"

"Walter, it can't be done. First of all, it's illegal. Second, if he's made up his mind it wouldn't matter if it *were* legal. Stop trying, will you? Anyway, as far as your father goes, it's none of my business. I couldn't force myself into his life. He didn't invite me. Maybe he wants the child."

"Sure. Maybe he wants to turn white, too."

"Maybe."

Walter sneered faintly, then sat heavily in the chair by the window and stared at the dark pane, his reflection clear and bitter. Then he slouched and leaned on his elbow on the sill. "No suggestions?"

"None."

"I got one."

"What?"

"First the old man, now you. What is this—let's be naïve night at the Bijou? Get rid of the kid or whatever it is at this point. After all, Doctor, we're living in the middle of just about the world's dandiest abortion mill."

"You could kill her."

"That might be."

"I said you could kill her. You find that an acceptable alternative?"

"No, I suppose I don't. Who's to say she'll die?"

"Go across the street to the clinic some night. Watch them roll in."

"You'll give me a key? Should I tell them Gregory sent me?"

"Be careful, Walter."

"Sorry. Then you do it. Nice and safe."

"You're out of your mind."

"Like hell I am."

"Don't mention it again. Do you hear me?"

"The old man can't handle a kid, or anything else for that matter."

"You're still out of your mind."

"Who isn't? Will you do it?"

"*I said no*. Enough."

"What do you want, another ratty kid running around the streets? Except this one will be *really* nowhere—an idiot mother and a grandfather named Uncle Tom. Look, I wish I had a nickel for every time I wanted to die or prayed it was all a bad dream, that I was never born. A crummy *nickel*. So why another one like me, only worse off? What is it you want? To find out if it's black or white or six thousand other possible shades? Come on, Adam, please. Wake up."

"Wake up? Do you understand what you're asking me? Here, flick a wrist, get rid of this nuisance. You're not having a boil lanced, you fool. You talk of nickels. I'd give you a ton of them if you could tell me what you're really trying to say. What's your investment in this—besides euthanasia for the good of society?"

"I can't stand this mess. Because it's crazy. Because, because, because. . . . Maybe you *do* want sociological reasons. Data. Did you know I'm a sociological freak? Here, in our thriving Negro community, statistics show that most children have mothers. No fathers however. Now with me, that's all turned around, a piece of data they throw out because it contaminates the study, the results of their dumb-ass research. So statistically I don't exist. Why should that kid, whatever it is, be given a chance to statistically not exist?"

Adam lighted another cigarette.

Walter said, "Look, I don't want to take Luce to some mainlining scum with a rusty coat hanger and a butcher knife. I don't want that. But I'll do it if I have to. I swear one day I'll grab her out of the house, and that's it. Now I've given you every reason I know, so can I have the abortion?"

"I don't practice."

"Then a clinic out of state. You must know some."

"I don't."

"For Christ's sake, don't make me beg. Look, I've known you for years. You have no regard for human life, not even your own. You don't even care if you smoke yourself into lung cancer. You don't give a Goddamn; you know you don't. So what the hell is this big act for?"

"Damn you, I'll hold you to that. All right, I have no regard. Then why should I even listen to your idiotic little miseries, your sister, your father's pride, your madness—any of it? Why should I waste two minutes of my time?"

"Because I also know you long enough to see that you can't be completely dead. That somewhere inside you care and you don't even know it."

"Don't tell me what's inside me. You can't walk all over me like you can your father, my friend. And you can't trip me up either,

53

not by wheedling or coaxing or spouting philosophical arguments. You throw a cheap insight at me and I'm supposed to act like a patient in a television soap opera. And then commit a crime as if I were running an errand. Well, think again. You're just an arrogant, bullying little bastard."

"What are you telling me now? That you're afraid of the law? That's a bigger laugh than somebody in the sack with Luce."

"One more time, Walter. Just one more time and I'll kick you out the door. It stupefies me that I've sat here for so long, listening to you, trying to talk sense to you."

Somewhere inside you care. A lie; he felt nothing. Yet the words bit into him and seized hold like the bizarre symptom of a patient he had not cared for: *My heart rattles when I bump into people.* He was suddenly whirled, perplexed and rootless, into Walter's anger, disgust, and frustration; and his fingers were slipping from his perch of inviolability, a void below, then quickly filled with a writhing torment of confusion and demands and misery leaping up at him like tentacles. *Somewhere inside you care.* Where?

"All right," Walter said. "I have no other choice. You won't do it; I know where to go."

"You're not going anywhere except home. Just give me time to think."

Walter paused, a squinting appraisal. Then, "Two months gone, Adam."

"Shut up. You want it all at once, on your terms, do you? Don't push me or you'll get nothing. Now get the hell out of here. As long as you've forced this on me, leave me alone to think about it."

He brewed a pot of coffee, strengthening it with an extra spoonful, then sat at his desk and gazed at the improbable arrangement of his books: the bulky reference works, remnants of medical school, many his father's, all seeded with tall art books which he used in place of museums and galleries. Here and there, like wedges, little clumps of detective and mystery novels he had once read in place of taking sleeping pills. He had not slept well in years, and at first he took to bed Conrad or Tolstoy or Thomas Mann only to discover a terrible paradox; the books kept him awake, absorbed him, but he retained nothing. Finally he considered it idiotic to read what were supposed to be masterpieces without a shred of retrospective recognition. The mysteries put him to sleep, yet he retained every plot, every major character, and eventually felt himself to be totally inconsequential. So lately he read nothing; he merely lay awake, smoking, and when sleeplessness pained him, he took a Seconal or two, self-prescribed. He wanted to drop the mysteries into the incinerator, but had never once made a move toward the shelves.

Drinking his coffee, he was suddenly aware of the bare walls, neither pictures nor prints. What he had of art was invisibly confined between the covers of the huge slick books.

Taking a pad and pencil he drew a tree, seeing the same old constriction that had never allowed him to paint freely or boldly. Medical illustrating was tighter, fed into his control, did not strain his limited color sense. He quickly sketched several foetuses in varying stages of development, drawing them backward in time until, almost stumped, he outlined a sperm cell and an ovum; then, like a cartoonist, he added several horizontal slashes, the sperm now in rapid motion, streaking toward the egg. Then he gave the egg a pair of stick-figure arms to which he attacked huge boxing gloves; finally features for the sperm, a cross-patch of adhesive tape on the cheek, and a determined set of the mouth.

With a quizzical tilt of his head he examined the whole sequence as if, forgetting he had animated the sperm and egg, he wondered how such an absurd configuration could produce a child. Himself, for example. Perhaps he would see no mystery in it if his mother had not died delivering him. He had always examined, appraised, asked for satisfaction from a parade of nurses, governesses, maids, and finally his father's sister, Prudence, knowing that they were only keepers with varying degrees of maternal warmth, none of them mothers. (Thinking of them in the streets as he walked, watching even the most appallingly vicious mother-child interchanges, he felt that he had been brought up with a kind

55

of aridity; his women had merely acted maternally, merely simulated the role they could not live.) Or perhaps he could understand if his father had not incessantly mourned his decision to place the delivery in the hands of another physician, as if he had remembered *post hoc* that by some miscalculation he had not provided enough sperm or magic in the act of conception and could have corrected the oversight at the birth. Or perhaps if he himself had married and become a father. Then, too, he could have become an obstetrician, a gynecologist, but that had always seemed an awkward, if not peculiar, business; he could never envision himself asking a woman to spread her naked legs and place her heels in stirrups; somehow he would always be driven to inquire, *What am I supposed to find?* And as for OB-GYN instruments, they always seemed like implements found lying about in shoe stores.

He tossed the pencil to the desk and leaned back, rocking, listening to the soft squeak of the chair spring.

Somehow Walter had drawn him into an absurd compact; he had made no commitment, yet on the other hand he had. *Leave me alone to think about it.* About what? A postponed trip to the dentist.

He found himself in favor of the abortion; it made sense in every way, except that he did not want to do it, had never done it, had never been asked. And he had lied to Walter; he knew of some clinics run by people who had a peculiar kind of conviction and acted upon it in the face of almost crushing risks. Why had he lied? Because Lucille was two months' pregnant? Because by the time a contact was made and credentials checked it would be too late to handle her with safety? No, he didn't think so; but he still did not understand why. He was annoyed by his confusion, tried to sort it out.

A clinic would probably not take her. It had to be done soon; now, if possible. But he wouldn't attempt it; quite simply, he did not know how, ethics and morality aside. Yet he could learn in a minute, with at least as much skill as the local witches, and with clean instruments. But less skillfully than the physicians who dabbled on the side for six hundred dollars a throw. Yet at two

56

months they especially would back off; they could not afford it, had no reason to try, not with such a secure bullish market in early pregnancies.

For all he knew, a physician who dabbled might sit opposite him each day in the cafeteria placidly eating his baked Alaska. Anyone on the staff; and through other eyes, he himself. He was wildly speculating and wondered why he linked himself with such a group, why suddenly it was so theoretically plausible that every physician in the world performed abortions, full- or part-time. Everyone—not just the quacks, thieves, or the men who sincerely believed in it.

It all hinged on his interchange with Walter; the question of regard for human life puzzled him. One man might be convinced that abortions were necessary because life was sacred and so should not be plunged, unsolicited, into a situation which might destroy it or maim it or overwhelm it. Another might consider human life purely a conglomeration of cells or dirt particles, and so have no feeling in ridding the world of another neutral organism. Where was his position on the continuum between these two poles? *Somewhere inside you care.* Said as if it were an incontrovertible fact, and he had opposed it, fought it as he might an unjust, vicious assault. Of course. Why do anything at all? *Somewhere inside. . . .*

He didn't know where he stood, and it was his perplexity that forbade Walter to label his feelings, because he might recognize a label and accept it by default, succumb to objective evidence. So if he did the abortion, even arranged it with a minimum of involvement, where on the continuum would his motives lay? He was certain of one fact: There was no science in this; he could not choose dispassionately.

It would simply be a favor for Walter. And Walter's father? Override him, usurp him, push him into the background; who cared? And if it were all so uncomplicated, if no one mattered, why had he bridled at Walter's decision to get an underground abortionist?

He seized the pencil again and sketched Walter's profile, then angrily crossed it through; who was *he* to manipulate, to force choices; who had given *him* the power to grab at a shred of wounded temperament and painfully tear it open?

This time he threw the pencil at the bookshelves. Why was he giving this even a single thought, much less sitting alone and ruminating? Wasn't it all simply a repetition of the girl on the quay or the stonefaced observation of his father's burial? It added up to a life of immobility where a yes and no was not only too facile, and hence impossible, but too obvious, clear-cut, invalid. He trusted convolutions and mysteries more than clarity; in clarity he was powerless; it dazzled him like a sudden explosion.

Somewhere inside you care. Impertinent, arrogant bastard. Snot. And he cursed himself for submitting to it, for being unable to utter that simple yes or no when common sense said no, a decision a child could make with little effort. He had allowed the obvious choice to be buried under a pyre of personal attacks and crippled (then why so potent?) insights.

Finally he surrendered, gave in. Confused, he needed a receptive ear and was annoyed by the need; a simple ear that would resist the temptation to twist its orifice into a mouth brimming with philosophical ideas and moral platitudes, that could discover in this complexity a simple thread of continuity and sense. Perhaps Arnold would know; his response, favorable or not, would at least be rooted in life, in reality.

He swiveled about in the chair, convinced that he would shout *No* if Walter suddenly materialized. He could shout it now, over the phone. Yet something within him said *Yes.*

He rose, swallowed two Seconal capsules, then a third, and undressed for bed.

He lay in the darkness, wondering at the strangeness of it all; he had no business becoming involved with mothers and children. Especially him, because he had simply materialized as a living organism, something chemically spontaneous bubbled up from a retort. Remembering that as a child he was convinced that he had never had a mother at all, at least before he came to know the irrefutable facts of reproduction, learned from his father in a sort of formal lecture series. Before that, he felt that his father had invented his mother; possibly it was the proper thing to do.

No, not really, only a thought in retrospect. Because when he was seven or eight he found a small room in the attic, its door almost hidden by sheafs of old calendars with faded bucolic scenes. Also a large framed picture of a man, either sepia or browned with age; the features were barely visible, but he could see that the head was bald and the cheeks blossomed huge tufts of hair.

He turned the knob and entered, immediately stubbing his toe against a steamer trunk vaguely outlined in the gloom. There were no windows in the room; the only light came from the attic proper. He tried the lid of the trunk; it lifted, and he was assailed by an onslaught of camphor. Holding his breath, he carefully extended his arm, felt, drew out what he recognized as a woman's hat, frilly and floral and beribboned with velvety streamers. Puzzled, he angled it on his head and was almost choked by a spray of dust; yet it should not have been dusty if it had been shut away in a trunk. Curious, but he had no time to think it through. His shoulder was tapped and, as if some hidden spring were loosed, his knees wobbled and sickled inward, butting.

His father said, "What are you doing in here, Adam?"

"What is this place?"

"I asked you what you were doing here." His father just then seemed to notice the hat, suddenly snatched it away, dropped it into the trunk, and closed the lid. "That was your mother's hat."

"No, it isn't. She's dead; she can't have any clothes."

"Come out of here. Now. You shouldn't be in here. There's no air. On second thought, I don't *ever* want to see you in here again."

Oddly, he began to cry; but there was anger in his throat. "It isn't. She's dead and she can't have clothes."

"Are you coming?"

"No."

"Then stay," his father said, his voice dry and toneless, and shut the door on him.

He blinked, sniffled, and tried to adjust his eyes; but there was nothing to adjust them to, so he warily accepted the darkness. He groped with his foot, found the trunk, and sat on the lid. When he was sure that his tears had run out, he breathed deeply and, precisely at the end of his exhalation, he heard a sound that seemed to come from his right, then from his left: a rustling of straw, no, more like the stiff rippling of his governess' skirt. And then it was gone; perhaps he had heard nothing at all. He trembled, just a murmur, and he quickly crossed his arms against his chest, pressing each hand into an armpit. Damp—but he blamed the heat.

He could no longer deny it, he had expected his father to reopen the door; he had accepted a threat, not an eventuality. He wished he had not rebelled, but it had been too spontaneous to control. He blinked again and strained his eyes, but there was still nothing to see. And then, on his cheek, a touch—light, feathery, moving with exquisite slowness up to his temple, pausing, softly vibrating, as if an itching had taken root somewhere inside his brain. He was afraid to touch it, to disturb it; he sat weightless, disembodied, then suddenly smashed his hand against his face, drew away wet fingers, slimy pulp. He screamed, sprang from the trunk, and again his face betrayed him; something delicate and wispy trickled across his forehead. He screamed until his throat ached, hurled himself at the door, groped for the knob and desperately, senselessly, twisted. The door opened. Light pained his eyes. The shock of it immobilized him, wracked him far more than the fear.

His father had not locked the door. He could simply have walked out, turned the knob and calmly walked through. No need to have screamed, trembled. He looked at his fingers: a tiny ball of something black—and sweat. Giddily, he realized that he had not slapped himself at all; he had reached to his temple and plucked out some hair. Now the spot stung.

He began to cry again because somehow it would have been better if the door had been locked. He didn't know why. Wheeling, he kicked the door shut, kicked it again, shivering the calendars and the picture, then lay on the floor, oblivious to the dust and heat. He could have simply walked through. Just walked . . .

Remembering now, he lay in the darkness, and before he could roll to his side he fell asleep, drugged.

60

Toward morning he woke shaking and soaked with sweat, his eyes searching for familiarity, his stomach calming only when he knew for certain where he was. He had just dreamed a dream which had crept into his sleep so many times that the count was past calculation. Occasionally the setting was grade school; this time it was in his old prep academy at term's end, he walking alone along a corridor, drunk with the knowledge that he had just received straight A's in every subject. Then, at a turn in the corridor, he panicked, fell back against the wall in horror, death in every nerve and tendon. Because he realized that he had registered for a course he had never attended; and so he had failed.

FOUR

✣ 1

What, Arnold wondered, could be so important so early in the morning? He had almost examined the phone for some visual clue. Adam's voice had projected a surprising strain of urgency, an almost palpable heaviness.

"How do you feel?" he had asked.

"All right. Fine."

"Then could you drop by later on? Take a cab? I have to see you alone. If you're not up to it, I can come there."

Well he didn't feel fine or even all right; in fact, he felt as if he had run two miles at the end of a sleepless month.

"No, I should get out anyway. About seven?"

"I'll expect you."

By noon he felt worse. He threw up the windows for air, driving Esther into a bulky wool sweater, then finally into another room. He was learning the game, the charade of illusion; he had first checked the radiator to see if the superintendent had gone wild with the heat. Not wild, but the pipes were warm, and so he could say, "Woof. Esther, the lunatic is at it again. May, and he tries to incinerate us."

"It's a cold day, May or no May. It's a crazy May altogether."

"I'm opening the windows. *Nach*, what a lunatic."

Cocking a wary eye at her, he was convinced that she suspected nothing: that his blood had turned to ice, that what he needed was purely the air. He leaned toward the window and gulped, then inhaled deeply until his nose prickled and his lungs pumped freely. (Amazing! Even with pollution the air comes straight through.) Then he sat and immediately found his fingers drumming the arm of the chair. He rose, went to the bedroom and dressed, feeling less an invalid out of his pajamas and robe, even a bit jaunty as he slipped on a pair of gleaming black loafers. Sporty, he thought approvingly, buffing the toes of the foot he could feel.

But his mood quivered and died; he made several false starts at a newspaper, a magazine, a book, then removed his glasses and switched on the phonograph. If he could crinkle his eye over a loupe, appraise a diamond . . . He had retired too soon; he nodded regretfully. Running his thumb across the spines of the record jackets he almost gave up the idea of playing one when he found an old album of Spanish war songs he hadn't heard in years. He set the needle on the record, wincing at the scratches and gargles, then sat at the window and stared out at the park, buttoning his sweater against the chill. Why wasn't May warm? May was supposed to be warm.

"The Peat-Bog Soldiers" played out, the German words jarring him until he settled into recognition; somehow he could never resign himself to the German words which proclaimed an orderly, almost armored massing of men and machines—which was precisely what the Loyalists lacked. There should have been more Germans on the Loyalist side.

64

Viva la quince brigada,
Rhumbala, rhumbala, rhumbala. . . .
Mercenarios y fascistas
Ay Manuela . . .

That was better; less drums and more guitar, a harmonica; that was a song he could always move with. Closer to home. They used to sing it at a summer camp in New Jersey, sitting around a fire and harmonizing until someone would cry. Not always a woman.

En el frente de Jarama
Rhumbala, rhumbala, rhumbala. . . .

There was Paul McCandlish with the crazy hair, an explosion of orange flame, like the bursting grenade that killed him at Jarama. And Harvey Siegel who also never came back, who left a wife and two children and simply never came back.

The voice of the city is sleepless . . .
How bitter the wind, how relentless,
It echoes our shuffling feet

Yes, that captured it; that was the continuity from the Spanish plains to the New York streets; continuity for the ones who returned, the changed names, the jobless, prey to the strange, mad hunt for the well-intentioned, a hunt meant to demolish what little idealism remained in the world. It had succeeded.

Bitter there; bitter here. Danny Locascio, who killed himself, an eagle's dive from the George Washington Bridge; Phil Engel, who fled into the anonymity of Mexico and once sent a postcard from Cuernavaca, written in pencil. And Arnold Goldman, who might have gone, who didn't.

When had these songs stopped making him cry? When had he played them last? Yes, thinking to share his nostalgia he had played the record for Adam. A chillingly bitter response. Adam sat and stared, indicating nothing by word or gesture, only a dull filmy cast to his eyes, sealing off his vision. He had not even tried to change the subject, just sat with those frigid hermetic eyes as if he were immobilized, helpless, forbidden to breathe until Arnold ended the torture. And so he did, lifting the needle halfway through *"Los Cuatro Generales,"* almost hiding the record, flushed with embarrassment.

Yet before that the songs had lived in him; shaving, walking, working, he hummed them. Lived in him throughout the second war which, he argued, would not have begun if Franco had been ended. Siegel and Locascio and Engel meant more to him (God, Moses, Buddha forgive him) than the death of six million Jews. Well, he knew them; he knew them; it was something he could touch; it was concrete, not abstract. And he could never feel himself guilty of living because other Jews had died; only guilty that he had not joined Siegel and Engel.

"Of course you can go, even with your leg. Do you think they give you a physical examination?"

"Bernard, my little brother, stop dreaming. I am what they call *inutil total*, good for nothing. How could I hobble around? I'm hardly any use to myself."

"Are you being honest?"

"I think so."

"You aren't. Let me tell you why. You might not be of any use, but that isn't the reason you don't go. You don't go because of your wife."

"Wrong."

"So if you went, you'd be crazy."

"I said *wrong*."

"Listen to me. If you have someone like Esther, you don't go. You don't have to go. You never have to go. Just admit it. Because you could drive an ambulance, work in a hospital."

"Bernard . . ."

"Admit it, Arnold—to you *and* me. It's important for you to know it. A man must choose. Your choice is to stay here. Say I choose to stay because I wish to be with my wife. It's the only true reason, the only reason that matters."

"You talk like a Freud. Every motive, there's something sneaky about it."

66

"No matter who says it, it doesn't make it less true. Arnold, could you leave Esther?"

"It would be hard."

"Impossible."

"Impossible? Am I a child?"

"Impossible—and the impossibility is what makes you use your leg as an excuse. We're all ashamed and guilty about our impossibilities. Like a child? Yes, because admitting them makes us weak and alone with ourselves. Know in your heart that you wouldn't go now even if you had six good legs."

"You're condemning me?"

"I'm happy for you. Why would I condemn *you*? I'm not going either."

"Then what is this all about? Why talk to me?"

"I have some need."

"What need?"

"To get something clear."

"So write a poem. Your clearness confuses me."

"And a need to respect you."

"Please."

"You don't understand, do you? I don't go to Spain the same as I don't go to a synagogue or even vote. I believe in nothing and I have nothing to believe in. You see? It's impossible for you to go because you have Esther. It's impossible for me to go because I have nothing at all. Because I'm the cripple, Arnold, not you. Because my impossibility *is* shame."

"Ah, my God, how you make me feel impotent. You tell me you have no beliefs, you have only shame, and *I* feel impotent."

"Yes."

"Bernard! Bernard, you talk like a dead man."

"That too, one day."

And in time he acknowledged it; he stayed because of Esther. Amen. But he could not understand why Bernard had chosen exactly that moment to disabuse him of his illusion. *That* he never came to know with time. Was Bernard merely crazy? There were moments, in fact many moments, when he thought so. Yet Bernard had always that need to respect him; he played it, with countless variations, a fugue, like a musical theme. Was it because he, Arnold the jeweler, a man of simple tastes (except in clothes) was a perpetual threat to bring shame on everyone? Maybe he hadn't been respectable enough even for Miriam? Obviously not for Joseph. Was he such a capricious danger to the stability of his world?

The needle reached the end of the record, bumping erratic sounds through the speaker; then it whooshed, leaped a groove, and slid with a cutting hiss onto the label. He rose and switched off the machine. Still burdened with the specter of Bernard, he followed his spoor to the bookshelf and took down a thin volume of poems. He flipped through the pages, reading isolated lines at random: "A touch like ashes in an August hearth"; "Its beak bloated to the sky, no bird's death." All about death, every one. So what was so gentle about Bernard? Being a poet, sensitive to death, was no definition of gentleness. No, he was gentle because he despised pain (or maybe couldn't bear it); more, because he could not bear to inflict it in the smallest measure —at least physically; his words could murder. He was like Nietzsche: embracing, in his madness, the neck of a flogged horse.

Somehow, though Bernard's presence had often been oppressive, few people avoided him; when he sang, he could sing like an angel. When silent, he would observe and detect in others some intention or feeling of which they were unaware; and so it was always necessary, for peace of mind more than resentment, to explain what had really been meant by a word, a phrase. And what he had divined in Arnold was a great measure of helplessness masked by frantic activity, and a deep confusion of thought and emotion that resulted in impulsiveness, rashness—not always to his own benefit.

"Think, Arnold. You don't think things through. You'll never understand."

He snapped the book into the space between other books, as if putting his little brother in his place, the child who long ago could not walk on a solidly frozen lake without finding and falling through the only thin spot on the surface, who got himself hopelessly lost in the subways, who couldn't turn the page of a book without inflicting a paper cut somewhere on his hand.

Pneumonia? In Hawaii? How could you die of pneumonia in Hawaii? Was there some cave inhabited by germs and he stumbled into it? Did he kill himself?

Feh. Nonsense.

So what was the importance he placed in this brother, his words like pearls? He tapped the book in line, thinking: When you die, you achieve respectability, profundity, even to those close to you. Yes, yes. In death there is respectability. They would even say, if they displayed you in the coffin, *He never looked better.*

And in some freakish way Bernard had led him to Adam, and Adam to Walter, and one day, after years of talk, coffee, and chess games, he unveiled himself, made his new debut, squared his hat, took his cane, and first walked, then limped, through the streets of New York City. A regular parade on a nippy March day. For a time he felt strange and creaky, not because he had never marched for causes but because it was not like the old anarchist gravity in Union Square, the labor rallies in Manhattan Center. The air was filled with laughter, nervous joy; he was surrounded by boys in beards dressed like ghosts, young girls, pregnant again, pushing baby carriages, young somethings—at times it was hard to tell. He felt dated, sediment in a bottle of antique wine.

He walked past the students to 92nd Street, where he had decided to assemble with the professional and pacifist groups. Then he relaxed; almost all grown ups—teachers, medical people in their white coats, writers. Even a famous actor. Thousands of people. He began to feel alive. Maybe none of this would have an effect, but he felt personally, privately alive.

And then it began, led by veterans, housewives, and soon a Negro carrying a sign: *No one in Vietnam ever called me a nigger.* He thought of Walter, checking a vague self-righteous anger. On Fifth Avenue the march moved slowly; he kept up easily, and the high point of his day came when a man dressed like a J.P. Morgan left the sidewalk and asked him to make a bit of room. Surprisingly, there were few hecklers. A sign: *Kill a Commie for Christ.* Unexpected applause for the marchers behind the police lines; he

69

raised his eyebrows. And then at 86th Street he saw three boys who looked like high-school basketball players, sneering, shouting, one dressed in a brown shirt and Nazi field cap, waving his arms like the blades of a windmill, each hand clutching an egg until they blurred in the violent spinning. He thought: one egg in his face, even half a yolk, and he would, *clunk*, land the head of his cane on a crewcut. But the eggs never left the hands, just whirled on, grinding some strange grist.

Small groups began to sing, and in Central Park there was more singing and speeches, and he was enjoying himself, he was with it again; it was almost like the old feeling. He even met an old Wobbly. Action instead of years wasted with words and parlor debates. Arnold Goldman, he thought, is out of retirement.

And then he was kicked in the heart.

He opened the window wider and was desperately chilled, but he needed the air again, his lungs hanging in his chest like stones. Stones, he thought, like the kind kids tied to cats destined for a creek.

"Arnold," Esther said, "enough."

"The lunatic with his heat. In May."

"There's no heat now."

He touched the radiator. "So there isn't. You're right." He pushed the window down to a crack.

The small effort winded him and he collapsed in the chair; he fought for breath and, breathing, pain touched his heart. Esther reappeared, wearing a coat.

"My wife is a comedian. I *shut* the window."

"Stop. I'm going for fifteen minutes to the A&P. Should I pick up a paper?"

"No, no. Listen, call Weinberg's. They'll deliver."

"Only for a five-dollar order. —Arnold, do you want me to stay?"

"*Nach*, stay. Go ahead. All right, get me a *Post*. And some oranges. I'd like an orange."

"We have apples."

"Elephants have trunks. Apples are not oranges."

I love you, he thought, watching her leave. I honest-to-God love you. The face and the body and the funny brain, everything. He was half convinced that she had not changed at all in her fifty-one years of life; at least not since seventeen. I trapped you in my memory exactly as I would have you, exactly as I would keep you, and I never let you change. Yes, yes. I love you.

But he could not say it now, not that way; he was truly learning the game and soon he would be very good at it. Sentiment was suspected in the best of health; in the worst of health its expression was a yardstick for fatality. Be regular, every day, a clock, a life put into tune by a laxative.

"Good-bye," he called, but she had already shut the door.

He immediately opened the window; as the sun bled into an afternoon haze, a chill increased, a slight wind stirred. He huddled in the chair, wanting a minute of rest. But the phone rang.

"Pa? Joseph."

"Hello, Joseph."

"How do you feel?"

"Like a million." Score three points, next volley. (Could he once, just once, tell someone *Lousy?*)

"Good. I'm sorry about Sunday. Muriel and I made up."

"Fine. Nice of you to call."

"Listen, Irving called me twice and I can't get him back. Do you have any idea what he wants?"

"He's selling something."

"Selling? What?"

"I wouldn't ruin the surprise."

"No, really. What?"

If Joseph really knew, if he were playing, he had just scored at least five points.

"I think he's going to sell you a plot."

"A plot?"

"Plot. *Plot.*"

"In the cemetery?"

"If there's another place I'd rather have it there."

"So you finally bought one. I think you made a good move. You see, with plot availability getting scarce, and with the cost of land . . ."

He slammed down the receiver; it leaped to the floor like a small frightened animal. He bent, cradled it, then fell back into the chair, into the cold. The phone rang again, but he didn't touch it; instead he poked a forefinger at it and said, "Ring yourself to hell, you stupid, idiotic, Goddamn . . ."

Why did they want him dead? Like the day of the march, walking out of the Mall in the park, the oddly rigid man who blocked his path, stared with beacons of eyes, and said, "Goddamn Jew bastard Communist." And later, Joseph: "You act like a *schwartze goy.*" Well, he *was* a Jew. But he was neither a bastard, nor a Communist, nor a Negro, nor a gentile. "The trouble is," he had said to Joseph, "you don't want me to be anything."

Again the phone rang. He extended his middle finger toward it, made horns at it, flicked his thumbnail off his teeth, menaced it with his fist—until it stopped.

So. The game was over; he was calling it off. Ask him *now* how he felt. If it was lousy, then lousy it was; miserable, then miserable; great, he would do a *schtick,* maybe a buck-and-wing. But no more games. He had lived a whole life to cancel it out like tictactoe? To hell with everybody's strain; he couldn't tolerate his own strain.

Joseph, stay in your *schul,* eat no flesh with dairy, and survive. But don't call me.

Irving, sell your goods to the Eskimos. Better the Arabs.

Bernard, lay quietly with all the dead poets of the ages. Don't provoke from the grave.

Now the chill was intolerable; against his judgment he shut the window, and the effort seemed to rupture some internal valve, releasing a pressure which smothered him like a blanket of steel. He gasped, breathing as if he had just been born, the slap in the buttocks, learning: in, out, in, out. His chest heaved with heat, then his stomach. Was he going to vomit?

"Oh, no," he said. Standing, he defensively extended his arms, holding back the encroaching walls, stretching until finally he drew a clean breath. "Oh, no no." What did fear and rage add up to? What was the emotion, its label? He didn't know; but whatever it was, he felt it. He went to the closet, put on his coat and hat, and stepped toward the door; but immediately turned back to the kitchen and scribbled a note for Esther: *Needed some air. Back soon. Me.*

Needing air he entered the elevator and was halfway down to the lobby when he realized that he had forgotten his cane. With or without it, he would still have stumbled into the lobby; and yet he was afraid without it, not to use it as a crutch but as a weapon, a lance. Sweat streaked his face, like liquid heat crushing his head; he tugged at his collar, then knocked off his hat. The walls, covered with smoked mirrors, reflected what seemed to him a whirling ritual of strange waxworks action; then stillness, watched by countless faces and eyes, all his. The images blurred, fused, and he breathed from somewhere deep in an ocean, trying like a fool to use his lungs when what he needed were gills. He tore open his coat and slumped into a chair, his legs bending inward, the artificial leg cracking into his live shin.

And then he was kicked; a lung was turned off.

In a lobby? How could his questions be answered now? Miriam? Joseph? Bernard? The whole of his life, his memory cracked into bits and pieces of a shattered mosaic, glinting, snowing. All a dream. Why hadn't he thought, only dreamed? Now he couldn't understand.

Arnold, you're an impractical man.

Oh, no—not in a lobby, scrutinized by a million mirrored images of himself. Watching himself die? A sacrilege. He rose and was convinced that he was making steadily for the door; but he was sniffing at the stuffiness of the carpet, felt its abrasive rub on his cheek, his hands clawing at the tufts which, so close to his eyes, seemed a sea in torment.

In death there is respectability.

How bitter the wind.

Genius! You knew! How did you know?

Not enough air in him to blow out a match; he scrubbed his face on the carpet.

Arnold, you're an impractical man.

Go home, Irving.

A lobby. At least I tried to go out. Oh my God, Esther, at least I tried.

Like a distant pistol shot, the puff of smoke preceeding the roar, an orange rolled toward him and stopped at his crying eyes. Only then the hissing rip of the shopping bag, Esther's scream of agony.

Before his dimming sight the orange looked like the sun; and then, sight gone, smelled like Spain, like warm nights. And then he no longer needed the air.

✿ 2

It was almost eight o'clock. Adam crushed out the last cigarette in the chain he had begun over an hour ago. He glanced at his watch again, tentatively touched the cigarette package, then pushed it away and dialed Arnold's number. Still busy.

He couldn't get through until nine, but this time the ring droned on for almost a minute. Then he didn't recognize the voice, pitched high and eerie.

"Who's this?" he asked.

"David?"

"David? This is Adam Gregory. Can I speak to your father?" Another eerie sound. "David?"

"Papa's dead." His voice rose to a whine, continued; a small thin signal of agony forced through the wires of the phone. Then, "I mean, he died."

"David, don't cry."

But he went on, his voice now like a jagged wet cough.

Adam was transfixed; he could not shut out the sound, could not hang up. He stared dumbly ahead at nothing, blinked, terribly intent on the weeping, as intent as if he were listening to a profound, eloquent argument. Then something mechanical ground in his throat, his lips moved. He said, "Don't *cry*."

FIVE

✻ 1

Was it Yankel, the green-gray boy who had saved Arnold's life, this rabbi who was saying, "He was many things to many men. To his children, a loving father, a model and guide through the vital early years of their lives, a mason of foundation stones on which to build a house of perfect construction, a temple in which to worship the God-given blessings and abundance he knew so well and appreciated so dearly.

"To his dead wife Esther, a loyal and loving husband, more than the rest of we ordinary men who content ourselves with bringing home our paychecks and our troubles, who make our houses merely footbaths for our tired feet, a hiding place from the slings and arrows of human existence. He was a true husband who

75

journeyed through life hand-in-hand with his beloved wife, who would not act or decide without pondering her words, without gaining her consent in his quest for a pure mutuality that raises man and his spouse to a state far beyond that of animal and his mate.

"To his parents, who long ago were called, he was a son. For them, he need not have been more.

"To his friends, he was again a model, a teacher of virtue, so that, in a manner of speaking, he was truly a rabbi. We who were his friends, who listened to the truth and wisdom of his words, felt ourselves bent to his persuasion in moral issues; for his morality was of the highest, and he became our rescuer when we fell into doubt and despair of the eternal wisdom. Like Spinoza, he embodied a principle: 'Minds,' said the great philosopher, 'are conquered not by arms but by greatness of soul.' Arnold Goldman possessed this greatness.

"His was a simple life. He walked a straight but not narrow path, pausing always to bestow his generosity. For he was a generous man, both in heart and purse. And he was a peaceful man, a man who valued peace more than the gold, silver, and gems which he examined in his profession. Peace was his character, not just an embellishment to it. He was gentle, never harsh. Although pained, he gave no pain. Impetuousness, the vice of the weak-willed, was unable to launch an assault on his constitution. Patiently and calmly he met and faced the world, weighed its meaning, and acted from the placid fountain of his knowledge and judgment. 'I think, therefore I am.'

"He inspired confidence. He was strength in the swamp of weakness which tempts all of us, seeking to drown us. He accepted: life, death, physical and moral suffering, a tumultuous world, good and evil, the wishes of others, the centuries of uprootedness and scorn which he sought to understand and overcome. He was a Jew. *Chochmah. Binah. Daath.* Wisdom, Understanding, Knowledge.

"And so, was he not human as well? Was he a man whose perfection maddened those around him, so that they were envious of him? No. Because he possessed what one is struck by in the great men who live in the pages of the holy writings: Isaac, the repentent Job. And in the great men of Jewish history: Herzl, Moses Mendelssohn, Dr. Weizmann. And what is this quality he possessed? Humility. And again we remember Spinoza, who said: 'I do not look for any higher worldly position than that which I now enjoy.'

"Had he *no* faults? I say to you, what man does not? Yet if one needs to find fault in a man, one must examine oneself deeply to understand the need and cleanse oneself of this corruption which reduces man to pettiness. Yes, he had faults. But they did not taint his character, nor those of the lives he touched. And that is sufficient. He who would look for faults and flaws which he considers heavy enough to negate the good works of this man, let him speak now so that we might all recoil from the words.

"He was taken from the bosom of his family.

"He was taken in the fullness of life.

"He was taken suddenly.

"But was he unprepared? When we weigh his life upon the eternal balances, we must say No. He was surely prepared, a preparation for which no man can truly prepare, but must achieve through the example and testament of his life. Because as Martin Buber would have it, Arnold Goldman was a man 'who has become a whole being, an activity that has been termed doing nothing: nothing separate or partial stirs in the man any more, thus he makes no intervention in the world; it is the whole man, enclosed and at rest in his wholeness, that is effective—he has become an effective whole. To have won stability in this state is to be able to go out to the supreme meeting.' "

✿ 2

The crooked man passed through Arnold Goldman's family, brushing them like vagrant flies to the rim of the path, saying behind immobile lips, "I am sorry for your grief." He lurched away with a slightly alarming off-balance hop, avoiding, as he crossed the grass, a grave protected by a huge stone, its freshly carved letters strong and dark: SEYMOUR RUBIN—DEAR FATHER. The crooked man sidestepped the grave, yet scattered the unveiling party with a threatening sweep of his fragile hand.

Standing stoop-shouldered a few feet behind Arnold's family, Adam looked away from Rubin in whom he was not interested and regarded the crooked man as he hop-skipped a row of plots on his way to the road. Crumpled at the waist, he labored over the limp, chain railing, his beard a clump of must, his chest hovering horizontal above the ground, a freakish victim of gravity. He wore a blue, almost green suit, shiny wherever it touched the world; on his head a sweat-dyed black hat; in his armpit a black dog-eared book. He stopped a passing couple and tapped the book, urging a prayer for the dead; his voice was raucous, the jostling of shattered glass: "You need me." The couple refused him. He jerked away with long angular strides, startlingly long for his folded body.

Near Adam a young man said, "Must be the golf pro."

"Groucho Marx," someone answered, then sang, "I'll always call you *schnorrer*. . . . "

Adam backed up an incline and gazed over the heads at the rabbi who had begun to intone, who gestured now with both hands, conjuring God over Arnold's casketed body. Lowering his eyes, Adam focused on the people: *yamulkah*'d men, hands clasped behind them; women in black, some veiled, a few inappropriately fashionable for a funeral, others passing handkerchiefs at their noses and eyes. All seemed poised for a signal—permission to unhitch emotion.

The intoning continued, rose in pitch and authority, a tincture of admonition. The rabbi in a stylish suit, with his firm nasal voice, tugged at Adam's remembrance; a sharp contrast to the minister at his father's funeral, ancient, his words aphonic and sepulchral. He blinked away the memory and looked again at the family.

Esther's face was tunneled into her handkerchief-draped palms, her shoulders trembling, her purse dangling awry at her wrist, her elbows held by Joseph and David. An old woman, bitterly old, whom Adam had never seen or heard of, sat in a wheelchair, her face vacant with senility, her fluted cheeks shaded by fuzz. She pulled absently at her ear lobe as if wondering whose funeral this was, who had exposed her here; suddenly her hand floated free, the bent wrist perched nowhere.

Chilled, Adam turned up the collar of his raincoat, stepping full up on the incline, unaware that it was a newly sodded grave, craning his neck above the *yamulkahs* and veils. Beyond the restless rabbi rows of headstones were planted like maloccluded teeth, bound by packed turf.

Adam's teeth clacked; he drew into his coat and moved slowly behind a tree. Calm again, he noticed the round middle-aged couple who had driven him from the chapel. The woman, while scrubbing powder into her cheeks and forehead, had said, "Did you know Arnold for long?"

"Almost twenty years."

"Oh. You knew him first from *schul?*"

"I'm not Jewish."

"Oh? Oh."

There had been no talk for the rest of the trip, and he preferred the silence; but twice he caught the man's eyes appraising him in the rear-view mirror; the second time he gazed back malignantly, held the gaze, until the eyes darted away. Had Arnold been such a mystery to them? They must, at least once, have heard him say, "*Schul?* A synagogue? Hocus-pocus. A rabbit from a hat."

It was none of his business, neither the man and woman nor what they thought. He leaned back in the seat and stared out the window for the duration of the ride to Beth David on Long Island. When they arrived, he walked alone to the plot, following them, using them as guides.

Arnold, invisible in his winding sheet and coffin, was being lowered into the ground. Weeping began, then several intense broken wails—except for the old woman who remained mute, somehow naked, unbearably invisible in her dusty ancient black, her hand twisting again at the ear lobe. Then, after Joseph and David had each cast a spade of earth into the grave, they led Esther through the parting crowd; her teeth raked her lower lip, her bruised red eyes swept the sky. The old woman was wheeled bumpily away, her face still befogged by some unfathomable puzzle.

Adam was barely conscious of the people filing past him; he was intent on a gravedigger tuning up his clawlike machine which began to tremble toward a mound of raw earth. He waited for some time, almost as if Arnold, now that the others had gone, would come sailing out of the darkness of his grave on wings of defiance.

Defiance is a way of life. When that ends, so does life. The only sin is giving in—forgive me the rhyme. You must be defiant.

"But it ends here anyway," Adam mumbled, "in a hole."

He watched until the machine began to scoop the earth, and when he finally turned to leave, the family, broken into small knots, were far ahead of him. It would be foolish now to run, to catch up for a lift to the city; perhaps they did not want him, or perhaps he should not have hidden himself behind a tree.

So he walked slowly and began an endless procession of buses and subways; and toward the end of the trip, staring at his reflection in a darkened train window, he wondered why he renewed his driver's license every three years but had never owned a car—with shiny M.D. license plates, a car he could park at bus stops and fire pumps, a car he could drive in magnificent isolation.

The door of Arnold's apartment was open, leaking into the hall the tinkling of glasses, rumbling talk, a shroud of cigarette smoke misting the blob of soft light poised on the doormat. *Welcome*, the mat said, furry dark letters streaking through the bristles. Exhausted by the trip, Adam entered the foyer, dropped his coat on a chair, and stood for a moment looking into the living room. The younger people, talking and holding glasses, stood apart from the older ones, a distance created almost by design, a clinging to some tacit protocol. Directly in the center of the room were those closest to Arnold, sitting in a semicircle, a space before them as though Arnold's body, or at least his spirit, lay or hovered in the empty patch of fading brown carpet. They were shoeless, seated on small boxlike benches; large graceless toads squatting on tiny toadstools, toes pressing toes, hiding, like private parts of the body, tips of socks and stockings.

Adam could not get directly to Esther without trampling feet, so he began at the edge of the circle, shook David's then Joseph's hand, and suddenly found himself standing before the old woman. Her ankles, extruding from the fringed hem of a plaid blanket, were bound in Ace bandages redolent of some sweet-and-sour linament. She was still manipulating her right ear lobe, which seemed fully an inch longer than the left, a tapering gray pendant that swung under her touch, dotted with a tiny, black-filled hole, once the anchorage for an earring. The back of her hand, like a wisp of old bark, trembled, prevented from disintegration by the roped veins. As he squinted, her face blurred to the shell of bone structure, the skin taut yet porous and flaky, as if the touch of it might be the touch of a moth's wing, leaving on the finger a crispy trace of bitter powder. He saw the milk in her eyes and realized now that she was blind; nevertheless, he touched her wrist and nodded.

Finally he reached Esther, took her hand and pressed it. At first she merely glanced at him, bobbed her head, then looked back at his eyes, into them, and they both remained that way, their eyes somehow joined in a kiss, until there was a peculiar shuddering in the depths of his ears, softening, cutting the sounds of the room. Looking up, he saw that he was being stared at. He quickly released her hand; she let it fall into her lap and turned away.

He left the circle and stood on a neutral piece of carpet, frozen, searching for support and order and banality in the rectangles of woodwork framing the walls, in the sharp angles of the windows and doors, then back to the blank carpet. And then someone forced a highball into his hand, and the woman whose husband had driven him to the cemetery paused before him, extending a tray. Slightly addled, he reached out reflexively and seized a small wad of browned dough, which nestled a diminutive frankfurter.

Bodies pressed him and he stepped gingerly into a corner; soon he was pinioned there by still more people who came at him like a solid wall, the darkness of their clothing suffocating him. The glass and frankfurter clutched awkwardly in his hands, he began to sweat but could not free himself from the corner. Finally he dropped the frankfurter into a pot of snakeplants and drank, wishing he could roll the cold wetness of the glass across his forehead. Then he heard, "I can't believe you *ever* took that seriously. My God, Arnold was no *atheist*."

"Well, I always thought so."

"Look, I heard he put a rabbi through school. This is an atheist?"

A slight quarrel developed, which physically separated the people; Adam stepped through the breach, moving to a space near a window. He parted the curtains and looked out into the dusky park. Then he placed the glass on the sill, leaned against the wall, and closed his eyes, feeling that the tension within him, if sprung loose, if he kept looking at them, would bowl them over like tenpins. Or he could throw open the windows and blow them away.

If I die, I'd like to be cremated. See? It's ready made. A little kerosene on my fake leg. Poof. The chumitz *burns up. But I won't be. They won't let me be. I couldn't even leave my corneas in an eye bank. Nach, that's life. Anyway, in the end how will I know to care?*

Close to his ear, a tight, urgent whisper. "Why on Sunday? Isn't it bad enough I kill myself day after day? Monday, Tuesday, Wednesday, Thurs . . ."

"Because Sunday everybody could come. How would it be during the week?"

"Better for me, honest to God. I could take a day off at least—*with pay*. Anyway, he should have been buried quicker."

"Those days are gone forever."

"Everybody wants to be a *goy*. Look, they don't even cover the mirrors any more. Sit on the boxes, but no covers on the mirrors. Religion is like a private club now, a little bit this, a little bit that. This we don't like, so we forget about it . . ."

"You won't miss Ed Sullivan, for God *sakes*."

"Am I worried about that? Do I look worried?"

Adam shouldered through them, hearing a young man with a fat body and a gaunt face say, "The psychoanalysts maintain that watching the coffin vanish into the ground provides a certain measure of relief. And then, a gathering like this allows . . ."

He leaned against a door, his eyes suddenly constricted, assailed and strangled by cigarette smoke; they darted painfully and nervously across backs and heads and walls, finding nothing peaceful to settle on. Finally they discovered a sacrilegious mirror hanging on the opposite wall and gazed back at themselves with infinite weariness, scanning the bleakness of the face, then discouraged at the sight, drooped shut. Immediately a sudden drop in noise forced them open, chilling him; because it had happened before, the almost silence, when he had looked at Esther; and he had just been thinking of her, and it was as if the thought had been laid bare to the room. But in the mirror he saw a young woman, a young Esther, with a beautiful face and large breasts coming toward him. Why was she approaching him, her arms outstretched? A young Esther; he felt close to madness and pressed back against the door.

And then he knew; he had been tricked by the mirror. The girl was not coming toward him at all; she passed by him, so close that her hip brushed his thigh, and entered the circle—directly, with none of the hesitation he had shown, kissing Esther. Of course it was Miriam, but he had not recognized her, had seen Esther in her even though the resemblance was only slight.

He did not know if the noise had abated because she had entered like some alien, or because the old blanketed woman had, with eerie deliberation, raised her hand and menaced them with a crumpled fist. The hand hung there, a twist of arthritic fingers. Yet she could not see; the gesture was ancient, undirected, practiced. Joseph Goldman left his bench and gently replaced the hand into the darkness of the blanket. Ice clinked in glasses again; talking resumed; but eyes peered furtively at Miriam, at the tiny gold cross hanging from a chain around her neck, as ostentatious in its smallness as a Byzantine icon.

David Goldman appeared to Adam's left, listening as he moved to a pimply man who was saying, "There's no sound reason why anyone should expect Israel to conduct itself along idealistic lines. It's *realpolitik* today. Idealism has no place in world affairs."

"But dealing with the Germans? Can't a line be drawn somewhere?"

"Germany is *the* European power now—despite De Gaulle's fantasies about France. If you deal Germany out, you deal yourself out. Israel is a *nation*. It needs an army and it needs to do business with former enemies."

"Arthur, forget it. I can't argue with you. I see I'm concerned with moral issues and you're not."

"Morality . . ."

"Forget it, Arthur."

In the impasse Adam plucked David's sleeve and drew him close.

"Who's that old woman?"

"My great-grandmother."

"Your mother's grandmother?"

"Papa's." Adam stared and David said, "No lie. She's something like a hundred and three, the best anybody can figure it out."

"My God."

"It's really something. —Adam? How did you like that scene at the funeral parlor?"

"What scene?"

"Joseph looking at Papa's body and breaking up like that. He just *had* to look, the big pain in the ass."

"What's the difference?"

"I thought it was disgusting."

"You were crying on the phone."

"Did I have to look at the body? I mean, making a grandstand play. What was his point?"

"No point."

"He's an actor."

"Do you have to be his critic? Is that David Goldman's role in life?"

"What's with you? Weren't you telling me not to cry? Over and over?"

"What's with me. Yes, I did tell you that. I'm tired is what's with me. I'm going home."

84

They shook hands. Adam went to the foyer and wormed his coat from the squirming chair, and as he poked one arm into a sleeve, he heard, "Listen, we ran out of herring. Go to the store, please, and get six herrings."

He turned. The woman from the car was holding out a five-dollar bill. Was she asking him to run an errand? Pray God she was, because he would . . . But she was speaking to a boy he had not noticed, standing there before him, visible, even a bit fat, but he had not seen him. He was even talking.

"Six herrings?"

"Six. Don't get the *schmaltz* because of the bones. Get the creamed fillets except without the cream."

And then he wondered why he was there; and in the elevator, why he had come; and by the time he was home, why he had wanted to come. Because, somehow, Arnold had not died at all, and he had just played out a charade.

❊ 3

Adam lay on the couch smoking. The far-off gunning of a car engine, the ticking of a clock—he twitched with each sound, strangely intent, like a trained Scrooge waiting for the ghost whom he would try to bluff, yet a ghost who could not be tricked by the subtlest mortal ruse. His thoughts wandered to the funeral, the crowded apartment, and yet he knew that he was not prowling in search of Arnold. Arnold was a fact; Arnold *was* dead and he was impervious to it, a confirmation of his belief that life was a sour joke gone utterly rancid, death its anticlimax. He remembered an old story of Franco's one-armed officer whose battle cry was *Viva la muerte*. A fool too, like himself.

He had forced the thought to drive out other thoughts, to transport himself to another time and place, but he always returned to Arnold's apartment. Thinking of Arnold—but that, too, was an evasion; he felt some vague, diffuse palpitation deep within him, a prelude to trembling. He lighted another cigarette, but the smoke tasted of burning rags. Yet he continued to inhale with a kind of desperation, and not even a new position on the couch could quiet the feeling which was now more than trembling; it was the arrival of the ghost, the throttling of his bluff, and he surrendered to it, to what he had not wanted to think.

Because the ghost was Esther; not a dead man but a living woman; and he shuddered again, heavy with the knowledge that he could not live in peace with the dead, and so was even less at peace with the living. She came and he relived the scene, his hand on hers, their eyes in an embrace, the stares of the funeral guests, the image of her behind his closed eyes—the image which made him fear that his thoughts had been read. And then he tried one last effort to wrench the memory away, focusing on Seconal and its promise of peace and forgetfulness; but it did not work. He lay on his back, staring, examining the lies in his thoughts; not even like other men who lied only to the world but remained honest with themselves; it made no difference that their private honesty might simply be self-loathing; it was at least some sort of truth. How many times had he lied to himself about Esther, about the vacation at Cape Cod so many years ago? And how long could he have pretended ignorance, obliviousness, if something—he could not grasp what—had not driven him into the cloaked corner of his mind where he discarded vagrant, unacceptable thoughts like so much rubbish? Yet he knew, had perhaps always known, that they were not rubbish at all.

Well, he would think them, controlling his decision, instead of letting them take him by surprise. And he was annoyed by the decision, which rang of perversity, as if he were defying someone, some edict or prohibition. And he was puzzled, too, because the thoughts, if nothing else, were bound to give him pain. Perversity in his own pain confounded him. And then he turned wry; his memories might not produce pain at all, not deep pain, because, God knew, he was entitled to pain and so might not receive it. No, there was something else in his ruminations that strained at the credibility of his life, that simply moving his mind was a defiance. Like a little boy's bad thoughts—exactly that— and he almost bolted from the couch, knowing that his image of Esther had somehow been revealed in the apartment, his closed

86

eyes staring at the mirror. The fear of a little boy whose most secret frightening thoughts, never expressed, haunted him with their sinful weight. That was the perversity; not in the self-infliction of pain but in the flaunting of his secret thoughts, inviting everyone to see and judge them, unconcerned about the consequences. He had held her hand too long; perhaps he *had* wanted them to see.

But who was *here* to see? Now. In a room that might as well have been a hermetically sealed vault, a room which usually denied access to even a street noise, a peal of thunder. Who was here to see? To see him sitting at the table in the seaside cottage, his hand curled around a cooling coffee mug, watching Esther caught halfway in some static, fragrantly ripe moment between girlhood and middle age, her hips smooth and firm despite the birth of three children. Leaning over the sink, washing—except for his coffee mug—the breakfast dishes, while indistinct sounds of Arnold, playing with his boys on the beach, floated through the curtains of the small window. It was perhaps the first moment that he had made a conscious, deliberate vocation of watching her, and he was as intent in it as if the power of his desire could encapsulate her in some exclusive possession. Leaning over the sink, her long hair was heaped randomly on her head and loosely bound by a scrap of red ribbon which struggled against the tiny wisps of darkness that tiptoed down the nape of her neck like a gloss of smoothness in the sunlight. She dropped a fork; and no doubt forgetting his presence, she bent without propriety to retrieve it, her skirt rising high over her knees. The movement lasted only a second, but as if he had trained himself to record and absorb minute detail in the span of an eye blink, the moment was long enough for him to take in the swell of her thigh, a flicker of lace hem, the maddening tumescence of her hips. And his hand would have crumpled the mug to dust if it had not been made of thick glazed pottery.

There were no sounds in the room then, just her movements, and he thought that he could hear the quiet hinges of her flesh. Her arms stretched from drainboard to shelf; the same glossiness as her neck, the skin not reflecting the light, but absorbing it. To paint her would require an ocean of pigment, heavy brushes, impastos; there was no surface to gleam with small, quick dabs.

And then she came to the table with her own mug of coffee and sat rather timidly opposite him; and he drank hurriedly, gazing obliquely at the rise and fall of her breathing breasts. He could say something; or get up and leave. But he couldn't leave, did not want to, so it was then that he said, "I'm not a warm person."

That time he had let it drop with a simple comment; but there were other moments, no matter how desperately he tried to deny them, no matter how theoretically trivial, purely the unavoidable intimacy of a shared vacation, the kind of closeness that guest and host must prepare for and accept. But the theory broke before the onslaught of evidence.

She emerged from the calm surf and walked along the beach, and he knew that he was observing her in various degrees, a progression, of nakedness; from the bit of thigh in the kitchen to the bathing suit, the long legs and complete thighs—on the left one, just below the elastic of the suit, a strawberry mark the size of a half-dollar. The blotch spoiled nothing; nor did the small varicose vein inside the knee of the same leg; nor even the raw corn on the little toe of her right foot. Knew, too, that he was hopelessly lost in her, that even his determined search for a flaw was of no avail; because his feeling for her was not simply a flood of pure sexuality where the flaw could be focused upon, pondered, swelled, finally to devaluate her. It was not simply that he wanted but could not have her; and so he had no need to diminish her.

He wanted to return to New York, to invent some pretext, but she was standing before him, his face prickling under the fine spray of water she toweled from her hair, and he needed to stay near her. He licked a drop of water that had fallen on his lip, salty, like a tear.

"The water," he said hoarsely, "must be wonderful."

So hoarsely, thickly, that she answered, "Did I wake you up?"

"No."

She lay on a beach chair, her face to the sun, her legs extended; and he tried to see her in individual parts: legs, torso, arms, head, hair. But it was impossible; no matter how great his effort, she refused to dissemble; he hadn't the power to disintegrate her; she resisted the device he had used for years to detach himself from whatever he did not wish to see or know. She shifted slightly, arching forward the mound of her pubic bone, and he was suddenly furious, wanting to shout: *What are you trying to do to me? Stop! For the love of God, stop!* But he said, "You seem uncomfortable here. At home you seem much more—comfortable." The words masked his feelings, his temptation to shout; but he immediately wished that they were palpable, solid bodies in space so that he could retrieve them, pull them back like a child's toy on a piece of string.

She did not turn to him, her face still engaged with the sun, her eyes hidden behind smoked glasses. She said, "I think you're right."

"Why?"

"It would be foolish to say."

He leaned toward her, propping himself on an elbow, his mind darting off in a thousand directions to an infinity of possibilities.

"No, tell me."

She laughed. "Alone, without Arnold, I don't know how to behave."

"Yes?"

Again she laughed, then turned to him so quickly that he recoiled slightly and almost lost the prop of his elbow. "At my age . . ." she began.

"Young."

"Thirty-five is young? Much younger than my husband, yes. But *just* young? No, I don't think so. At my age, a woman with three children—I still don't know how to act with a gentile."

He gaped; his mouth snapped shut; the possibilities smashed on their own delusion; he almost cried in frustration. A bit roughly he said, "You can't be serious."

"I can. Any time I can be serious." She turned away. "It's what I thought when I first met you. I can't talk, I said to myself. I don't know how to talk to a gentile, a Christian."

"I haven't been a Christian since I was fourteen."

"Never mind. I said it was foolish; I'm a foolish woman. The first time you were coming, I said to Arnold, 'How do you talk to a gentile?' He was angry. 'How do you talk to a gentile?' he said.

'Are you a lunatic? You've talked to a hundred gentiles.' Well, so I must be a lunatic."

"You don't know *how?*"

"I don't know how."

"Then it's me. You can't talk to *me.*"

"I wouldn't like to think that."

"But it's true. If you've talked to a hundred other gentiles, then it must be true."

"I hope it's not."

"No, you'd rather think you couldn't talk to your own children. You'd rather that than telling the truth, that I'm impossible to reach."

She was silent for a long while, then said, without inflection, "I think so. Yes."

He despised himself then; the sun could burn his flesh to embers and he would not care; if he removed the support of his elbow he might fall to the sand, sink beneath it, and he would welcome his obliteration.

"I would have wanted to agree with you," he said quietly. "I didn't want to think it was me—even though I knew it was."

Looking at him, she said, "I'm very stupid. I hurt you."

"Yes."

She bit her lower lip, then, "But I don't think it *is* you."

"But you're not sure."

She said, after a reflective pause, "No, I am not sure."

And then he seemed to step out of his body, move several feet away, sat, and observed himself; because he did something he was not aware of until an eternity after it ended. He reached out and removed her sunglasses, and they looked at each other; and although her shoulders drew back and her legs locked with tension, her whole body pulling away, fleeing, her eyes did not move. They stared, seared, and he tried to look into her, penetrate her; but all he saw was the diminutive reflection of his face.

"I wish to God," he heard himself say—but he was stopped by the disappearance of his reflection. She had shut her eyes with the force of a blow; he felt dead; she had just killed him.

When she looked at him again he held out the glasses. She took them, then rose and walked to the cottage, and he could no longer watch her.

"*Hoo!*" Arnold was calling from a boat, a speck in the eye of the bay. "*Hoo!*"

Then he would surely have left, but in three days they would all leave; a sudden departure meant the consolidation of his shame. And (*Hoo!*) he was caught up in the life of this man, this friend whom he had just tried to cuckold, whom he had cuckolded in his thoughts and dreams for almost two weeks.

So he stayed, but even in the few days left the cuckolding continued, intensified; because now he could not watch her without pain and guilt, could not even ask her to hand him a spoon or pass the bread without fearing the touch of her eyes, her expression which could only radiate contempt. Intensified, too, because once during the night as he lay in bed in the room next to theirs, he heard them making love—or was aware of it for the first time. He lay there and listened to it, an unbearable creaking of old springs, a snapping twang like the breaking of green bones, small cries of inanimate pain, a mattress gone mad with the lack of sleep. And it was the last gasp of rage, of murderous anger that he was ever to permit himself to aim at Arnold, or at her. He wanted to smash them both, to break through the thin wall and strangle, crush them, No, just Arnold. Only Arnold. Instead, he hammered his temples with his fists; and ringing echoes shocked him into immobility. In a moment he fell into a stuporous sleep, pounded himself into unconsciousness.

On the last night at the Cape he avoided them; he walked over two miles into Provincetown and drooped along the garish, bulging streets, and impulsively entered a shop advertising old-fashioned candy. He bought some Mary Janes, chocolate whips, and slices of cloying sugar shaped and colored like watermelons; and later, embarrassed, shaking his head, he threw everything into a trash can. He left the main street, already wretched from watching girls parade in explosions of color: tight slacks, like coats of paint, cut below the navel; some in shorts with sinuous legs tanned a deep orange. And he cursed himself for wallowing in an agony that had remained a constant throughout his adult life; wanting a woman but not knowing where, or how, to get one.

An odd thought, but it struck him that way; odd, because once he had lived with a woman for a month or two, but he could not remember what she looked like, except that she was half Jewish and half Italian. She spent their nights in bed knitting him a muffler. But she was an accident; he had not sought her out; she had found him. And so it was all a miracle of consistency; he had never known what to do.

He bought a pint of rye and walked out to the far end of the public dock where he sat on a mooring pile just outside the oval wash of a boat's dim lamp. He watched the dark bobbing shapes of the fishing and excursion launches; and after half his bottle was gone, he saw a couple leaving the cabin of a boat, emerging from the interior where they had probably just made love. They scrambled to the dock and, as they passed close to him, he saw through the weak light the girl's white slacks streaked and smudged with dirt. Her hair hung over her eyes like the crown of a bizarre poodle. The whole world, he thought, everyone on earth making love. Screwing in dark places. His eyes followed her tight, muscular buttocks until she merged with the night; and then he wondered at the criminal injustice of his creation; how he could, all at once, be consumed by such fierce desire and such a profound inability to satisfy it.

I reached out and took her sunglasses. In her eyes I saw . . . But it was someone else who had done that; the someone else who, if he kept sucking down the burning rye, would borrow his brain and body and go wild.

He threw the bottle into the bay and left the dock, and before he returned to the cottage was propositioned by a boy wearing pants as tight as the girl's, as white, and, strangely, just as smudged. He did not sleep in his room that night; he crumpled up on an old porch sofa and was kept awake by dreams.

As he was kept awake now, chain-smoking, the dreams threatening to prevent sleep forever. Arnold. The funeral. All leaping to other places, other times, and yet to the same time. Esther. The kitchen in the cottage. The beach. The stifling apartment; their eyes.

He rose to get the bottle of Seconal, and in the bathroom felt a tingling in his back, a prickly vibration; and when he reached toward the medicine cabinet his hand stiffened and warped to a claw suffused with a paralyzing electric tension. He could straighten the fingers only by jamming the hand between his thighs. Suddenly his left armpit throbbed; and then it was all over and he stood in frozen perplexity before the mirror. Quickly turning away, he wondered if the spasm had really occurred; perhaps he had dreamed it.

To be sure, the next morning he had himself examined at the personnel clinic, but there was nothing wrong with his heart. There was nothing wrong with him at all.

SIX

❧ 1

It was almost ten o'clock and one of the more rotten Monday mornings of Walter's life. Twenty-six years of bad Mondays, but this verged on the worst. "Black Monday," he moaned, lay quietly on his back, and, as always, stared up at the ceiling, wishing he were somewhere else, someone else. He traced his thoughts on the ceiling as he might sketch for a painting, but the white plaster usually became a movie screen for gaudy subway posters: Buy a share of sea-swept Majorca for $18 down; Jet to the Riviera for twenty-one glorious sun-drenched days. Monday was escape day, an invitation to fantasy land; and he would lie there, his thoughts wheeling and spinning in broad strokes, treading barefoot on foreign beaches, a one-man show at the Parke-Bernet Galleries, a rumble of guilt about his father, a conjured and fabricated image of his mother.

Her image often drove him out of bed, shaking his head, causing him to pause for a moment during his shave, contorting his face and blubbering, "Goo. Goo-goo-goo." He wondered about her, at times sure she lived somewhere in the French Quarter of New Orleans in old-world splendor in silks, laces, and baubles, a dusky romantic face peering sensuously through the filigreed grill of a balcony. His father he saw as the face on a box of Uncle Ben's rice, with maybe a small bale of cotton perched symbolically on his shoulders.

Or if he had time to kill, he would switch on the television set, bought in a moment of impulsive love for old movies, and watch an advertisement or two: especially, if he could find it, the one in which a teenage girl horrified her grandmother, who was loafing in the dining room, with the suggestion that the entire family used the same deodorant, then magically converted the horror to rhapsody by squealing, *It's a spray!* Or another one he was fond of: a mother's intense veneration of a toothpaste, looking at the half-inch of white gop with the rapture of a genuine religious ecstasy. Other mothers were not as devoted as this one; their faces implied only that the gop might cure cancer or leprosy.

Or he would catch a morning soap opera, hoping that some Negro actor would offer himself for study. Once there were no Negroes, and it was like watching the denial of his existence; when he watched now, he preferred the denial. Now they were beautiful, sturdy, sincere, clean-cut types at whom he would eventually laugh through tight lips, seeing a new breed of Amos and Andy and Kingfish—except nothing was funny. He could visualize a concerned woman, perhaps the one in the toothpaste ad, sitting before the desk of a distinguished Negro physician, the TV audience biting their nails, and the mother would say: "Please, Doctor, please tell me what my boy's chances are." And the reply: "Oh, he ain't got nothin' a'tall but a touch ob de poxes. Don' you worry none, ma'am, he gonna be fahn soon's ah hones up mah razor an' cuts it out."

He ran through some of the ritual, then left the apartment,

stopping for breakfast and a ham sandwich "to go" before heading uptown for Adam's. He remembered Lucille, the abortion, wondering if the thought of it, lying asleep somewhere in his brain, had caused the particular pall he had felt earlier. Shrugging, blanking out his mind, he walked along 8th Street toward the subway on Sixth Avenue. As he neared the corner Nedicks, he saw a young Negro man, slim as a pencil, selling newspapers; only that, until he got closer, the face clarifying, growing familiar, larger, finally recognizable. He stopped, held out his hand, and a newspaper touched his palm, then snapped away.

"Why, Lester honey," he said, "you ain't even lookin' at yo' customers."

"Well, well."

"Yeah, yeah, Lester. It sho am me. Good mawnin'. Say, why yo' layin' down all over the street, man?"

"Can it, Walter."

"*Can* it? Now what kind of talk is that?" He bent his neck and jerked his head from right to left, his eyes darting along the sidewalk, the curb, back to the sidewalk. "Lester's cool, now you come on back here. Where you off to, a big fat cool like you? Stop shuckin' around so's I can grab aholt of you." Then, "I mean, for Christ's *sake*, Lester, I heard about this but I never believed it."

"Well, you're looking at it."

"I sure the hell am. Anyway," extending his hand again, "how you doing?"

Lester appraised the hand through slitted eyes, his face suspicious of some devious trick; then he took the hand, pumped it quickly, dropped it.

"I'm doing fine."

"I'm not putting you on, but you look weird out here with those papers—in your uniform." He touched Lester's black ribbon tie which lay almost shellacked on his white shirt; then he stepped back a pace and pursed his lips at the deep olive suit and pebbled shoes.

"No uniform any more, Walter. I quit."

"You quit?"

"Yes, man. I quit."

"You're out of your mind."

"Okay, man. Fine. Now I got business."

"No, look, Lester. I'm serious."

"So am I."

"Lester, no crap now. Let's get a cup of coffee."

"I said I got business."

"Take a break?"

Lester raised his eyes to heaven, then tucked the stack of newspapers under his arm, wheeled, and walked into Nedicks. They sat at the counter farthest from the corner door and, after their coffees were brought, Walter said, "Why'd you quit, Goddamn you Lester?"

"You wouldn't understand."

"I might."

Lester cocked an eye at him, then shrugged. "I was playing with the Man . . ."

"Playing? Lester, you just don't talk the same way."

"Look, I'm sick of this shit. You want to hear or not? I ain't sitting here for kicks."

"I want to hear."

"Well, I was going great. I came off his bass, off some chord that hit me hard, straight into big business—just like that. I could feel it under my sticks like I was beating the skin on my own self, and then he lays in with the bass again and Everett blows for two minutes like you never heard. I moved them, man. I did it all; just that once I was the leader. I could see it in the Man's eyes. He knew it; everybody knew it.

"And when the set ends, this fat man, this very fat man with red hair starts to wave his mixer and yells, 'Let Philly Joe do a solo; you got a real drummer boy there.' The Man laughs, see, and he says to this fat man; we never had Philly Joe up here, no Philly Joe ever blew with us. And then the fat man yells back he knew it all the time; he didn't think it was a good as Philly Joe, but who's this here boy? The Man looked real evil and walked away, and the fat guy keeps yelling out who am I? Shaking that fuckin' mixer and yelling, for his money he's going to know who am I? And I said, 'Mother, you'll never know. Not till one night you dragass uptown and run into me. Then you'll know.'" He drank some coffee, then said, "Yeah, I quit. I had it. That fat mother—a million of them. I just had it."

"You can't quit."

"I can do anything I want to."

"You're twenty years old, Lester. You haven't even started moving and already you copped out?"

"Copped out on what? On just *what*? I can't take being stared at in rooms no more. I ain't going to kill myself for those fat men like Richie and Clifford did, blowing my brains out for a pair of beady eyes looking at me like I was a freak without a name."

"I never stared at you so hard as I just did outside."

"Yeah, well that's your troubles. The misery's all yours."

Walter leafed through one of the newspapers, pausing at an ad for a mosque cafeteria and a column on dietary laws; then he returned it to the pile, sipped some coffee, and said, "Lester, you really believe in this?"

"You ain't much different than that very fat man."

"I'll take the chance for five minutes."

"Yeah, well if I didn't believe it I wouldn't be out there."

"Why?"

"Because I had it. Because I ain't going to blow and blow and blow for no fat white cat who tells me who I ain't." He tapped the newspapers. "Because they're right."

"No they're not."

"Makes no difference to me what you say."

"It used to."

"Lots of things used to."

"What's Harriet think about this?"

"You can leave off Harriet."

"Is she going around with somebody?"

"I don't hear you one note."

"Yeah, Lester, I guess you have to quit. One note."

"Look, don't come around again after Harriet. You gave her enough shit."

"She's over twenty-one."

"We're still blood, man. She worked you out of her, stay out."

99

"We broke up, Lester. That's all there was to it."

"Uh-*huh*."

"She wanted me to marry her. I didn't want to marry her."

"Yeah, nobody's good enough for you. Man, you're black. Same as me, same as she is. You ain't squared off to that fact in years. Maybe you never have."

"Sure."

"I'm telling you, you never have. You want to be one of them, you know that? But you don't belong to them; and when you go with them and blow the shit they tell you to blow, you don't belong to us even more. Jesus, man, why don't you knock off this phoney crap and look at who you are?"

"So I can quit like you?"

"I quit what I don't need."

"Jazz is nigger business."

"I ain't a nigger. That's the whole thing you don't see. You don't see it at all, do you? There's a difference between a nigger and a black man. *You're* the nigger, not me. You put one foot in their shithouse and you're a nigger, because they ain't going to let you be white. I don't know no niggers any more."

"What are you doing for bread?"

"I'm making it okay. You don't listen, do you?"

"No, Lester, I don't listen."

"You got to listen." Averting his eyes, he began to toy with his cup. "Yeah, it still matters to me—what you think. Outside of this," jabbing his thumb at the newspapers, "I haven't had a good idea since you walked on Harriet. You know, I tried what you said. To be me. No more grass, like that. And I came up with nothing—except that one time I got the feeling in my own skin, a leader, something, maybe something. And then it had to happen, it just had to, because that fat man been sitting out there for all my life. Well, they ain't about to let me be me. Nor you, you, Walter, read the paper. Take a copy home. Please."

"Man, don't whine. Please don't whine at me. What am I supposed to do; change my last name to X? I mean, I can't do something crazy like that." Then a fleeting memory of Arnold Goldman's remark—seizing it, he said, "Do I go up to some mosque and learn karate and stop eating pig and make it with some whacked-out chick in a white robe? Jesus, Lester, I couldn't even have a nightmare that bad."

"You're scared."

"I don't want the government to put me on a reservation like a dead Indian. Man, I don't *want* the Goddamn state of Texas."

"Every day we get more people with us. Every day."

"Hell, yes. You got every nigger-hater in the world in your corner—the very fat ones."

"Well, what do you want to do, Walter? Kneel down in the street and let some cop stomp you? You want to carry a sign?"

"I don't do that either."

"You don't do anything."

"Bug off."

"It's going to be our way, Walter, because we don't fight ourselves no more. And you're going to get hurt, baby, right along with them. One day there's going to be an explosion uptown, so big the city'll break in half. Not like the last one. This time it ain't going to stop; nobody's going to stop it—not the cops nor the National Guard nor the preachers. *Nobody.*"

"So that's the way you'll try it. After all."

"Believe it."

"I always have. And when you win, Lester, what'll you do with me. Fry me just like Stalin did to the old Bolsheviks?"

"Yeah, Walter, that's right."

"Lester? You're crazy."

"Yeah, well that don't bother me no more. Say it ten more times it still won't bother me."

"So why waste my time?"

"So why waste it?"

They left Nedicks and went out into the street, Lester not looking at him, immediately unfurling a paper and thrusting it toward a Village girl with two children in tow. He said, "Care to help the cause of the black man?"

She batted a dubious eye at him, smiled in a vaguely seductive way, and walked past. And Walter vanished into the subway.

✿ 2

Almost at Adam's street, Walter approached the medical-school dormitories, glancing over at the low concrete wall beyond which the Hudson River twinkled in the sun, running into darkness beneath the George Washington Bridge. He looked straight at Barbara Ramsey, and his first impulse was to run, flee from another chance meeting on the street. Too late—she waved to him, the flaps of her long white lab coat crinkling back in the wind. He raised his arm, then let it fall, and crossed the street, passing an adolescent girl who sat on the wall, her legs dangling, her heels kicking against the concrete.

"Hi," Barbara said.

"Nothing like a day in May."

"For what?"

"Who knows? Sounded like a good thing to say."

"How are you?"

"Good. Off to class?"

"In about five minutes."

He pointed to her clipboard. "Armed to the teeth?"

"To the teeth."

Then they were silent, looking at each other awkwardly, half smiling. Uneasily, Walter said, "How was the exam?"

"What exam?"

"You had an exam the other day."

"Oh, *that* exam. Fine. And you? Off to Gregory's?"

"Also armed to the teeth."

Again they were silent, and his discomfort deepened; he wanted to count down the minutes. Turning slightly, he saw the girl on the wall staring at them intently and unabashedly, her legs crossed now, her arms folded across her chest.

He looked back at Barbara and said, "Well. This is quite a day. I've been running into all sorts of people I know."

"There are days like that."

"I guess."

And then the girl on the wall said, "*Jesus!* What a pair."

They turned to her; she was shaking her head in absolute help-lessness.

"I mean," she said, her voice brilliantly musical, "don't just stand there and *blah*. What a sad sight you two are."

"Now just who the hell are you?" Walter asked playfully.

"That's my town house," she said, tossing her head toward Psychiatric Institute, her hair whipping across her face, then back to her shoulders. "Of course, I share it with a few brethren, but what the hell. I always sit out here on the wall. Fell off the Goddamn thing once, but who wants to give up a nice wall like this?"

Walter peered over the wall—a drop of at least twenty feet to a shrubbed rocky slope. "Yeah, yeah," he said, "a regular Humpty Dumpty."

"So don't believe me. But I have the cracks in my head to prove it."

"Okay, so you never learn. What are you practicing for, an-other dive?"

"Counterphobic, it's called."

"Counter *what?*"

"Literally, against fear. Learned that in a group therapy ses-sion. Like facing something you're scared of—like a lion or a mother—so you can be better than *it*. Dig?"

"Dig."

"But I really do it because I like the wall."

"Okay, nice to know you."

"Lizzie."

"Lizzie." He turned back to Barbara, more relaxed now that he had spoken to the girl, wondering what had upset him in the first place. A bad Monday, Lester, perhaps the mention of Harriet.

The girl said, "For God's sake, you miserable square, kiss her or something. What are you going to do, stand there like a six-year-old and keep on saying nothing? 'Hi!' she mimicked. 'Off to class? How was the exam?' *Jesus*, fella, even my shrink can do better than that."

Barbara laughed; then, after a moment, so did Walter. But to hide his embarrassment, he said, "Little girl . . ."

"Lizzie. That's twice I told you."

"Lizzie, if you don't behave, I'll help you pull another Humpty Dumpty."

"*Yaa.* If you can't kiss, how can you hit?"

"Such profundity."

Ignoring him, the girl said to Barbara, "Look, Miss someday doctor, what are you hanging around with this fugitive for? When he pulled that jewel of a line about a nice day in May, and you said like, for what? Well, I had great hopes for you. But now, I just am not sure."

"I—" Barbara began, but the girl scrambled up and stood on the wall.

Walter lunged toward her and she said, "One step further and I'll plunge to my doom." She raised her arms, palms out, silencing an audience. "Okay, Jack, assuming your May line stands up. So how can you two waste such a day blabbing about nothing? Throw yourselves into each other's arms, run down that sunny beach toward each other. Clinch. Embrace."

"Look, Lizzie, get the hell off that wall."

"In due time. Now hear this, both of you. Kiss yourselves hello or off this thing I go, off into existential emptiness." She leaned toward the edge.

"Come on, get off there."

"Please," Barbara said.

"Ohh—*both* of you. You're not worth saving." She jumped lightly to the sidewalk and assumed her belligerent, arms-crossed stance. "Be ashamed. Go ahead."

"I'm ashamed," Walter said.

And Barbara, "Me too."

"Well, at least that's something. Anyway, *ta.*" She whirled and walked off to the Institute.

And when she entered the front door, Walter said, "Good God, she was serious."

"Didn't you think so?"

"I guess I didn't."

She touched his arm. "I have to go; I'm late now."

"Take care," he said, smiled, and crossed the street.

But at the corner he looked back at the wall, then at Barbara growing smaller in the distance; not as far away as the distance he had put between them when they were no more than two feet apart.

Walter worked for several hours at the drawing board, stopping near two o'clock for lunch, going to the kitchen where Adam's cleaning woman was scouring out the oven. He opened the refrigerator, plucked out his ham sandwich, then paused a moment and surveyed the inside of the gleaming white box, noticing its emptiness for the first time: two apples, a half container of milk, a can of tomato juice with a top rusted solid from the drippings of a previous defrosting. Still angry at Adam's vacillation, he wanted to reject the milk, but he took it in preference to the juice, poured some into a glass, sat at the table, and unwrapped the sandwich.

"Annie? Don't you ever go shopping for the good doctor?"

She turned from the oven, pivoting on her knees, a red kerchief tied tightly under her chin.

"No, I don't. I ast him once did he want me to, but he said no. Ain't nothing in there, ever, except my sandwich and soda."

She was about fifty, large and soft, and when he thought about her it was as a perfect companion for his father—more logical and appropriate than the woman he imaged as his mother. Women like Annie never abandoned their men; women like her did all they could, would even connive with the devil to hold their men; the kind who scraped up bond money to bail out a husband gone half blind on whiskey; who pleaded the goodness of their delinquent boys to impassive, apathetic desk sergeants. A pillar of the community, a member of the legion of maids he often saw early in the morning walking along Fifth Avenue below 14th Street, opening ranks, turning into apartment lobbies by twos and threes, all with kerchiefs and shopping bags from stores they could not afford to buy in, ambling gaits and coats with a single button mysteriously missing. When he was running hot on the exploitation issue, he

105

had had bitter thoughts about Annie working around him while he sat like a white master at the drawing board, directing silent accusations of hypocrisy at Adam for being a Simon Legree. Absurd, he felt now; but a residue of the feeling found an outlet in a bantering humor.

He said, "Annie, why don't you cool it for a few minutes and have a cup of coffee. Coffee I know he's got around here—by the ton. And I got half a sandwich if you're hungry."

"No, I ate. Tuna fish." She pointed to the drainboard, to an empty Pepsi-Cola bottle, illustrating, as if he did not believe her.

"Annie, sit a second. I got a problem. Everybody says I should join up with civil rights. Everybody says I should be a Muslim. What should I do, Annie?" He gnawed at the sandwich, aware that he was fooling with her and expecting her to fool back.

But she said, "I don't know enough about it. Was up to me, though, I say stay away from all of them."

"Why?"

"They's enough misery without them. They all up to no good."

"Well, now, down South black folks are getting the vote, getting in the white schools."

"Maybe colored people don't belong in no white schools."

"They're getting in."

"I know. I know that."

"But you don't think it's right."

"That's something I don't know."

"And the vote?"

"Well, I voted once; but to tell the truth, I don't think they count them up."

Yes, he thought, she would be perfect for his father. He said, "Don't you get tired working for white men, cleaning up their mess?"

"What else I got to do? They don't make no mess; I don't get no pay. I can't *do* nothing else."

"You know that better than I do, Annie."

"You see," she said intensely, "I'm saving up, me and my husband. So's our Charlene and Alfred. We going to buy us a house out to Long Island someday."

"That's nice."

"Yes, because I'm scared here; been scared for years. Charlene, she comes home late sometimes, and I can't sleep for fear something'll happen to her. Them men hanging around, all them dope fiends and all. And they always trying to get Alfred in trouble; and sometimes I look at him and think how long's it going to be before he can't hold out no more. I'm just plain afraid of the colored men, Mr. Ford. Down in Dalton, Georgia, I *never* was. I was afraid of the white men down there. But up here you walking in the street at night, the colored men all in the doorways looking at you. Just looking. Ain't one night something don't happen. One morning I come out of the house and there's blood all over the steps, and the first thing I says to myself is, where's Charlene? Oh yes, she's upstairs, thank God, because I just seen her. Well, I guess you know all that; ain't no sense telling you about it."

"I haven't seen it in a long time."

"There ain't no reason to it. There ain't no reason to being scared all the time." She reknotted her kerchief as if girding herself against the fear.

Walter said, "They tell me all this is going to change when the colored man gets his rights." For a moment he was about to call himself a bastard for leading her on; then found that he was suddenly intensely interested in her logic, almost fascinated.

"Mr. Ford, I ain't got the time to wait. I got to go home in the dark tonight."

"Can't your husband meet you?"

"He works. No, when I go home all I got's God. I pray."

"Some people wouldn't think that's good enough."

"Yes, and I heard people say God don't care, and that ain't good because I don't know no other way. I ain't got God in them streets, I ain't got a thing. Oh, there's times I think does He really care, but that's a bad thought; it don't do no good thinking it. Alfred, he says it, that God don't care. He says that Jesus is a white man, so He don't care at all. Well, I tell him to shut his evil mouth; but I got to thinking on it, and Jesus *is* a white man, all right. Look here." She rose stiffly from her knees, went to the cupboard, opened her purse, and placed before Walter a colored picture of Christ, His features Semitic as usual, but His face tinted a tawny brown. "Now that don't look right, does it? Some woman give it to me on Manhattan Avenue, and it didn't look right then, and it don't look right now. I ain't got any idea why I keep it, because it makes me feel funny."

"I suppose you could get used to it."

"No," tucking the picture back in her purse with great care, "Jesus is white, and that's the way it is."

"But does He care about the colored people then?"

Resuming her position at the oven door, she said, "I sure hope so. Anyway, two, maybe three years we can get us that house."

She began scouring again, and he returned the remains of the milk to the refrigerator, threw away the wax paper, then rinsed and set his glass on the drainboard next to the Pepsi-Cola bottle.

He worked through the rest of the afternoon, said good-bye to Annie when she left, and waited impatiently for Adam. At seven o'clock he was furious, feeling like a beggar caught in a buyer's market. And when the telephone rang, he almost knocked over a lamp.

Adam said, "I'm not getting back for a while."

"Well, have you decided anything?"

"Can you come tomorrow?"

"I'll wait for you tonight."

"Come tomorrow."

"Now what the hell, Adam. Why all this *mañana* crap?"

"I can't talk now."

"I'll come to the hospital."

"I'm at Arnold's."

"What the hell are you doing?"

"I didn't say when, did I?"

"Look man, Luce is getting far gone, and this is no time for a social visit. You knew I was coming; you could have . . ."

"Arnold's dead."

Walter caught his breath, paused, then said, "Jesus, I'm sorry about that. When did it happen?"

"Last week."

"Oh. Last week. Yeah, yeah, I'll come tomorrow."

108

He slammed down the receiver and began to pace the floor, clenching, unclenching his fists, not knowing exactly what he was angry at. Perhaps at everything. Finally he slumped to the couch, sick of the whole oppressive day: Lester, Annie, Adam, his sister and father—all capped off by Arnold's death. He was lucky he had even heard of it; sneering cynically, he almost spat on the floor.

He wouldn't stay at Adam's and he couldn't face the loneliness of his loft, nor could he work or go to a movie. Suddenly he thought of Lizzie, the girl on the wall who, in her craziness, might not be crazy at all. And before he could involve himself in arguments and counterarguments, he called the dormitory and asked for Barbara Ramsey. While he waited, he decided to ask her to supper in the Village, then to his place for coffee and a drink and a peek at his paintings—which were zingier than etchings. Perhaps she would say no and he could focus his anger on her, aware that he was setting her up, not caring. But when he reached her, she didn't say no. In fact, she sounded pleased, even happy; in fact, she sounded a bit excited. And Thursday night couldn't have been better.

3

Not wanting to go to Arnold's apartment again Adam had tried to fight off David Goldman; he had held the receiver almost a foot from his ear, as if the distance would make refusal simpler, as if the voice were a recorded message, lifeless, inhuman. He was tired; he wasn't feeling well; he couldn't tolerate another crowd. But he relented when David said that Esther wanted him to come, that Arnold had left something for him, that there would be no crowd. Relented, he realized, only because Esther wanted him, and he could not resist. He was a bit frightened by his gravitation toward her, and guilty because he had promised to see Walter; and both feelings merged began to confuse him. And worse, for the first time in years he was avoiding a confrontation; lied to avoid it. Because he had called Walter from a pay phone in the hospital lobby, praying the operator wouldn't cut in and give him away, hoping his peremptory, authoritarian voice would keep the call under three minutes. Knowing that the voice was, of itself, bluff. Perhaps it had always been bluff, a sham; but this time he knew.

He knew it and hunched his shoulders as he left the hospital, hoping he would not meet any of the people to whom he never spoke, the people he passed with a frosty impersonal nod. Outside, his uneasiness deepened to fear that he would run into Walter even though he had just spoken to him. Or that they might meet on the subway platform, his lie revealed, his feet shuffling like a trapped child's. So he hailed a cab and buried himself in the back seat; and while looking at the driver's license, he trembled, almost bolted when it occurred to him that the name beneath the grizzled face was Saperstein, the same as Arnold's physician.

He felt claustrophobic in the cab, and his sense of oppression barely lifted in the apartment; there was no crowd, but some fifteen people were milling about and the family were not clinging together as they had the day before. There were no boxes.

Esther greeted him; her eyes, burning in her grave face, were raw and swollen, but not as demolished as they had been at the funeral. She said, "You were his closest friend. I thought you might want to eat with us—and with some of his other friends."

"Thank you," he said, seeing the trace of a smile at her lips before she turned and went to the kitchen. Then David took his arm and introduced him to a number of people, all of whose names he immediately forgot; but he noticed that the snippets of conversation were less complaining, less like whining monologues than they had been last night. Yet Joseph Goldman seemed to have filed a formal complaint, sitting far off in a corner, talking with an old man.

David steered Adam into a bedroom and shut the door, saying, "Hurt your leg?"

"Leg? No, I didn't hurt my leg."

"I thought you were limping."

"Limping?"

"Outside."

"Why would I limp?"

"Well, that's what I mean, why I asked you if you hurt your leg."

Puzzled, Adam glanced down at his feet, then shrugged.

David said, "Adam, my mother is a great woman."

Wary of any attitude he might express toward her, Adam said nothing.

"Except for one or two," David continued, "all the people out there are Papa's friends."

He left undeciphered David's connection of Esther's greatness with the presence of the friends and simply thought: *So many.* So many and he had not met a single one before tonight, and for a moment he was struck by the absurdity of something he had accepted, perhaps wanted to accept, as fact: He had assumed that Arnold, like himself, had no one else. A wife and family, yes; but no friends. Why hadn't he at least met one? Had Arnold deliberately kept them away?

"Close friends?"

"They range; they all knew him, not just acquaintances. But my mother? A great woman, I tell you. After everybody left last night she was so depressed it was making me nervous. She sat wringing her hands, and then she went to the kitchen, picked out one of her good cups and heaved it against the wall. Joseph was scared as hell; he tried to stop her; and she yelled, 'Your mother is *not* insane. Your mother is *mad*. She is *furious*.' Then she broke another cup for good measure and said, 'When I die, there will be no sitting *shivah*. My spirit couldn't stand it. *This* is to comfort the grieved? *This* is insanity.' I tell you, it was like Papa back in action again. This morning she called the funeral parlor to come pick up the boxes and had me tracking down all Papa's friends who weren't at the funeral."

"Why weren't they there?"

"Because Joseph, my *brother*, forgot—in quotes—to tell them. The ones who came saw the obituary. Anyway, Mama said, 'They're also my friends. I'm putting life back into this house.' Then she cried like hell—she's been crying off and on—but I don't know, it's hard to explain. It's not like yesterday or the day before. She's upset, but she's full of life."

"Good," Adam said, wondering if he really belonged here with the people in the living room; apparently Arnold had not thought so. Without bitterness, he found himself accepting Arnold's judgment. He suddenly felt morbidly tired and sat on the edge of the bed. *Limping?* "You said your father left something for me?"

"Well, he didn't leave formal instructions or anything, but I know he wanted you to have it." He opened a drawer of the dresser, removed a small ledger book, and handed it to Adam. "He wanted to give it to you for a long time, but for some reason or another he never got around to it. A couple of weeks ago he said you were definitely to have it when he died." His voice dropped; he shook his head. "He said it like a joke. I thought he was kidding."

"What is it?"

"A journal my Uncle Bernard kept in Hawaii."

Adam ran his thumb over the binding, yellowing, gray-green, rough like sailcloth. He almost opened it, then merely placed it next to him on the bed. "I thought it might be something else."

"What?"

"You'll think I'm foolish. His cane."

"Would you like it?"

"It seems I would; I don't know why. Maybe it's because I always knew he was coming by the noise he made with it."

"It's yours."

"I'd appreciate it."

"I'll get it."

"No, don't bother now."

But David left before he could object again; and alone, he regretted that he had asked; perhaps he should refuse it; such a peculiar request. Then David returned, clattering into the room with the cane clutched in his hand, pursued by Joseph who slammed the door behind him, saying at the top of his voice, just short of a shout, "What do you think you're going to do with that?"

"I'm giving it to Adam."

"Over my very dead body!" He swiped at the cane, but David yanked it out of reach.

"Joseph, you lay off me."

"It isn't yours to give, you little *putz*. Hand it over."

"Forget it," Adam said. "David, never mind. It wasn't right for me to ask."

"No, he just wants it because the silver might be worth a few sheckels—Goddamn Fagin."

Puffing, his face dangerously engorged, Joseph moved with startling agility for his bulk and backhanded David across the mouth, shouting, "You little bastard son of a bitch."

Rising, Adam said, "David, give him the cane."

"And you," Joseph wheeled on him, "keep your nose out of this. You don't even have a right to be here, never mind a right to ask for the cane—for anything."

David threw the cane onto the bed and began to rub his cheek.

"Get out of here," Joseph ordered him, adding without a pause, "You heard me—get *out*."

He left, his body drooping like a whipped dog's, and when the door closed Joseph said, "What do you want here?"

"I was asked to come."

"Well, now I'm asking you to leave."

"I'm not going to leave."

"If you weren't an old man . . ."

Adam waved a hand at him, the brushing away of an annoying fly, then sat in a chair. He said, "Stop behaving like a fool, will you? You make me tired, and I'm tired enough as it is. Take your cane and go away."

"This is *my* house. Stop giving me orders in my own house."

"Sonny, this is your father's house. And now it's your mother's. If she wants me to leave, I'll leave."

"You always were a superior being, weren't you? A real representative of the master race."

"Go away. Go read your *Commentary* in some corner and don't pull that manure on me. I once wiped snot off your nose; I see it's still there." He lighted a cigarette and spun the match into a wastebasket.

"Why don't you go to your own family?" Joseph said. "Why do you come around here? Who's asking you to come around here?"

"What's eating you up, Joseph? What?"

"Please." He drove the heel of his hand into his forehead. "What an actor!"

"Now listen. I tell you calmly, with all the reason and common sense I can dredge up; your life has nothing to do with mine. I never touched your life except as a passerby. I came to this house to see your father, never you. Never. We have nothing to do with each other. If you have some agony in you, get rid of it in some way. But not on me. Because it doesn't make sense; it has nothing to do with anything."

"Never touched my life? Didn't you? You can say that and my father sitting around with you for years, attracted to you like a magnet? Adam this, Adam that, according to Adam . . . Because of you, he went on *peace* marches. Right out on the street, rubbing elbows with beatniks and bums."

"It was his own business. I had nothing to do with that."

"And the year before last, when he and my mother went to Florida and I got his mail redirected to me, what turned up in my mailbox, delivered by *my* mailman, to *my* home was Communist *newspapers.*"

"Oh, stop with your Communist newspapers. He read lots of things."

"*The National Guardian?* He had to read *The National Guardian?* Delivered to *my* house? One of those other rags, it actually said Vietnam was like Spain, that people who were fighting for the Communists in Spain would be fighting for the Viet Cong! So don't tell me you never affected my life. My father making a spectacle of himself, a fool; reading propaganda, because he sat at your feet and listened to you. And all of a sudden even that wasn't good enough; he starts talking about some *schwartze* named Willis or something. What do you have up there in Washington Heights? Cell meetings?"

Adam stared at him balefully, extinguished his cigarette, but did not interrupt.

"It was sickening to see him doing this. Here's a man, over sixty, with a wooden leg, a wife, three children, grandchildren— out with beatniks and Communists, doing something almost *illegal.* It was ludicrous, a man like him."

114

"That's the man he was."

"He was absurd."

"No more than you, Joseph. Hardly more than me."

"Oh, stop it. But now you mention it, why *you*? Why couldn't you be like all the rest of the doctors in this country? Why can't you love the AMA? Why can't you be against Medicare? *Medicare!* He wouldn't sign up for Medicare because he heard somewhere that they'd ask if he was ever a Communist. *Principles*, he tells me. But you know the real reason? He didn't sign up because he didn't need it. Principles." He slapped his forehead again. "Why did you have to make such a mockery of his life? The only doctor in the world who was in that Goddamn Spanish civil war, and he has to turn up at *our* doorstep."

"I was in *what*?"

"Don't be coy. —And you pumped his head full of it; you couldn't let sleeping dogs lie. You *knew* he was bugged on that Goddamn thing, and you had to stir it all up again." He looked as if he were addressing the wall; he had turned squarely to it. "For years he lies quiet, all those crazy ideas gone; then all of a sudden —*bang*. Communist newspapers. Not enough. A peace march. *Schwartzes. My God!*"

Watching Joseph's one-voiced dialogue with the wall, Adam was muddled. Had Arnold said that he had been *in* the war? He was dimly aware that Joseph had just turned back to him, volatile with abuse, but he ignored him, addled by perplexity; had Arnold *said* that? Or had Joseph heard it that way, wanted to hear it that way?

"You misheard. I wasn't in the war."

"*Misheard?* Misheard at age fourteen, fifteen, sixteen—all the way to over thirty inclusive? Monday through Saturday, maybe an hour of peace on Sunday?"

And now, strangely, he wished that he had not denied it; wished, even, that it had all been as Arnold had said, that he could be responsible for every point of Joseph's accusations. But why had Arnold built this lie? Perpetuated it? For what? Was that why Arnold had kept him apart from the people in the living room? Because he had told them, not just Joseph?

And Joseph was saying, "What effect do you think all this had on us, his children? On me—criticizing everything I did or wanted, despising his own son for being a *Jew*. And David, a punk who's going down the drain, no respect for anything. Everything for his friends; for his family, nothing. Oh, not to mention Miriam who spits at her birthright and becomes a Catholic, *marries* a Catholic. I have twin nieces I haven't ever seen, that I can't even call my flesh and blood.

"All the way back, in those lousy left-wing camps in New Jersey, grown people sitting around campfires and plotting the overthrow of everything—but he couldn't plot the simplest guidelines for his children. *He let us down.* And my mother goes along with him; yes, Arnold, yes, my husband. A girl who was raised in a family where women went to the *mikveh* after every period, where they wouldn't wipe themselves in the toilet with their right hands. She goes along with him every inch.

"Then for years it gets better. He loves my kids; I have a *briss* and he comes without question. I look at him and I see I love him; so what, he was a nut when he was young; he's different now. And then he starts, out of nowhere, no warning—the way you wake up one morning and see a foot of snow outside. He starts: When the kids get bigger, you wouldn't have a *bar mitzvah*, would you? Why do you keep a kosher house? Your politics stink. Why are you like you are? I see I love him, but he despises me. The whole world—crazy, in pieces, no values, no meaning. You finally got to him; you finally made it. And you tell me I *misheard?*"

Adam did not want to deny it again; he couldn't understand it, but he fought against denying it. Why destroy the illusion Arnold had needed to lay before this son? Why the illusion was needed at all he couldn't fathom; why *he* was chosen was also a mystery. He perceived the irony, but was confused by it. Then, looking at Joseph's face (was he going to cry?) some source of black joy sprung loose within him; he wanted suddenly to build on the illusion, on Arnold's foundation, brick by brick, until the entire edifice of Arnold's lie, with himself forever threaded through it, would become complete and immutable.

But he couldn't; he could only curse himself, that all he could give to a man he loved was a cloud of deception. Arnold had attributed to him a life of dignity and meaning, had had to pour substance into his emptiness and smallness.

Cutting through Joseph's newly begun tirade, he said, "You didn't mishear anything. I was at Teruel, Madrid, Jarama—the Lincoln Brigade. I belonged to the Marxist Workers' Party for Unification. I even changed my name." Joseph stared. "And, of course, I'm an atheist. In Madrid I set fire to a church and beat a priest to death. And my name is really"—he groped—"Vasiliev, Boris Tomashevsky Vasiliev. I'm really a Jew, and I'm wanted by the FBI." Suddenly he sprang from the chair and roared, "You Goddamned idiot! I don't know what your father made of me in his private life, but if I was half that—*whatever* it is—I'd be grateful. Whatever he did, he did it by himself—right or wrong or foolish. You? You haven't got the stomach to stand by what you think you believe in. Your father didn't care who accepted him or what anyone thought of him. But you do; so much so, I can't even see you. You know only what you are by what others think of you or tell you. So, maybe he failed you. Maybe he hurt you. Maybe he was a rotten father. But it doesn't change one thing, Joseph; you haven't got the means to overcome it. You're a small man. A very small man."

Joseph still stared, but his face sagged, his eyes gazed dumbly.

Quietly, Adam said, "Now I'm going out into the living room of your father's house and eat something with his friends. Your mother invited me and that's what I'm going to do. What *you* do is your affair."

He took Bernard's journal from the bed and left the room.

Later, as Adam was leaving, Esther said, "David told me about Arnold's cane. Forgive Joseph, please. I would like you to have it."

"No, give it to Joseph. He wants it. I think he wanted it all the time."

He went home, slowly, walking a great distance before he took a cab; and as he left the elevator at his floor, Vasiliev, one foot wedged into the door of the incinerator room, glowered and said,

"Adam Gregory. 'For these be the days of vengeance, that all things which are written may be fulfilled.' "

Clutching the journal tightly, Adam hurried along the hall, then a few steps away from his door he caught himself up in amazement. He was limping.

🐾 4

Bernard Goldman's journal was hardly a journal at all. The ledger contained only a few entries, undated, scrawled in a tight waspish script, so that even under a powerful light Adam was forced to lean close to the pages, half afraid that the writing would pale, vanish.

I was a tourist yesterday and saw Pearl Harbor. Wreckage still there, ugly horrors, rust-slimed spears thrusting through the skin of the sea. The wreckage of everything, not only the husks of ships. I was eyed curiously by a sailor, himself a brown study, his chin a fine advertisement for razor blades guaranteed to satisfy, wedged deep into huge crusty-knuckled barnacles of hands. Until he noticed my trussed-up arm and nodded respectfully, throwing out a half salute.

—Makes you mad, doesn't it? Makes you want to blow those little slant-eyed bastards to hell, don't it? Where'd you get it?

His eyes attacked my arm.

—The Solomons.

I said it, but I wasn't sure, and still am not, where I was wounded. I left. I couldn't talk. I didn't agree. The sight of the ships hadn't maddened me, aroused no murder in me. I am not like that sailor and I could almost feel, part by part, thought by thought, the difference between us. Because I was sickened, and it made me sad; the wreckage reminded me of other wreckage, all wreckage and waste. The sailor could feel something beyond himself, the transcendence of rage, something beyond the fact. I feel nothing but what is within me. My arm twinged.

118

My poetry is trash. I am a rotten poet. I sing not of the world but of crying and ashes, and so the song is a sob, the catch in the throat of a bad tenor who fakes emotion. I sing of despair as though it were holy, yet despair of holiness because my song is a sob. My poetry is a gigantic masturbation. I am afraid of being discovered in the performance of either.

("It troubles me," Arnold had said. "It's none of my business naturally, but . . . Forget it."

"What?" Adam had asked.

"You never laugh."

"Not true."

"There's laughing and laughing. You know what I mean?"

"Yes."

"So—you never laugh."

"There's nothing to laugh about."

"Nothing?"

"Not for me. No matter. I can't help it anyway."

"Maybe that's the worst thing; you can't help it."

"Let's play chess."

"I'll take white."

"You need the advantage tonight?"

"No. But I thought to open as long as you're defending already."

"Arnold . . ."

"The Nimzowitsch Defense, the Yugoslav Defense, the French Defense . . ."

"Arnold . . ."

"The Goldman Opening. No, gambit. Obviously no good for a middle game.")

Ours was a strange family because it remained so old. Yesterday I saw a crumpled, wizened native and he reminded me of Uncle Nissel—and on and on, and for some reason I thought, almost as if I were watching a play, of tables and food, of knishes

119

and kugels, of schav and challah, of mice and men and the braised cheeks of a cow. Of Passover and Chanukah and the syrupy wine and a bit of matzoh, of my bar mitzvah when, despite my stammerings, protests, and screams, they proclaimed me a man. And of paychecks and Friday afternoons, Mama presiding at the cleared and solemn table, transformed by her presence into an altar; Irving, Arnold, and Bernard, in that order, placing before her the homage of their pay, searching for that coveted smile, the benign mood which elevated one to goodness and meant an extra fifty cents. And it was always Bernard who received the first pay cut, the first pink slip, the first who inspired Mama's comments to Papa: See your son? Again! A nothing. So? *I could never hold a job; sometimes Bernard even forgot where he worked. He liked to ride ferries to Staten Island and commune with the gulls.* Sue me, *Arnold might say.*

That first poem—that very first defective link in the chain of formidable mediocrity—but a special link that day, defect unseen, visions of the whole chain set in type on a real page in a real magazine. My gift, standing behind Irving and Arnold, no money but the poem. I forgot that she couldn't read English. So I read it to her and she twitched her shoulders, duly noted the absence of the paycheck in the vast debit column of her mind, and said to Papa: Your son, not mine. *Oh, yes yes yes yes; my father's keen ear discovering in the middle of some middle verse the word God. He took the poem and found the word with his searching finger, his nail as sharp as the knives he used to cut his furs, and tore the page to shivering slivers and snowed my hopes in banks and drifts upon the carpet. Because I had written G-O-D, not G-D. I had confronted the Creator that day, stared Him defiantly in His glorious sacred O, and was cast from His side.*

I raised my hand to my father. I did not bring it down. I wished him dead with the small flame inside me; and then it went out.

It was the end of that line. I ran away, a boy with a stick aslant across his shoulder, from whose tip, like an errant tear, dangled a red sackerchief filled with—nothing. Nothing of use to anyone. Except to my brother, who pursued me. Arnold who, paying some incomprehensible, mysterious debt by surrendering a leg, came to possess more with a part missing than he had whole. Because he was a nasty boy once, silent and passive in his nastiness, who suddenly traded in, bartered the weakness of four limbs for the power of three. He no longer stood on that line pretending to get anything. He hobbled off with a dazzling, brilliant speed, outraced me, and I lay in his wake filmed by the dust of his departure. This, he said to Papa, is ridiculous.

But he had the good sense, my brother, not to say absurd. He located what was ridiculous in the center of that circle, the five dim rooms, Mama and Papa. He did not generalize the ridiculousness of that life to all of life. Somehow he knew not to.

Yet what a blessing absurdity might be; how tolerable life would become; what a fine escape from it all. The philosophies that hold this as central: drunk with the delusion that life is absurd, committed to absurdity to palliate death and pain, the extension of nothing to nothing. If all is nothing, I do not need to face my nothingness, do not need to look into myself, can laugh at the best and worst parts of myself, laughing only because I cannot tell the best and worst apart, cannot separate what I have from what I have not. The laugh of absurdity is only a hysterical giggle in the darkness—to render what is meaningful outside my power to see it into a universal nothing. Killing and destroying with envy, fear, and contempt the substance of those whom we hate because they live.

But it is not nothing, nor is it meaningless, and that is my pain. My emptiness is mine, the fault of no one else; I simply cannot choose otherwise. No, my little dealers in absurdity, there is more in life than you can face. An aged man is but a paltry thing, but powerful enough in his scarecrow majesty to confound your cheating and cheated vision.

("Stop working on me, Arnold. Let well enough alone. You missed your calling; you should have been a rabbi."

"Not my style."

"More than you think. Or at least a philosopher, the lens-grinding type. One pose is as good as another."

"Pose? What pose? Is that the way you beat me off? You can't fight above board?"

"I don't want to fight at all. Can't you see that?"

"You have too many rules. I was always a rule-breaker."

"All right. Then a simple question: Why do you want me to be someone else?"

"That's not what I want. If it looks like that it's because I have to guess—like a wild man."

"What do you mean?"

"You make me feel like a trespasser, like a fisherman sneaking a trout out of season. You walk; you talk; but who are you? Sometimes I have to invent who you are. You don't think that after all these years I'm entitled to ask you personal things?"

"I never ask them of you."

"*Nach.* I gave up an eye for an eye the day I left *schul.* I *want* you to ask me personal things. Who are you going to offend? Maybe you don't care? Maybe you're afraid? You understand what I mean? You don't let me come close. Every question about your life is like I put a noose around your neck and twist. So that's why I have to guess who you are. Maybe I'm wrong, always been wrong. How can I know?"

"Who have you made me?"

"Nobody. You just remind me of someone."

"Who?"

"He's dead."

"A dead man; it fits, why not?"

"I didn't mean it that way."

"Let me tell you, my friend, what's wrong with being a dead man? The only difference between me and all the other dead men in the world is my fingerprints."

"So kill yourself."

"You miss the point. I don't have to kill myself. Because I know I'm dead."

"You know something? You enjoy it. That's your pleasure in life."

"Pleasure? There's no pleasure."

"Are you God? You're above it?"

"You're an old fool."

"Adam, I'm afraid for you."

"Should I see a psychiatrist? Should I lie on a couch five days a week and examine my lesions? Well, I've thought of that."

"Then go, lie down."

"Thought of it for twenty-five years. I could give you a catalogue of reasons why I didn't go. Logical reasons. But I'm going to tell you the truth. Mark it down somewhere that you got a straight answer from Adam Gregory, something you don't have to guess. I never went because I was afraid of what I might find in those lesions. I would rather live as I do than take that chance. Mark it down, Arnold."

"What are you afraid of finding?"

"Let me set you a scene. A cellar, damp and musty, and there's a door at the bottom of it that you were never to open. One day the lock rots off and you remember how you were never supposed to look. You tremble, maybe the hairs on the back of your neck prickle up. You're going to open it, but you stand back from it, do it at arm's length. Maybe spiders will pour out or the stink of dead bones. Then you open it and look inside, and you freeze with horror. That's the scene."

"What's there? Behind that door?"

"Nothing, Arnold. Nothing at all.")

In the mess hall I saw a watery streak of blood escaping from my bandages. I blinked, looked again, but there was no blood, not a trace. I lost my appetite.

I was given some tests this morning. Ink blots. One image I saw still haunts me and perhaps there's material for a poem in it. It was black and deep, tones of black upon tones of black, a shadow with frayed, crumbling edges. As I stared, feelings of footlessness, falling. I held the table. The shadow grew before my eyes and I wanted to enter it, walk into it.

123

Shadow peeking at shadow of me,
Enter the darkness of light,
Washing wounds as Christ washed feet.

I dreamt of Arnold last night. I forgot the dream but I remember him—somewhere there. Or here. Perhaps even here.
Why does he pursue me? Why can't I tell him the truth and have him hear it as truth? Why won't he listen?
A letter: to be opened at the Second Coming.

Dear Arnold, my brother:
Why couldn't you allow me to be just another scribbler of verse? Why did you pay one thousand, four hundred, six dollars and eighty cents to publish a volume of my excretia? Perhaps the question should be: Why did I let you? Did you owe me something? If so, the debt escapes me. I could have vanished, ended up as a distant shadow that stirred some diffuse memory. I can't bear the burden of what you try to make of me; I go for the door and you block it. I try to tiptoe off and find you have chained cymbals and cowbells to my feet.
Not your fault, but I never really left home. I still remain in those five little circumscribed rooms, life beginning there, generating and flowing there, the outside purely an interim, an unreal interim, the part of my life that didn't matter. Inside, at that table, was all that importance and urgency from which I was omitted (by my own doing), that pay line, hoping to purchase Mama's smile and Papa's benevolent nod. Did you think that I could finally receive that smile, that nod, because you paid for the engraving of my name on a volume of senseless poems? I don't know. But I let you; I could never resist you—you, some strange mythical beacon more powerful than the Sirens. I hovered around you like a crippled moth. I believe you love me; I believe I love you; but your beacon is far from here and I cannot see its light.
I've repaid you—with merciless scalpels, with criticism, with strange pronouncements, capitalizing on the wisdom and power you have created, invented, attributed to me. Can't you take your own advice? Must you follow a drummer—one you've created—who really tells you what you can tell yourself? You're a follower; rebellious, yes, but a follower nonetheless, and no different from a poet who is afraid to sing directly and so sings through written words, once, even twice removed. You, my Arnold, turn people into poems; and you follow your own voice in the mouths of others.

A poet, you are—and a rescuer, too. But you rescue everyone, everyone from those five rooms to which you, too, are still attached, but in a different way from me. It required an amputated leg to set you free. Another repayment; another slap in the face.

Yet I cannot accuse you of practicing some black art. You made of me only what I wanted to be. You misjudged; the very practical part of you misjudged, because once I was given what I wanted, I no longer wanted it, could no longer use it. You can't make the dead walk.

You don't think enough. How many times have I tortured you with that? Well, don't listen. I wail from the misery of my immobility and stagnation; think, don't act, weigh issues, don't act. By thinking I mean no honorable thing, no higher process of man. By thinking I mean to say: Be afraid; crawl in fear; use thought in the service of ornamenting and prettifying self-disgust. Because I have myself firmly planted in those five rooms, symbolic of the only world I can understand, and I am afraid to leave them. And where once I saw them as holding me back from everything, I see them now as something to which I cling, something I despair of releasing. I am mired, held fast, in that war; I cannot exceed its boundaries.

If I could leave them, abandon them, then I, the dead man, would walk; you would have done your miracle. But I clutch them with more than one completely, entirely expendable leg; to free me would require endless amputations; and the shreds left would equal little of value. As it is, I am like a piece of ancient oriental pottery covered with deliberate tiny cracks carefully put in the surface. But that process has been lost, and hence a larger crack cannot be repaired.

So I stay there in the dimness of that room, on line, looking for the smile, hoping for the nod, and adjusting the broken stretchless elastic at the knee of my knickers.

—Yours, & etc.

I have lost track of the times I have wondered what I was doing here, in this uniform, pulling the trigger of a gun, aiming in the darkness at a dark enemy, myself assailed in the darkness. I find that I may be medically discharged. Unfit again even to die.

—Did you ever think of taking your life? the doctor asked.

—It was offered to me at birth and I didn't take it then. Why would I try now?

(He sat before Landau's desk, watching the scraggly gray tufts vibrating at the orifices of each ear.

"In exactly one year," Landau said, "I'm retiring. I've set myself a date finally."

"Sorry to hear it."

"Are you?"

"I imagine I am."

Landau rose and went to the window, patting his paunch with both hands, then tracing its perfect roundness with his fingertips.

"Last week I thought there was something in here. Woke with pain. Began to sweat. That was Monday. I found out what it was on Friday."

"What?"

"Gas." He smiled. "My father was a GP in Berlin. A poorman's practice, lots of petty clerks. If a patient complained of stomach pains, he used to say: 'Do deep knee bends; twenty. If you fart, go back to sleep. If not, you will come to my office immediately.' I wonder how that sounded in German?" He turned from the window. "Anyway, you get the idea?"

"No."

"Took me a week to check the gas. I was afraid I was going to die."

"Physicians always have peculiar attitudes toward death."

"They usually take a more constructive turn—like healing. I was willing to die rather than find the . . . 'truth.' That it was real—which it wasn't. But you see what I'm driving at."

"What will you say on your letter of resignation? Reason: gas"?

"No. Age. We'll leave it at that. Besides, it's the truth. It's time. So, what I asked you in for was to offer you my job."

"Why me?"

"Because you're ruthless—a necessity in this office. Aside from matters of competence."

"Ruthlessly competent?"

"That's good."

"Glad you liked it. I don't want your job."

"It's your last chance."

"For what? I never wanted your job."

"Last chance, period. You haven't published in years. And you're almost too old for the job now."

"Too old to be your protégé, anyway."

"You've squandered a great career."

"So have you, for that matter. One course, then sitting up here the rest of the time flapping applications. Why would I want to be little more than a high-school dean?"

"It's an important position."

"I don't want status; this profession stinks with it."

"I'm sorry."

"Are you?"

"Honestly? Yes."

"Landau, I don't want your job. I just do *not* want it."

"Fine. Settled. Why get angry?"

"I'm not angry."

"When a voice is raised, I assume anger."

"I don't like to be pushed."

"I wasn't pushing."

"Good-bye, Landau. I hope you find the right man.")

I am going to leave here, another mad poet loosed on the world. Beware, Arnold. I come to subvert you, to give you no peace, to remind you how much you possess and how little is mine. Hide.

I returned to the wreckage in the harbor and stared and wondered how many of them—caught with orange juice in their hands, a spoon of oatmeal in their mouths—are still down there. Lithe skeletons quivering in the salted winds of the sea. I see the truth of myself, what I am, have been, and know that down there they are no different from me. Fleshless, we quiver. I watch the water.

Water. Poor Keats, whose name was writ in it, was wrong. Truth is not beauty, nor beauty truth. I am the truth, and I am not beautiful.

Adam closed the ledger, slumped back into the corner of the sofa. How wrong Bernard Goldman had been—Bernard Adam Goldman Gregory. How wrong and yet how paradoxically correct. Arnold, who lost a limb and left and yet followed, the compliant rebel. Because now he knew that he and Bernard had fused in the tunnels of Arnold's brain.

But there was something, a clarity obscured by its dazzling simplicity, that Bernard Goldman had not seen. That Arnold had left those five dim rooms, yet spent his whole life trying to re-enter them. And Arnold never knew how hard he tried, knew only that Adam and his brother Bernard were the missing limbs.

Poor . . . Whose name was writ in it.

SEVEN

⚜ 1

When the doorbell rang Adam was playing chess by himself, keeping to some semblance of a poor, sloppy game, moving pieces into positions where they could easily be captured.

"Come in," he called, his throat rebelling at the words, rasped dead from smoking. He went on with the game even though Walter stood above him for several minutes. Then he moved the white king and, looking up, said, "Check. Wouldn't you say?"

"Check. Sure."

Adam met his eyes, his head thrown back, smiling mirthlessly. "Did you hear what I just said?"

"I heard you."

"I said 'Check. Wouldn't you say?' Arnold used to say that."

"I don't remember."

Adam laughed shortly, eerily. Then, with exaggerated care, he placed the chessmen in the compartments of a leather box, knowing that his slowness must annoy Walter; tucking the pieces away, one by one, side by side; but he didn't care; let Walter be annoyed. Somehow he had to do it as he was doing it, slowly and ritualistically. Finally, closing the lid, he leaned back and looked up again.

"Well?" Walter said.

"Well."

"Look, what are you trying to do to me? You want to slice me up like one of your bodies?"

"No."

"Then what about it?"

"I haven't given it much thought."

Walter slapped his palms together and said, "You haven't given it much thought. You just haven't *thought* about it."

"Neither have you."

Walter tried to speak, but he produced only a thin squeak deep in his throat, throwing up his hands in frustration and stalking about the room. Suddenly he whirled. "Why didn't you tell me before? The phone last night—you could have told me on the phone."

"I didn't have time."

"Doctor, am I shit? Am I such shit that you can't even take five minutes on a lousy telephone?"

"You're not the only human being with troubles."

"*You* have troubles? Sorry, sweetheart. You're the man who sees things straight; you're the man with the inside track on the world. I can't see your troubles."

"I'm sorry."

"Okay. Just give me a simple answer now. Yes or no?"

"No."

"Uh-*huh*. So that's that. What did you have, a real old-time religious experience? Flashing lights, thunder, the whole works? All of a sudden you get filled to overflowing with the spirit of life? Yes, sir and oh, boy."

"I was going to speak to Arnold . . ."

"Yeah, well he's dead. Sure, Arnold. You and Arnold. Think big, prod the mysteries of life. Sit around and talk about some war you weren't even in—sentiments and principles and causes. I listen but don't even get the courtesy of knowing the old man died. I listen about a war that wasn't mine, that I only read about—and even if I was old enough to be in it, they wouldn't let me."

"He talked about it, not me."

"Just another white man's war, Daddy, and you fought it all at your chessboard. But when the streets really run with blood, like now, like right under your nose, you just duck. You just take a fast freight back to Spain and duck."

"What are you talking about?"

"All about you."

"He wasn't like that."

"I said *you*."

"Are you trying to tell me something I don't already know?"

"Who, me? Not me. You know *everything*. Right before my eyes, in your infinite wisdom, you've turned humane and life-loving."

"That's not the reason."

"Okay, we'll just advertise in the *Times* for some eligible bachelor, hook him up with Luce, and they'll live happily ever after."

"I said there's nothing humane about it. I'll tell you something I *don't* know. I don't know anything. Can't you understand that? What you're asking me—I can't handle it. I don't know what to do about it, so I'm letting it alone. I'm ducking. You're right. I can't help you, Walter."

"Why? Just why?"

"I don't know. I see your point and then I don't see it at all. It has nothing to do with ethics or morality, any of that. Maybe it has to do with you. I've never let anyone badger me the way you do. "

"Makes no sense."

"Doesn't it? I don't know. Right now I just can't think of life and death and abortions. Your father wants the child; let him have it."

"My father's been senile since the age of reason. He's got some

131

muddy idea that doesn't check out any way you look at it, some Holy Roller mentality that's so confused in its simple-minded craziness that you can't even dope it out. Can't even come close. He can't see what it means—another drooling little nigger carrying out slops from a Harlem chitlin' house."

"The way you say 'nigger' sickens me."

"Why? Because what you really want to say to me is 'Get lost, nigger. Beat it'?"

"You really make me sick."

"Oh, that's right. I forgot. Among everything else you haven't got, you haven't got any attitudes toward niggers. You're color blind. What it really is, is I'm just like everybody else to you and so is my father—just one big blob of nothing. You don't even know I'm black. At least people who holler 'nigger' have a little blood in them. You're color blind, Doctor, because you can't even *see* the black. I bet you didn't know Arnold was a Jew either. We're all the same as your corpses. People are for slicing and explaining, but not for seeing or hearing. Well, I'm black; so look *at* me, not over me or around me, and stop measuring my heart for an incision."

"Please go, Walter."

"Not yet."

"I don't want to listen to this."

"You'll listen. You see, I could make you listen; I could beat you up. Because you're old and tired and you've had it; there's nothing left. You want it that way?"

Adam was retreating, felt it, searching for that place within himself, the soft cave in which he would find numbness and immunity; but now it was as if he had lost his maps and charts; the cave was harder to locate this time, or narrower, or less accessible. And then he could not find it at all. He listened, dazed and strangely panicked, afraid he might hear something that he had truly not known, become burdened with a knowledge he had forbidden himself because it would fetter and not free him. Almost reflexively he opened the leather box and removed the white king, surrounding it, hiding it, in his fingers, clutching until his knuckles blanched and a small cluster of sepia liver spots stood vibrant on the back of his hand.

"No," Adam said, eyes trained on the hand, the pain alive in his fingers. "I don't want it that way."

There was a pause, Walter staring, his eyebrows arched high, as if surprised that his threat had been taken so literally. Then he quickly faced away and said, "I want you to look at me because I want you to know what's so lousy about being black, because as long as you don't see me, you think of abstract crap like a bunch of slogans at a sit-in. It's not the lack of good schools or a decent suit of clothes; it's that a Negro can't dream big like you or Arnold. He can't dream except if he's on junk or maybe asleep. But he can't dream big awake. White kids can be president; a black kid can't even dream of being a cowboy. Maybe an Indian, only an Indian, and that gets him to the same place, nowhere. And he doesn't *have* to dream about nowhere because sooner or later he'll get there without a try.

"You're black and the only thing you can dream about is a certain kind of white man, the one with a house in the suburbs and a car and a charge plate at Saks. There are no wings on a black man's dreams; he can't think past what anchors everybody to the ground. And that's all he can dream of—the property scene and maybe a good school. Where he can learn to be shifty and how to cut his neighbors dead and to fear people because they're after what he has. And he can learn to love the great middle class and go to PTA meetings and get up plans to keep Puerto Ricans off the block. And he can learn to vote for the right people and try to stop unions from infiltrating the schools and sooner or later invent himself a Red menace. He can learn it all so fast your head will spin, and one day he'll find he's still a slave—of a different kind, in a different place. What the white man let him into is the white man's prison.

"There should be a better dream than that, but there isn't—and maybe *that's* too big. A Negro wants to have what isn't good enough for a white man: a cast-off society where a Negro will always be a step behind, never quite making that dead wingless dream; but the dream gets swollen, just because you can't grab it. You can move into a white neighborhood, and if you stick, one day you wake up and it's a black neighborhood. They give it to you for twice what it's worth and slip away some place where you

133

can't get in but where you feel you *have* to get in. And so it starts all over again, and then you begin to see something very clearly: You have to want whatever it is they don't want you to have. You never want something just because it's there; you want it because you're not supposed to have it."

"And you?"

"Me? Well, like my father says, I'm too big for my britches. My dream is on a canvas—no white, no black, nothing else except just Walter Ford. At the end of it all, I don't know what it is I want; but I have to have a dream, whatever it is. And the least thing I want in this world is to be called a *Negro* artist. I won't be reduced that way, like a good end man in a minstrel show. *I paint,* man. *Me.* I don't paint with black genes." He sat heavily on the couch and tapped his teeth with a knuckle. "Yeah, I know I'm loused up in contradictions. I'm black, but I won't be called a Negro artist; and I wish my old man was capable of even the most broken-down dream. But he's not; he's too scared to think of a steak, he's so rooted to chitlin's and second-hand chicken parts. He can't understand what Luce really is—never wanted to put her in a home, can't see what this baby . . . Every time I think of that it's like some weird idea that makes me feel I'm going crazy, like my mind is slipping away for good."

"He wants the child."

"*Wants.* It's crazy."

"It's *his* dream."

Walter said nothing for a time, then, "Thanks."

"Why do you want to deprive him of it? Is it just meanness?"

"I knew it. Somehow I knew if I started to talk this thing out it would end up this way, I'd drown in words. I knew I'd be swamped."

Adam released the chess piece; it has left deep purple dents in his fingers.

"But you made me feel like garbage," Walter said. "Not a word on the phone. Arnold dead, and who knew?"

"I'm sorry for that."

"It adds to the misery, Adam. —Listen, you ever talk to Annie?"

"Not often."

"Somebody gave her a picture of Jesus in blackface. She can't accept that; for her, it's all wrong, impossible. Do you know why? Why it scares the hell out of a Bible-thumper like her? Because when you get right down in the gutter, a Negro doesn't feel just economically or culturally deprived—some stupid phrase like that. And he can't buy that sex bit the headshrinkers run off at the mouth about. A Negro feels dirty is what it is—black is dirt. No matter how hip you are, how cool, that fact crawls around inside you, that *must be it*. Because, Doctor, everybody—*but everybody* —says so. Now if I straighten my hair, if I run right out to the drugstore and get that jar of skin whitener, I won't be dirty. I will be baptized white and pure into the human race. Then no one will accuse me of being a dope fiend and a rapist and a killer, which I have come to half believe I am—got that way by the process of birth. —Can Annie believe Jesus was dirty? That he was *bad?*"

"You . . ."

Walter waved his hand. "No, you don't have to enlighten me, because I see it plain and clear, because I don't want to be black, because I say 'nigger,' because I can walk down the street for maybe five minutes and feel just fine, and then I see a black man and he *reminds* me—and he can be a wobbly bum with a pint of horsepiss in his hand or a snappy dresser with an attaché case, and I still say 'Nigger, you've just ruined my day.'

"Years ago I used to wake up in the morning and indulge myself in a little magical thought: I'm not black; it's all a bad dream. I wake up now to find I have been white all along. And tease myself. Put on the coffee and fry up the eggs, and eat, and feel a little tenseness creeping up on me, like, what am I really going to find when I shave? And then I stand in front of the mirror with the razor in my hand and laugh at the whole fantastic business and say, 'Howdy, *boy*.'

"No, it's not really a feeling that I may have to run elevators or bus dishes all my life. You just can't scrub that color off, the color nice white people never ever mention when you're with them. You get tricked ten times a day, thinking it's not there. They don't talk about it; maybe it's not there? Who am I? At any given moment, who am I?

"Funny, but just now I remembered something—when I was about eighteen. I needed two bucks bad and I went down to the Met to be a super in *Aida*. The Ethiopian prisoners are always Negroes, but most of the time enough don't show up and they use white guys, paint them black from head to toe. In the dressing room after the second act, all I had to do was get out of my little loincloth, and there was this white guy in the shower trying to get his black paint off. He looked at me and like he was really agonized, and he said, 'You colored guys are lucky; you don't need to make up.' 'Yeah,' I said, 'yeah, yeah.' Everything to that guy, just for that minute, was relative to the stage, to *Aida*. Outside, where it's real, he wouldn't even remember saying it. I spent a lot of time in fairy-tale showers like that, scrubbing and saying to white men, 'You white guys are lucky. You can play Rhett Butler; you can even play W.C. Fields.'

"So Arnold always wanted to know why I can't get what he called 'committed'—whatever that means. Because I am not going to do anything for my *race*, that's why. I am going to do something for Walter Ford, who is very dirty but smart enough to know that skin whitener and split-level nightmares aren't going to do the job. There is no use in looking for the fountain of purity."

"You hate Negroes."

"Yes, Daddy, lots. Lots and lots. Civil-rights workers and Uncle Tommers—all in the same pot. And myself. Might as well throw me in too. Anyway, why should *you* be surprised? You hate white men and you're white. Except for white men it's called misanthropy; for me it's called a lack of commitment, self-loathing." He rose from the couch. "Luce can't have that baby. It's disgusting."

"Another reminder? Like the bum in the street?"

"Maybe. Maybe so."

"Let your father alone."

"No."

"You left his house years ago, by your own choice. You left his life. You have no say in it now."

Walter was silent, clenching and unclenching his fists, and Adam said, "You treat him like an empty-headed son."

"Only a fool heaps more misery on himself."

"He must get something out of the misery, something we can't see."

"You must be joking."

"All I know," Adam said, his fingers stroking the chess piece again, "is that if I were him—but the way I am—I'd want an abortion."

"I don't understand."

"Because"—meeting Walter's eyes—"because I'm not capable of understanding what the life of that child means, that it means something to your father no matter what happens to it someday. And I don't understand *his* life, what it is that makes his hands stretch out to clutch at something potentially alive. In his position I could only see the necessity of death; the necessity of life would escape me."

"I," Walter began, but he could not go on, suddenly sitting on the arm of the couch.

Adam said, "You're not yet thirty. Life must have some necessity for you. And me?" He examined the white king and finally stood it upright on the table. "Never having lived, what can I say to a man like your father?" He chuckled hollowly. "I don't care about the abortion. I'd do it. It wouldn't matter. But I'd be ashamed to look at your father. If I had just one idea of what it was all about, what I was all about, I'd face him."

"I'm sure you'd dent him."

"You see? That's the point. I *could* dent him. I really feel I could. And that's what I'm afraid of, that he couldn't stop me from doing this thing. Afraid no one could stop me. No one."

Aware that he was drifting off, that he could no longer communicate anything meaningful to Walter, he let his head sink forward like a massive weight on a broken spring, saying almost to himself, "What will you do?"

"I don't know. The way I feel—well, there's no sense talking about it any more. Take it easy, Adam. See you around the graveyard."

"Walter," he said, but he must have said it minutes later, because when he looked up Walter was gone.

✴ 2

Adam could not stand another assault because it was impossible to fight. For years he had lived in the expectation of attack, but he saw it now as a stance, an abstraction, a game he had created as a way of driving others away. And the attacks now—from Walter, from Joseph—were real, delivered directly at him, at vulnerable soft spots that began to open like dormant ulcers. This was no game; he was truly being assaulted and he could not handle it; he was weak, all his strength a suddenly tottering illusion.

He felt dangerously cast adrift, alone, hated, foundering; feeling that Walter had, consciously or not, hacked away the last cord that had anchored him to some rotten piling of a pier. His anger at Joseph Goldman had drained his supply, the last burst. The anger had not stirred with Walter; he had sat and absorbed punishment, and whatever he had said, anything sensible or reasonable, had been squeezed from him with unbearable effort, with hesitance and tenseness.

Caught on a light breeze, a curtain stirred, trembled into the room. He turned toward it almost as if expecting something to appear at the window; like a cheap horror film, the specter's entrance announced by the sudden snap of a lock, a tinkling of glass, French doors blown apart, the draperies billowing, flowing. Then the breeze died; the curtains fell quietly back against the sill. Yet he had turned quickly, eagerly, a spasm, and now his fantasy of something supernatural became only slightly less unreal, thinking that Arnold might come tapping through the door, the door exploding from its hinges. Squinting, he could almost see him, saying again, as he had said prophetically almost a month before his first heart attack: "I find myself thinking of death."

"Why?"

"It must be premature old age. I woke up this morning and my thoughts were full of it."

138

"Why now?"

"I don't know; I can only guess. It hasn't happened in years. Maybe because everything seems good."

"I don't understand."

"Maybe I don't want to lose what I have. Maybe. Maybe I want something I can't get."

"I'll make some coffee."

"I could use some coffee."

When comfort was wanted, when understanding and confrontation were asked for, he had offered coffee. On his way to the kitchen to plumb the humanity of the coffee tin, he had touched Arnold's arm, felt it. The solidity beneath his fingers negated death: the arm was whole; Arnold was sitting there alive—as Adam wished he were sitting there now, his eyes squinting at the vacant chair.

He had touched the arm to deny death, the magical touch of flesh a wish for immortality.

But Arnold had pressed on. "I let myself grow flabby—in the head, everywhere." And when Adam had plugged in the coffee pot and returned to the living room, Arnold said, "You won't laugh if I tell you something?"

"No."

"I'm going on a peace march."

"Where?"

"Down Fifth Avenue to the Mall in Central Park. Do you think I'm foolish?"

"No."

"But you're thinking: How is what I just said—what does it have to do with thinking about death?"

Adam nodded.

"So I'll tell you something profound: I don't really know, but it does. Last night I couldn't sleep, and when I can't sleep it means something is eating at me. But last night I couldn't see what it was. I sat and stared like a *mishugah*, and then it all came clear to me. I had no investment any more in anything outside of my four walls. I retired early in my life to do the things I always wanted to do. So what happened? I just sat down and reread my old books and remembered old memories, and there it was. I didn't have a past that entitles me to just sit and reflect on it. What's there to reflect on? Somewhere back there, God knows, I stopped living; I was dreaming awake. I read the paper in the morning; it could be fiction. Where is myself in this fiction?"

"It's not true what you're saying."

"It's true. I got to a certain age, I laid down with my memories; but I see that all my memories are just wishes, dreams of how it should have been, how I could have changed it. My life stopped—maybe after Spain, maybe after Auschwitz, I don't know. Seeing it start all over again, everything was going the same way all over again, I crawled into bed with my wishes.

"I was so guilty when I didn't go to Spain I actually thought of becoming a Communist. Repentance. The little boy in Russia on top of that cabinet. My common sense stopped me from that; I couldn't destroy my family or myself. But I thought of becoming a Communist even when I knew, right here in front of my brain, that I hated their GPU and NKVD, that Stalin made my hair stand up. You see? I'm crazy. Because all the while I also knew that I would never join them. So why did I think it? Besides the guilt, I'll tell you why. It excited me. I could get people very excited. I could be me, Arnold Goldman, a walking controversy. For a hundred years I could scream and make fists about some cause, good or bad, and then make it all into a dream."

"Arnold, don't talk like this. You're punishing yourself for no reason."

"*Nach*, it's all a lie. Do you know what a liar I am, what a mouth I got? I wanted to change the world. That was the first lie I told myself, the first illusion. But I can say, well, I could have changed it—if I didn't have this leg, my wife, my children, a size fifteen collar. I could never satisfy myself that I was just a man, that I could do something but not everything. You know what? You can always aim high as an excuse for hitting nothing. You aim high; you miss; and then you fall down and break and look that somebody should pick up the pieces and glue you up again. —Anyway, I'm not punishing myself; I'm telling myself the truth.

"And the second lie? I wanted to die a hero, die bravely—

sometimes I think I was born with a Spanish temperament. That was on my mind when I wanted to go to the war, not fighting to win as much as dying with some banner in my hand. Isn't that funny? Another repentance. And for what? Why are all my penances ways to hurt myself? If I knew what, I wouldn't have to dream of dying as if it was some great accomplishment. Because one thing I know now. I tell you this: Dying stinks. The dying you can't help is bad enough, but the dying you go to meet like a whore in a hotel room with VD, it stinks. Because when I was thinking about it today, it struck me all of a sudden; the understanding came through my window on the rays of the sun. I don't care how I die. I can get hit by another trolley car, fall off a ladder, die from a chicken bone in my throat, or from a mosquito bite. They can do anything they want with my body. Say *kaddish* over it or throw it in the gutter. Who's going to care? Me? What matters is the way I live, not the way I die. Only the way I've lived."

"You've lived well."

"Not to my satisfaction. I lost myself some place. I'm going to find myself now, before I *do* care how I die."

"In a peace march?"

"You *do* think I'm foolish."

"I didn't mean it that way."

"Anyway, yes, in a peace march. For the first time to do something without thinking of dying, or what cause it fits into, or to play around with it. Just one real thing Arnold Goldman can do—not as a Loyalist or a member of the NAACP. Just one thing to make the blood run in my veins, to feel it inside of me, not to shed it in a dream. I want all my blood in *me*; I'm not giving it and I'm not letting anyone take it. I'm just going for a walk—for *me*. Because that's what I can really do—walk. I'm a good walker; I can walk miles. I can't change the world, but I can walk in it. If I saw that years ago . . . Well, I didn't. So now I'm going for a walk."

"You talk as if your life has been a total loss"

"Total loss? *Nach*, total loss. Who said anything about a total loss. I have Esther, my children—if they'll have me. No, not a

141

total loss in that direction. In other directions, well, maybe not a *total* loss ... "

You have Esther, Adam had thought; and thinking it now, he felt that it was she they had talked of, not wars and death, not purely Arnold's self-scorn, his torment and disappointment. Possessing her, somehow one's vision expanded; in her light a personal salvation was possible. But he possessed no Esther, and yet just once he might have come close, in Hawaii, sharing some bleak part of an island with Bernard Goldman—a nurse whose hands touched his one day in surgery; finding her fingers when he had asked for a knife, and even through the gloves he had felt a tremble of emotion. Both lonely, they came together, but he killed her with his loneliness, drove her away with his fear, his accusations that he was not worth loving, that she hadn't the strength to love him. And eventually she came to believe him; even in bed with him, or because of it, she came to believe his conviction that one day she would leave him, that he could not hold her. She vanished into the velvet obscurity of all the other women he had known or touched. He had forgotten her name, her face.

And Arnold had said, "Will you take a walk with me?"

And he, "No. —No."

Rising now, he glanced at the various places where Walter had stood or sat, then went to the bathroom for Seconal. He paused by the mirror, his hand on the knob of the medicine cabinet, thinking: Through an almost occult power he had assumed Arnold's characteristics and mannerisms as easily as he might borrow his raincoat; knowing it when he had used Arnold's checkmate phrase, when he had grinned coldly at Walter. And the limp, the delusional pain in his chest when he had thought of Esther, Arnold's pain, the pain that streaked through his dying. Arnold had somehow entered him, and he gazed into the mirror wanting to find more of him.

But instead he saw the dour features of an old man, yet miraculously preserved, as if someone had long ago placed him into an airtight jar, snapped a rubber ring in place, screwed on the lid, and set him on a shelf—yet not like a specimen trapped in the smells of a laboratory—something that reminded him more of plums and rhubarb in the must of a cellar.

He might have been fifty, sixty, six hundred; he was gazing at his father in the glass, the compressed forehead dissected by a thick scarlike furrow, his jowls grouted deep by lips perpetually turned down at the corners. And more than simply the features and lines, the entire set of the face, the imperviousness and scorn. His father presenting himself to the world, his portrait.

He turned from the mirror, pressing the small of his back against the sink, blinking, as if all the while he had been standing behind his father, as if his own face were not to be found in the mirror but projected on the blank wall. Perhaps that was what Joseph Goldman had sought during his dialogue with the wall: himself. Or Walter, when he had turned to the window. And then Walter's words: *See you around the graveyard.*

A graveyard was where his father was supposed to be, not in the reflection of his face, a graveyard in the hills of the Berkshire Mountains. Suddenly it was necessary to see him, the spot where he lay immunized and perpetuated by a monument of stone.

He laughed, cringing the moment his mouth opened; but he could not stop, and finally muffled his voice with a towel.

EIGHT

❦ 1

He had almost broken the date with Barbara Ramsey; he had twice begun to call her, each time cradling the phone, the last after dialing only the first two numbers. He had projected his miserable mood that far ahead, foreseeing more convoluted talk, more confusion, more unnecessary burdens. In a fleeting moment of intense bitterness he wondered what she wanted from him, almost hearing Lester's philosophizing voice: "Now when a white chick eyes a big black buck, why all she wants . . ." Except that he had called *her*, had made the first move from the start, and he was no big buck; and yet he felt a strange urge to mobilize anger toward her, to cast a deep pall on what was simply an ordinary date. The only threat to its banality might be a quizzical stare, a sidelong glance; but he knew that no one would stare; Thursday was not visitor's night in the Village.

He was always angry at the wrong things, he decided; because somehow he was unable to find an object he could focus on without equivocation or reservation, and the anger swelled and oozed out of him like paint from a tube trod on by a heel, and he ended up by splattering himself. Part of the anger he tried to direct at Barbara sprung from his realization that he had called her because he needed her; but when he examined the need, he had no idea if it existed because she was a white woman or simply a woman.

And then he switched it. He began to mistrust her quick acceptance; perhaps she had flung out some subtle bait and he had snapped and was gaffed and she would play with him. But he repudiated the thought; if he needed it, he was placing himself almost beyond humanity, denying his manhood; there were enough people who tried that on him; he didn't need it as his own invention. Yet perhaps he believed it, because he knew that if he let himself, he could build suspicion to the point where he would listen not to her words but, like a third-eared psychoanalyst, ferret out hidden meanings in every syllable, wedging them into a theory whose only maxim was that you must hear only what you wanted to hear, eventually forcing her to accept a position in which he needed to place her. It was a simple theory, and the rules of its practice even simpler: Kindness was patronizing; fondness masked manipulation. Always the given and self-assumed fact that he was an animal in a zoo without visible bars, under constant observation. With such a theory it was impossible to lose.

And then he had gone to that damned analyst. Only nine sessions, not even prone on a couch, but enough time to lose a centimeter or two of head. After hearing the theory, the analyst had said, "It sounds as though you're really saying it's impossible to win. As though you say to yourself: 'With my belief in how people are, I can always know that their rejection of me is only a matter of minutes. And the closer I listen, the quicker I can get that first clue; and then I can reject *them*. I'm the rejecting one then, the powerful one. I know their game; I won't be hurt.' But what you really feel—and I think this is very much conscious—is a fear of getting close to them, a fear that you may be accepted, not only rejected. An acceptance you can't face for some reason. Perhaps because you need the power you somehow link up with rejection, with the rejector. Perhaps because to you to be an equal in any relationship means to be inferior." And he had answered, "I'm a black man in a white world." And the analyst, "I'm not talking about white people, Mr. Ford. I'm talking about *people*."

He had left; paid his bill and left; not because he doubted the man's competence, because he violently disagreed, but because the interpretation had jolted him with the electric force of a spinal tap. The structure of his theory had cracked; he did not want it to crumble; he needed it too often.

But the trouble was, he could not repair the crack. The interpretation had tiptoed through his mind when he met Barbara that evening at the dorm, and he resolved to listen less intently, play it easier. He had too many troubles to create more. She looked slightly bedraggled, but after a bottle of wine and a plate of lamb wrapped in grape leaves, she came to life; and when they went to his loft for coffee, she became almost excited, clapping her hands like a child because the elevator of the old factory building opened directly onto his studio. She threw her raincoat on a chair and began to cock her head at his paintings while he made coffee in the kitchen alcove. After a time she called out, "I don't know a damn thing about art, but I've never seen such fantastic color." He didn't answer and she said, "Walter? Is that the wrong thing to say?"

"You should see them in daylight." He caught the contentment in his voice, realizing that she had complimented him, concentrating on the color and not troubled by the absence of recognizable objects. "Some people get upset, quote because they don't look like anything, a nice horse or tree."

"Who cares about a horse? I can't keep my eyes off the color."

He grinned; non-artists were rarely attracted to the paint itself. With an air of celebration, a flourish of his arm, he poured two small glasses to the rim with brandy.

"My God," she called, "what's *this?*"

"You found it. I should have hidden it."

147

"What *is* it?"

He stacked a tray with the coffee pot, cups, brandy, and glasses, and carried it out to the studio. She was staring at a large unfinished canvas on which had been glued a blow-up of a red Honda motorcycle. Perched on the seat was the Kellogg tiger, his teeth clamped on an ear of corn with a woman's bust, her upraised hand holding the torch of the Statue of Liberty.

"I thought I might make a buck on it. I gave it up a long time ago."

"Thank God," she said seriously.

"I like you. You know what you're talking about."

"Like how?"

"Your remark about color."

"But I told you I don't know anything. I don't even know enough to know what I like."

"You know more than you think. Ten dollars say you'd go wild in a museum."

She wrinkled her nose at the Honda, then sat on his bed, made up like a couch with a corduroy cover and heaped with pillows. He put the tray on an old paint-spattered table and sat next to her, watching her face; it was almost clouded again by the vaguely tattered expression.

"Something the matter?" he said. "With museums?"

"No. I'm just reminded that I'd rather be in one. Or anywhere else, for that matter." She looked quickly at him. "I don't mean here, now. I mean, I think I want to quit school."

"Had enough of the medical establishment?" He poured the coffee, then leaned back and examined her profile: strong determined lines, almost harsh, which miraculously softened and became slightly childlike when she turned full face.

"Walter, I don't know what it is—not really. I feel blah. Just like the girl sitting on the wall at school said."

"The bodies?"

"Not just that. Somehow I can't get with any of it any more; it's soured. It's like I've exhausted whatever dole of energy I had for it. I'm tired."

He tacitly agreed; small lines laced the corners of her mouth, vanishing as she drank some coffee, then chased it with a sip of brandy.

"It'll pass," he said. "These things never last too long. I wish I had a dime for every time I wanted to stop painting."

She waved toward a painting and said, "But see what you can look at when you feel that way."

"On certain days it's when I look that makes me want to quit."

"What makes you hold on?"

"A pot of gold at the end of a rainbow."

"Money?"

"No. That's only a possibility, the way you bet on a long-shot horse just because you like its name. Some other kind of gold. Who knows what? What's in your pot?"

"It's empty." She was silent for a time, then raked her teeth across her upper lip and turned to him, her profile shading, melting into softness. "I've come a long way from putting splints on a pussycat's leg. Grumkin was her name; never did break her leg but I taped her up anyway. The fact is, I'm having the kind of daydreams I had when I was fifteen. They're all about rose-covered cottages—oceans of roses—and wearing an apron and making supper, hearing the front gate creak, and rushing out to meet *the* man." She blushed fiercely, jerking her head away. "I mean they're just that way—no subtlety, no sophistication. Just like that. Some professor starts to talk about bones or catheters, and I'm gone. The notebook turns blank and I dream and I can't get back to the lecture until it's over; and I haven't got a word written down." She pursed her lips and suddenly rapped a spoon against her cup. "I want to be a little girl, or at least something female. Look at me: straight dark skirt, a sweater like a sack. On Sundays I go through the *Times* and ogle all the dresses with lacy edges. And then I study, just as I used to, hour after hour, and my mother telling everybody that Gray's Anatomy was a guidebook for the bagging of a rich medical student. It could be that's the real reason I went to med school."

"You sound like you were sent."

"No. Yes. It's all mixed up and I'm weary; and the wearier I get, the more I dream my adolescent dreams. I think to myself:

149

apply for a leave. But then I know I'll never come back because down deep I want to quit."

"Can't you be female and a doctor at the same time?"

"No."

"No one?"

"Me. *I* can't. A woman is different from a man by absolutely irrefutable facts of biology, chemistry, and visual inspection. But a woman—all right, maybe just me—a woman can only feel like a woman if a man lets her or makes her feel it. I simply can't go out any more with medical students. I don't want to talk medicine a hundred hours a day, not when just once or twice a week I want to feel like a girl and not a member of our country's most honored profession. Oh, and then there was the young man who put his arm around me and before he even smiled at me asked if I used a diaphragm or took Enovid. Very seriously. Everybody, but *everybody*, has been in school too long. I'm dying of school."

"Are you really serious? Not one man treats you like a girl?"

"No, just as an inferior. Maybe it's my fault. Probably is. The loneliness I told you about, it's in my blood. Maybe I want too much; maybe I beat them off. —Look, I should shut up. This is one hell of a pleasant evening I'm giving you."

"You are."

"Well, when you called me, I said to myself: Girl, this is no schoolboy. This is one guy who isn't going to see me as a competitor or a nothing. A guy who might understand that I want to get out of this business without accusing me of selling out. A guy— forgive me, because I guess I *must* have planned it this way— who'll let me unload."

"Forgive you? I'm flattered."

"And I'm sorry."

"Don't be." He poured more coffee. "I know how you feel. You're a little like me—always involved with people you can't unload to, so you carry it around like a lead sinker. I once went to a shrink to unload; trouble was, he dumped my mess right back on me. That I can get anywhere. The way we're different is that I just want to dump—period. Don't want any comment back, any advice. Just an angry, sore-as-hell dumping." He nodded, then, "I read a book once. Negroes are supposed to be more aggressive." He said it to snap a cord of tension he had felt stretching painfully through him; irrational or not, he had needed to say it, say that she was white and he was black, as if she could not see it, or worse, that she had seen quite clearly and was doing something intensely personal and strange with the information. Yet he also regretted saying it and actually nibbled at his tongue, saddened that his attempts to clear the air only cluttered it.

"Yes," she said. "Well, I read a book that said men are supposed to be more aggressive than women."

If there was innuendo in her remark, he could not grasp it; then he drove it out of his mind and said, "You want advice?"

"You said that as though I asked you."

"I thought you did."

"All right, advise me."

"Have another drink."

"You want me to quit school, don't you?"

"Why do you say that? How could I possibly have an opinion about it?"

"Be illogical."

"I don't know you well enough to say anything about it. I have no idea who you really are, or what would happen if you quit. I don't even know what would happen if you *didn't* quit."

"I won't be bound by what you say. Just say something."

"All right, quit. Don't ask me why."

"Why?"

"Because I think it's what you wanted me to say."

"Was that the advice you had in mind?"

"Maybe."

"I'll have that other drink."

Smiling, he said, "I don't want to lug home a lush." He refilled her glass, them hammered the cork into the bottle with the side of his fist.

"So I'll sleep here."

She kicked off her shoes, tucked in her legs, and leaned her head back against the pile of pillows. He tried to appraise her expression, holding his thoughts in abeyance, and, like a boy counting cracks in a sidewalk, decided that if she kept her profile toward him, what she wanted was sex; if she turned to him, she simply wanted company for her loneliness.

Not turning, she said, "It would be lovely, just once, to get up in the morning and have coffee with someone who was right there with you. No dressing up to the teeth, no cafeteria line. Just to sit for an hour and wake up into yourself, not into a robot."

"You *do* have a powerful loneliness, don't you?"

"Didn't you believe me?"

"Funny. There are mornings I get up and run outside and deliberately eat in a cafeteria, just so there are people around."

She tilted her glass against her chin and dribbled the brandy through her lips. "*Can* I sleep here tonight?" And when he didn't answer, she said, "What are you thinking?"

"I'm thinking *no*."

"What's the thought behind that thought, O aggressive male? Anyway, no murderous thoughts. I haven't felt so comfortable and good for years. God knows, I'm ripe for seduction; but that isn't what I had in mind." She laughed brightly, then finally faced him. "I think I read that somewhere. I think we read too much."

"It didn't sound like you."

"It isn't me, at least not that glibly. But honest to God, I would like not to get up to those four institutional walls and the institutional grind. A few weekends ago I rented a hotel room just to fold, mutilate, and spindle the routine. But it didn't do much good; there was nobody with me. No, I don't belong in this business. I belong married to someone, a membership in the Book-of-the-Month Club, those roses . . ."

"You'd get sick of it."

"Sure, I would; I know that. I'd want to walk out on that too. It'd be too much like my family, the ones who sit around."

"Is it always so extreme with you?"

"Always. The way I daydream now, you know? If the daydream turned real I'd dream about something else—quick. Maybe even medicine. I want both, I guess, but I'm scared I can't ever have both. One thing though, I've been a medical student even if I've never been in love."

"You have."

"Never."

"Like the song goes—in love with love."

"Of course. How about you?"

"I don't think so."

"Everybody is."

"Not like you. Roses? In Harlem, the Village? Maybe that's what's in the pot of gold at the end of my painting, but I doubt that too. I have no dreams about it."

"Let me give you a few of mine," she said, leaned suddenly toward him and kissed his cheek.

He snapped his head away and stared at her, wanting to be enraged, unable to. Softly, he said, "Don't come too close."

"You don't want me to like you. Why?"

"Like me all you want, but not that way. I don't want your daydreams; I don't want my back broken." He left the couch and stood almost halfway across the room. "I don't belong in your rose patch, and I don't want to be your buffer against that God-damn school."

"All I did was kiss you. Friends *do* kiss."

"Sure, and they also want to sleep in your pad. Look, are you nuts? Do you think I could sleep a minute without wanting to crawl in the sack with you? And what would I find there? Rosy cottages, a creaky gate, and a kiss on the cheek? I'm not saying you're bitchy or two-faced, anything like that. We're both lonely. Except let's not feed off it. You invite me into those daydreams of yours, I accept, we're both through. I mean, coffee in the morning, all that. How long would it be before you needed to change my color? Take a look. It's black, and I'll make you see it, and I'll never let you forget it. And once you get the message, what's left for me? Waiting around until I become your private, white man's burden? Both ways it's crazy. I'd look really natural swinging through that gate in Darien, Connecticut—or absolutely in place picking you up at the hospital."

"Did I say one word about living with you or loving you? Or anything like that?"

"No. —No, you didn't."

"Then just shut up." She turned her head, then quietly said, "I know I'm an idiot for kissing you, for wanting to sleep here.

Somehow I didn't want it to be a date, you know? A *date*. I wanted to say or do anything I pleased. I just thought you'd accept it, let it go."

"I don't want to be felt safe with. Didn't you say that only a man can make a woman feel like a woman? Okay, so I want to feel like a man, not a big brother who'll tuck you in and peck at your forehead."

"Make up your mind, will you? Anyway, that's another thing I never said." She sat on the edge of the couch and slipped on her shoes, saying, without looking at him, "Well, anyway, Mr. Ford, you tried to read my mind, and I don't like it read because that's cheating. Of course I had sexual fantasies about you, and you knew I did, so what is it for you to expose them, a triumph? I just thought how nice it would be to lie in your arms, in your bed, and let whatever happened happen. I *have* done it once or twice before; it doesn't altogether repel me. If you want to keep away from me, it's not my fault; and God knows it isn't my wish. Only it would have been nice just to act like people."

"Why me? For God's sake, why me?"

"Just because."

"That's not good enough."

"Then you'd better find out why. It should be plenty good enough."

She rose and was almost past him when he seized her arm and twisted her toward him. He began to speak, but she cut him off.

"At least tell me one thing. Why, when both of us want it, can't we have it together? Why do you have to break what might be into little pieces? Break it and smash it up before it can even get started?"

"Because *I* don't want to break."

"But you are. A little twig at a time. And one day you'll be cut in two and swear it never happened."

"You don't know what it's like. You can't know."

"I'm seeing it now, aren't I? Right this minute? Seeing it work? And don't pull a Negro thing on me because you'll just be talking to yourself. If it's your way out, take it; I don't want to know from it."

Looking into her eyes he saw her honesty and wanted to grout

154

it out and crush it to bleeding dust between his fingers; she was
going to make him cry; he felt it, the scalding in his throat.

He said, "All right. You can stay. You can sleep here. But no
daydreams. No commitments."

"Just a pair of bodies."

"Yes, that's all—a pair of bodies. You go your way, I go mine.
When we come together, then it happens. No more. No tenderness
or compassion or Hollywood crap. Just convenience."

"Right now I had another one of my fantasies. That I could go
back to the lab and cut into a corpse as well as Gregory ever did.
Maybe better. Right now, maybe a damn sight better."

He loosened his fingers and she left him, took her coat from the
chair, and entered the elevator. After a time he sat on the edge of
the couch, plucked the cork from the brandy, and drank from the
bottle. And before the meaning of his fury could crystallize, he
bolted up, still clutching the bottle, and kicked a hole in the painting she had admired. Finally he seized a torn strip of canvas and
ripped it down, dropping it like a rag to the floor.

❧ 2

Pounding the door panel with the flat of his fist, Walter
clenched his teeth, for a moment afraid he would rouse the entire
block; then wallowed in his half-drunken freedom and pounded
again, the plywood buckling, almost cracking.

And then a shrill, but muffled voice, "Who's there? What do
you want?"

"Sur . . ." Almost losing the word in the twist of his thickened
tongue. He lurched against the door jamb, steadied himself. "Surprise!" he bellowed.

"Who?"

"It ain't a Cadillac and it ain't a Buick . . ."

"It's a Ford!"

A chain grated, the door swung open, and he strained to see the
dark face against the darkness of the room; he caught the gleam of
silver fingernails clutching a fold of sequined robe.

The voice said, "Well, damn *me*."

"Dark girl, put on some light. I can't hardly see you."

He staggered through the door, she sidestepping in time to avoid a collision; and he bumped into the opposite wall. He heard the door close, the chain, then felt an arm around his waist and let himself be led into another room.

Sitting, focusing his eyes, he saw her sitting on the corner of a sofa-bed, then smiled thickly and waved. "Loretta. Hello there, old Loretta."

"I'll 'hello there' *you*, come busting in on me first time in a year, two o'clock in the morning, and drunker than hell. What you want, Walter?"

"A drink."

"You drunk enough."

"Shee-*it*."

"You going to be high and mighty? You out to make fun of me, Walter? You going to make fun of me, you best get out of here right now."

"Ah 'pologizes."

"You keep on, I'm going to pick up this lamp and swat it off your head."

"Sorry. —Look, let me have a little something wet. I'm not that drunk. Mostly tired."

"You sure?"

"Yeah."

"All I got's some gin."

"Any ice?"

"It ain't hard yet. Takes a month in my fridge."

"No ice is just fine."

She took a squarish bottle from a table next to the bed, hooked a finger into a glass, rose, and poured for him. He drank a bit, gagged, coughed, then set the glass on the floor.

Sitting on the bed again, she said, "What do you want with me, Walter?"

"I won't put you on, Loretta. Come right to the point. I'm never going to put a nickel on a white man's word again. Him speak with forked tongue. What do you think of that?"

"It sure took you a long time to figure *that* out. I guess you just come by to tell me that?"

156

"No. I am only a big black jackass." He extended two fingers above his head and wiggled them, then tried to bray.

"Hush up! The Goddamn cops'll bust in here, you hollering like that."

"No cops, no cops. Listen, okay? You remember Florence or Frances, whatever her name is, and that boy friend of hers? The orderly? Fellow used to get Lester the goofballs and do the abortions?"

She squinted, said nothing, slipping a cigarette from a crumpled package on the table. She struck a match, inhaled, then leaned back on an elbow.

"Well?" he said.

"Frances. Yeah, I remember."

"I got to look that man up."

"Herman."

"Herman? *Herman?* Christ!" He giggled, then, "Where's he at?"

"What you want him for?"

"An abortion. Where can I get him?"

"Don't know. Ain't seen him around. She puffed on the cigarette almost as if she were eating it, then sat up stiffly, her voice edged with anger. "You knocked somebody up, didn't you? Knocked somebody up and you come around here. Walter, you a good-for-nothing son of a bitch."

"I didn't knock anybody up. If you have to know, somebody put it to my sister."

She stared.

"Yeah, yeah," he said. "Don't look so whacked out. *That* sister. I ain't got no other sisters."

"Jesus," she half whispered. "It ain't a fit world for a pig to live in. A girl like that."

"Amen. That's exactly what I figured. So can I get in touch with that man?"

"Walter, I don't know where he is, but there's somebody else'll do it."

"Thank you, Loretta."

"Sounds like you mean that."

"I do."

She tore a strip from the edge of a newspaper and scribbled with an eyebrow pencil. She came to him and pushed the paper into his shirt pocket, saying, "Call that number I wrote. You tell her, 'Harold's got to work overtime,' then give your phone and wait till they call back."

" 'Harold's got to work overtime.' "

"Yeah, that's it."

"So easy, isn't it?"

"Ain't anything to it. Only don't use my name."

"I mean, it's just so effing easy." He grinned savagely. "Just like that."

"Who done it to her?"

"Don't matter, does it?"

He tried the gin again, then gave it up and returned the glass to the floor; as he straightened up, he ran his hand along her calf and thigh, resting it in the socket of her hip. She looked down at him, imperious but soft as the hip; then as he circled her waist, her expression grew even softer, the haughtiness purely an ineffective wish, and then that, too, vanished into a vague sadness while she rested her wrists on his shoulders.

"Why'd you go away?" she said.

"I don't know."

"Staying this time?"

"Yeah." He moved his hand from her waist, stroking the small of her back, feeling for the softness beneath the robe.

She urged him out of the chair and they lay on the bed, she saying with a tone as unconvincing as her cold stare, "I really guess I shouldn't, the way you . . ."

He began to fondle her ear lobes, then reached out and fumbled with the lamp, finally switching it off.

She said, "It sure is good to have you back. Don't matter how bad you are. Just good to have you back."

"Well, this is really where I belong, now ain't it?"

And when his throat began to clog, he quickly turned to her and pulled open her robe.

158

NINE

✻ 1

On Saturday morning, wedged into a small rented car, Adam drove out on the Taconic Parkway, following the arrow marked UPSTATE. He began to pick up speed. Because he had not driven for years, he had been careful, almost overcautious on the more crowded city streets and parkways; but now he held the car between fifty-five and sixty and leaned back less tensely. His mind was clamped as tightly as his hands on the wheel, needing at least that much control, feeling that instead of driving he was being driven to Massachusetts, as if his car were inside a larger vehicle, his steering and braking the useless actions of a child sitting in a toy carseat at a toy wheel aping the motions of his father. Driven along the twisting ribbon of parkway by some emotional force he was half afraid to admit, yet sought to hold firm, his brain rooted into it like teeth; knowing that if he examined it, dissected it, it might dilute, disintegrate. And he would be left a fool, driving purposelessly halfway to nowhere under a broken roof of trees, the toy wheel still a toy, but the reliable father gone. A heap of blistered smoldering tin crushed against the trunk of some tree, a pop-art gravestone.

He rolled his window full down and inhaled the air: light and fresh, a medium inviting and sweetening travel, a voyage through it, not palpably heavy as in the city, suffused with murderous acrid and sour stenches with a grainy texture that fought his lungs and eyes. He breathed deeply again, yet immediately lighted a cigarette, somehow reminding the air that he was an alien, that his body must reject its promise of cleanliness and sanity. The cigarette perched between his lips, it burned smokeless in the rush of the wind; yet he squinted from habit.

Soon, strained by almost two hours of driving, he turned off the parkway into a state campground, eased the car along a narrow road, then cut the engine outside a log-cabin restaurant. Inside, he sat with a cup of coffee at a crude plank table cut to match the cabin, hacked out in an attempt to wedge all the pieces into the natural pattern of the surrounding woods. In several places the table was etched with initials, the deepest of which he felt, then traced with a forefinger.

Leaning back, he observed several couples, young, dressed in slacks and sweatshirts emblazoned with academy and college seals; one broad athletic chest was adorned with the scowling face of Beethoven. Students, he guessed, heading for promising weekend dates, freedom from parents meaning freedom of sex, the fifth freedom; fresh, bright faces redolent of soap and toothpaste. One couple, joltingly different, almost bizarre in the setting of the cabin, caught and held his eyes, and he furtively watched above the rim of his cup. They seemed in their late twenties, dressed almost in deliberate defiance of the logs and planks and rolls of bark: the man in a dark gray suit, white shirt, striped tie, sitting opposite a girl with the face of a secretary or junior editor, half-cooked on lunchtime martinis. A pleasant face framed by dark hair which hung, teased at the ends, below her ears, all well in place, groomed and polished with special care. Yet it was a bit damaged by the tender purplish crescents of a sleepless night, supporting heavy, weary, lusterless eyes. Her mouth was turned down; at the tip of her nose, the small red blotch of a recent cry.

They toyed with the ears of their cups, between them an untouched pair of sugared doughnuts atrophying on a strip of wax paper. They did not speak, did not look at each other; two hostile armies unwilling to enter the no-man's land separating them. Adam thought: *As if.* As if they were together; as if one word mumbled by either would shatter the world like a crystal globe with a hidden defect; as if the sugar of the doughnuts were the poison in a suicide pact about to be forfeited, the forfeiture creating a deeper disillusionment than life. He watched; and soon the man leaned toward her and said, voiceless but with a precise movement of his lips, *I'm sorry.* She shot him a look of utter contemptuous disgust, hatred, a brutality of expression that accused, judged, and condemned him of a crime past atonement or reparation. Like a glob of spit exploding against his face, her glance drove him back; he jerked away his head, yet he seemed almost to have expected it; his movement was sharply defensive, but there was no surprise in it. She held the expression, there now to stay, at least for him, never to vary or waver; and for a moment his lips trembled. Then his face hardened with a wrench of jaw muscles. He stared away, somewhere through the wall.

It was so obviously the end for them, so very obviously the end of whatever they had begun or culminated or merely spoken of. The final death rattle was his own new attempt to engage her eyes, then his sudden turning back to the wall. A fly spiraled down to one of the doughnuts, joined in a moment by another, perhaps his mate.

He left them sitting there, the flies and the people, left them to the profound loneliness that only a broken man and woman could create like a diabolical invention, left them and set out again on the parkway.

For a time he pondered their relationship; what might have

happened the night before in some sterile motel room where, if they had not consummated their love, had conceived a monumental hatred. And then he thought that between a man and woman there was never hatred but only the breakage of illusion, a seeking not found, an expectation unfulfilled, the tormenting persecution by reality. All shot dead with the same surprise and shocked disbelief of an archer who aims at a target and unwittingly pierces a bird in midflight. The tolling of fate. Vast depths of disillusionment, a psychic and emotional disembowelment that sprung to the face in the shape of loathing and rage; something perceptible, identifiable, to fill the bleeding emptiness of a great loss; the emptiness itself never revealed because it would clearly say: *I am dead.* The emptiness hidden, the face said: *I don't need you.* A killing look—kill before the other saw the deadness behind the look. A lie, a killing lie. Yet he felt that the one who lied, the one who showed the illusory power of rejection, was always the weaker; the one who, with an inner perverted triumph, sealed off a more profound emptiness with an ornate lock of self-sufficiency. *I don't need you* would come to mean *I don't need anyone.*

The loser, back in the cabin, had been the girl, protecting herself with maniacal desperation. It was she who had denied her loss, who could understand no more than the dubious fact that some great fantasy had foundered, listed, sunk. The man, as unwittingly as the archer, had demolished a dream of which he had no awareness, and she would never forgive him. He could only frame the single mute, ineffectual word: *Sorry.* About what, he might never come really to know.

And then a memory of Arnold, denting the top of a table with a violent swipe of his cane. "I can't watch human waste. I look at it, I suddenly want to throw up. You can swear all you want, but there's no wound people inflict on each other that can't be healed." "You believe that?" "I want to believe it. All right, so I *want* to believe it."

Then a memory of Esther, the day on the beach so long ago, a shaft of pure pain.

Why was that girl still sitting at the table if she hated him so intensely? Because. Because. She needed a ride back to the city. She wanted to kill him, but a lift was a lift.

Shaking his head he drove onto a long stretch of blacktop, the tires humming steadily, no longer punctuated by the *thunking* sounds of tar strips binding concrete. Then turning off the parkway he slowed and drove on pocked roads through a short scrubby section of New York countryside, past diners and billboards, until an almost circular sweep led him into Massachusetts. Within minutes the landscape brightened: greener, fuller, heavily treed, every so often a sign advertising a dude ranch or last year's music festivals. On through Great Barrington, a careful, snug town with a movie theater whose name was unpronounceable, a great inn badly charred by fire, the straight main street tucked in on both sides by stores and stone churches, finally an old abandoned factory, a façade of smashed windows. Past the factory he turned right and across a short bridge, through another, rather seedy amalgam of stores and gas stations, a sudden rush of motels, then out again on open road. Towns he had not seen in an eternity, yet altered only by a growing legion of signs and motels so new that their lawns were not yet sodded.

Halfway between Stockbridge and Lenox he drove with the speed of a cantering horse, searching for a small turnoff; and then, ahead, he saw the large elm, the striking serpentine trunk which, like the towns, had neither altered nor fallen but seemed merely to have grown. Suddenly he braked, a moment of intense confusion. The mouth of the road was flanked by two whitewashed boulders; behind one was a post from which hung a pair of coachlamps and a sign, a replica of signs attached to Yankee inns, unpatterned sawtooth edges, yellow Old English lettering against a brown background:

Inn of the Olde Armourer
Luncheon: 12-3   Dinner: 5:30-10

Dangling from the sign by two screwhooks was a small panel: OPEN.

It was certainly the right road, yet he gazed up the highway as if there might be another, lying hidden, smothered in the brush. Finally he turned into the gravel drive and coaxed the car softly up a hill, its steepness eerily familiar. At the top of the hill, emerging from a dense tangle of slim-trunked trees, he saw the house in which he had been born.

He parked in the unpaved lot, then eased himself from the seat, stood, looked, absorbed; the house was huge, twenty-rooms, if he remembered accurately, the full flowering of his father's and grandfather's Midas-guided scalpels. It was still white and apparently freshly painted, with a deep green roof and eaves and shutters, its tall columned entrance the pivot of two symmetrical wings which melted softly into cascades of willow trees.

He began to walk; the windows of the east wing hurled back the sun with a sparkling intensity; he blinked. Blinking again, he noticed the long broad lawn fronted by lengths of black chain strung through the rings of iron posts set apart at precise intervals. Posted on the lawn was an impressive array of ancient cannon, pyramids of balls, antique American flags draped from a trio of tall, white, eagle-topped staffs.

It was not yet twelve, so he skirted the chains to the back of the house, deliberately searching for familiarity—a bench, a tree— finding nothing until he came upon a small dipping valley of trees beyond the rear lawn, a corner of which was sentried by a line of shiny galvanized trash cans. He was aware now of what he sought: a large tree with initials carved deep, permanent, forever in the trunk. He walked, tapped trees with his fingers, but he could not find the carving; and after half-an-hour he spread his handkerchief on a stump, sat, lighted a cigarette. The initials: EH-AG. Enclosed, he remembered, in a rough-hewn heart; and a date: 1923? Perhaps all that remained of the tree was the stump he sat on. He looked up and gauged the distance to the house; it seemed far too close to the stump; he would have gone deeper into the woods to hide the initials from prowling eyes. Yet he had already gone deeper and found nothing; perhaps not deep enough. Suddenly he was convinced that he might search all day without success, the tree always elusive. What became of such carvings that were done to outlast time, to extend to perpetuity? Did time obscure them after all, or did the trees grow new bark to repair the insult to their integrity, caring nothing for human motives? Or did the carver somehow know, as he laid knife to wood, precisely how

164

long his message would remain, some occult inner knowledge that guided the hand, the depth of the cut, the size of the letters, even the genus of tree?

He sat for some time, smoked another cigarette, then stamped it out and rose, shuddering slightly from the damp chill of the shade. It was past noon now and he bent forward as he walked, counterbalancing his body against the incline of the hill; and at the top he paused and panted excessively, a vague ache deep in his chest. He circled to the front of the house and entered the door. A wall had been removed immediately to the left of the entrance hall; glancing into the gloom he saw a short polished bar backed by stacks of bottles, a scent of old whiskey. He waited, then was suddenly joined by a handsome woman dressed in trim black. The dimness softened her face, even the white teeth of her smile, so that her age was perplexingly indefinable. But as she plucked a menu from a lamplit table he noticed the slight shriveling of the skin on her hands, the prominent corded veins, all quickly obliterated by the brief explosive spectrum of a large diamond ring.

"Good afternoon," she said, an unrelenting smile. "Are you one, or are you expecting others?"

"Just one."

"This way, please."

He followed her down the long hall with a growing sense of unreality, caused not by some spectral chain of memories but by the incredible emptiness of the rooms, the cleared tables and rows of captain's chairs, the absence of diners. She seated him in a room flooded with sunlight, its glare muted by floor-length curtains; windows stretched the expanse of one wall, smooth eroded bricks beneath his feet. Again, no people, and their absence helped him to recognize the room immediately; he could almost see it brimming with his aunt's jungle of plants, could almost smell the hothouse stuffiness.

She extended the menu, her back to the light, so that although she appeared somewhat older than she had in the hall, he could still not guess her age accurately. He thought that she must have carefully manipulated herself into this position, using her surroundings with consummate skill as an ally in her battle against

165

time. Taking the menu, as large as a newspaper, he said, "I feel like an intruder."

A practiced quizzical smile, a flash of the ring on fluttered fingers.

"I frankly don't see how you make ends meet."

Her smile broadened. "We've just reopened. You see, we're seasonal."

"Seasonal."

She seemed impatient now; as if, despite the emptiness of the rooms, she had much to attend to and he was nastily detaining her.

"After the skiing and summer seasons we have our hiatus."

He thought the word peculiar; he repeated it.

She said, "We close from March 1st through May 15th. And from the first week after Labor Day through November 15th. —Would you like a cocktail before lunch?"

"No."

She nodded curtly, the smile only a vestige; her heels clicked away on the brick. He felt that he had crucified her smile by committing some faux pas of which he had not the faintest understanding. Shrugging, he looked about the room; useless trying to remember its former color, where things had been, so he concentrated on the menu; and when a waitress appeared, he ordered New England clam chowder and roast beef.

The food was dead; not as steamed out as hospital fare, but somehow thin, without body, vaguely off, like a sedimented wine. He ate quickly, without hunger, his thoughts returning to the young-old woman, her so easily quenchable smile. Her face held a kind of familiarity, resonated some quality behind the gash of lipstick, as if she had once smiled a more genuine smile that had frozen to a mask through some dramatic trauma; now an obligatory, permanent smile, never genuine, warm, or joyful, but thin and without body like the soup, the meat. And drinking his coffee, absently poking a fork at the wedge of nesselrode pie, he realized that he was searching for recognition in her as he was in everything else, as if those who had peopled the house in the past would people it now—perhaps older, yet still there, unable to leave, prisoners. Foolish, he thought, idiocy; but he could not help it.

When he had paid the bill and lighted a cigarette, he left the room, walked into the hall, and almost paused at the staircase against the wall; then, reflexively, he veered to his left and climbed the steps to the upper landing. He stood, gazing down the long, crabbed passage, then knew that by "seasonal" she had meant to imply more than simply the operation of a restaurant; he was standing in the main corridor of a hotel, brass numbers attached to the doors, a wheeled canvas hamper heaped with sheets. He walked along the hall, his feet almost repelled by the steel-like carpet runner, arrived at his old room and tried the knob. Locked. Then on to his father's room, judging that its size must make it the most expensive in the inn. The door opened with a quick twinge of the hinges; entering, he gaped.

Nothing had changed, except for the wallpaper which he remembered as dusty rose or mauve, now a rather florid lemon yellow planted here and there with stylized sprigs of Sweet William and bluebells. The same bed, high polished posts, fluted knobs, the fireplace crowned by a gleaming mahogany mantel, the three broad windows set slightly away from the room in a curved bay, several braided oval rugs, a pair of overstuffed slipcovered chairs which may or may not have been originals; his father's chairs, probably a trace of his mother's taste, had been draped with delicate tatted antimacassars. Recovering, walking fully into the room, he realized that he had expected to see a renovated motel style, corrugated concrete swirls on the ceiling, repellant porch-type chairs of blond maple, a gooseneck lamp, a television set. Yet of course it was all as it should be: the genuine article, the authentic complement to the modern trumpery of affected old New England—the sign, the lettering on the menu, an eighteenth-century spidery scrawl with small *s*'s that resembled *f*'s.

In a corner of the window bay, as if introducing some down-to-the-sea-in-ships motif, lay a coil of knotted rope—the fire escape. For some reason it jarred him.

His cigarette had gone out, burned down to the filter; the ash had fallen off somewhere, perhaps in the hall. He threw the scorched filter into a wastebasket and sat in one of the chairs, leaned his head back, and closed his eyes, and saw again the tree he had not found, the initials EH.

They spoke in those days, *sub rosa* and immorally, of Negro jazz and Charlestons and goldfish-eating and secret drinking. In public, in the big houses of the neighborhood, they spoke, openly and moralistically, of good manners and the necessity of preserving the dignity and decency assailed by the corruption of the post-war world, of girls "coming out" and attending finishing schools, of boys growing to gentlemanhood in pre-Harvard academies.

Throughout the year there were parties for the "best" young men and ladies—back-to-school parties, spring dances, Easter and Christmas parties. The neighbors specialized; Adam's father, with a battery of hired maids, arranged the September pre-school "gala," chaperoned it—though in a peculiar way. Against the apparent grain of his character, and the characters of the local families, he encouraged kissing games.

Typically, Adam's father and Aunt Prudence would greet the boys and girls as they entered, and they chaperoned with exuberance and obvious glee, their high mood remaining constant straight through to the conclusion of the kissing games. In Adam's group it became a taboo to mention the games to parents; some illicit quality begged for preservation, a vague immorality made so much more immoral by the stuffy protocols of other parties at which, in glorious anachronistic splendor, someone would play Sinding on the piano or caterwauls on the violin; perhaps a poetry recitation, invariably by a girl with buckteeth or braces; dancing to proper melodies, bodies separated by such a vast distance that boys' fingers were perpetually slipping from girls' waists, like men dangling from the brink of precipices. At Dr. Gregory's it was different, and everyone aimed to keep it so.

Adam had never dreaded the parties, though he would often cock a wary eye at his father or Aunt Prudence, suspecting that they might be slowly accumulating overwhelming evidence of concupiscence and would one night drive everyone from the house like Jesus clearing the temple. But they didn't, and yet his quiet fear remained. He wondered, too, why it was that whenever he looked in a mirror a single thought recurred: No girl could like, or want to like, the mildly pimpled image that gazed back at him; girls could only kiss him at parties, his father's parties, but never because they wanted to.

Just once the image in the mirror lied. In the summer of his sixteenth year he fell in love with Ellen Hale, whose mother was particularly prim, whose father was a huge bearlike attorney who spent most of the week across the state in Boston. And as Dr. Gregory's back-to-school party loomed close, dread finally set in. He could not face the kissing games; he could also not avoid his own party. Because the kissing had over the years evolved from a kind of naïve, confused, fearful enjoyment to a nerve-jangling tension of anticipation; silences began to follow the games, averted eyes, harsh breathing.

He could recognize each girl in the darkness: Heather, who sought out lips with her nose; Laura, whose hair cascaded into her partner's eyes, always one strand left in his mouth, worth an hour's torture until some excuse could be found to leave the room and spit. And others, all with their revealing movements or words. But Ellen was unique; she first felt her boy's face, then warmly circled his neck, kissing his cheek, his lips with an abandon of sweetness and sincerity.

What Adam had come to dread was that inevitable moment with her in the darkness, because it had all ceased to be a game; he wanted her for himself. And if she only played, he would be mortified; he could, with vague alarm, see himself drowning in tears he could not stop.

That summer, despite the fear caused by his face in the mirror, the fear that plagued him like an unwanted hair shirt, he clung to her. She knew nothing of the fear, did nothing to perpetuate it; she spoke softly and intently, and never teased—not even when one day, bicycling, he heroically released his handlebars and coasted into a tree.

Lying flat on his back, an odd mystical sensation of perfect stillness after a sudden painless accident, a feeling of having defeated destiny, he stared unbelieving at the sky, creating shapes and profiles from the billows of clouds. He did not see her wheel back and come to him, only felt the gentle lifting of his head into her lap. Her face was above him, and he thought that he had pierced the clouds and had seen heaven, a fleeting sacrilegious feeling, watching the gold of her hair, that the idea of locating God in heaven above had come to a man while he gazed up at someone he loved.

"You're not hurt, are you? Please say something."

He was aware only of his euphoric smile, his desire to lie there forever, even if he must concoct a story that his death was imminent by minutes. He focused on her face (could God be a girl?), small and serious with a crescent of faint freckles dancing across the bridge of her nose. The sun glazed her left cheekbone, deepening the brown of her eyes. And for the first time he noticed what she wore: a yellow dress, a high neckline trimmed in white, small pleats that expanded calmly and wistfully under her small breasts, the softness of her thigh beneath his head.

"Please say something."

How simple it should have been to reach up and kiss her; instead, he groaned and said, "I'm all right—I think."

His statement got him no more attention; she simply helped him up.

And he could have kissed her once again that summer. On a cool evening she bicycled to his house and sat with him on a lawn swing; silently, until she spoke.

"What do you want, Adam? More than anything else in the world?"

"I don't know."

"To be a doctor? Like your father?"

"Sure. I suppose so."

He didn't know why he had agreed; he was mysteriously opposed to medicine but could not produce reasons when lately his father had begun to press. He had taken to avoiding the issue—and his father as well, because the man and the issue were inseparable.

The sunset dimmed; the grass grew pallid and gray, and, as if the dusk had silenced the world, he was suddenly conscious of the creaking of the swing, the nervous sexual rhythm.

"What else do you want?"

He could have said *You.*

"I don't know."

"You must."

"Well, I really don't."

"Would you like to hear what I want?"

"Yes."

"Actually, I *don't* want more than I *do* want."

It sounded cryptic; but afraid that he was simply too stupid to understand, he would not risk questioning her.

She sighed and rested her head on his shoulder; their fingers had already come together. The second opportunity, and this time an invitation; but he declined, flushed with embarrassment, and withdrew his hand. And then more than embarrassment, fear, petrified that his father might be watching from a window. His confusion swelled like nausea; he could not explain his fear of discovery when he considered the freedom of the kissing games. He was painfully adrift; he needed the structure of some clear-cut, well-defined rules. He tried to steady the swing.

When she left, he loathed himself, but the next day carved their initials on the tree.

On the morning of the party he lay in bed and gazed at the ceiling and wished he had run off somewhere—before the summer, before the bicycle ride, the few minutes on the swing. How could he avoid the party and her arms, and a kiss that had suddenly, in two short months, grown to be a burden of confusion and portentousness? He could be ill, spoil the party; he shook his head.

Looking for roads of escape, he dressed, ate breakfast, and, swept up in an amazing compression of time, found himself poking at his lunch. He burned to leap at the clock and tear away the hands, yet he was immediately standing on the porch flanked by his smiling father and aunt, hoping that some miracle might prevent her arrival. And when she walked up the steps he prayed that still another miracle might keep them apart during the games.

And as she said hello, Prudence, too bland to recognize authentic color in anyone, asked, "Lipstick?"

"No, ma'am."

He watched it all and hung his head. He would never be a man, but he no longer cared; it was simpler not to be.

They milled about through the house, girls in party dresses and boys in stiff suits, eating tiny sandwiches and drinking a strange enticing punch that tasted of alcohol but contained none. Everywhere he went he stumbled on a clock, each whirling on in a progression of time so swift that he was afraid of being transported into some future world. He saw Ellen wherever he turned: by the windows, the buffet, prophetically by a grandfather clock. He avoided her but was inexorably drawn to the hair falling almost to her shoulders, the small pouting lips, the faint iridescence of her pale blue dress.

In the sorrowful throes of reluctant avoidance his spine stiffened as his father stepped into the middle of the room, clapped his hands, and summoned them to attention. With a peculiar excitement, he said, "Who's for Spin the Bottle?"

Everyone chattered and buzzed approval while Adam stood in abject misery, trapped, for a moment convinced that he was really becoming ill, wanting some sudden assault of fever or plague.

"As usual," his father said, "Adam will begin the game."

Pleadingly, Adam looked at Prudence, who seemed far less delighted than his father; nevertheless, her expression provided no support. He stepped into the center of the quickly, automatically formed circle, took the old wine bottle from his father's hand, and gave it a violent twist. Holding his breath, he followed it to its prolonged, suspenseful halt. Its neck drifted past Ellen; gratefully he straightened from his squat, took the girl's hand, and led her into the pitch-black hall which contained the love seat.

"Thirty seconds," his father called.

Adam kissed her peremptorily, awkwardly, and they returned to the circle. The game proceeded, outlasted its novelty, and despite two more turns at the bottle he did not pair up with Ellen.

Soon his father snatched away the bottle and distributed small numbered cards, then he copied each number and the name of the owner into a notebook, finally collecting the cards and dropping them into a pocket.

"Now for Post Office," he said. "To start off, Adam will whisper the first number in my ear. Adam?" Adam obeyed. His father said, "It's . . . Mary Calloway." They marched off to the hall, his father's voice following: "Forty-five seconds for Post Office."

"I should think thirty would do," Prudence said; but his father reiterated, rather sharply: "Forty-five."

Adam was struck; for the first time he realized that he always began the games. He was puzzled, then decided that since he was technically the host by someone's logic it must all be appropriate. The puzzle rationalized, he began; he kissed Mary Calloway; and as the game went on, his father whispering names and numbers, seething with secrecy, Adam praised his luck: He had not been called again. He might never be called; and if he were, he would escape her. Then, once convinced, his mood saddened.

He was called almost when he sensed the end of the game; he entered the hall and without groping went directly to the love seat. He sat next to Heather, who could not recognize him, and dutifully placed his right arm around her shoulders. He closed his eyes against the thrust of her nose, then received her kiss.

"Alex?"

He said nothing; she kissed him again, her mouth more exploratory.

"Come on, Alex."

"It's not Alex. It's me."

"Oh," she whispered, dismayed, then moved away. "Goodbye," she added, and left the hall.

Immediately his father craned his neck into the darkness.

"Number?"

"Six. No—no, four."

"Four."

His eyes had grown accustomed to the dark, seeing a figure enter through the grayish archway. It came forward, sat next to him, and tentatively placed its hand on his arm. He felt breath on his cheek, inhaled it: Ellen's.

She knew as well as he that they had lived a summer of missed opportunities; she surely knew, because she moved no closer, only whispered, "You don't have to kiss me if you don't want to."

His stomach contracted with a new fear that he would lose her; and he said, without quite knowing why, "Yes, I do. I do want to, but not here. I can't here."

"Neither can I."

"I swear I'll kiss you later if you let me."

She tightened her fingers on his arm, a trace of verbena. "After —I'll let you know. I'll . . ."

His father's voice cut through. "We don't wany any engagements to be made."

He rose and returned to the parlor, maddeningly jealous of the next boy called, yet calmed by a sudden assurance, bolstered by his bravery in speaking, discovering during the next hour that time could also be capriciously interminable.

When the game ended, the last of the sandwiches and punch were attacked with the energy of unfulfilled sexuality diverted to a more easily satisfied hunger. His father began to fascinate them with stories of medical anomalies: two-headed Siamese twins, hundred-pound goiters. Occasionally a couple left; Adam waited, inconsolable, knowing that she must be the last to leave if he were to take her home. He began to practice clairvoyance, concentrating on the suggestion that everyone leave, happily watching her refuse escorts.

And then, with complete propriety, he told his father that he would walk home with her. They were silent on the way, he slightly chilled by the late dampness, feeling himself dangerously on the brink of a retreat into his little boy's trembling world. Could he kiss her?

They were sitting on a garden bench at the side of her house, and the moment had arrived with a sudden intensity, the culmination and consummation of the summer; he must simply touch her. He leaned to her, his head giddy, throbbing, wanting and compelled to say, because it was always said, "I love you. I really do. Honestly."

She circled his neck with her arms and, although the verbena had magically vanished, he was half-dazed by the scent of her hair.

174

"I love you too." A catch in her voice.

They kissed, kissed again, the first tentative touch of their lips growing into a more assured, comforting firmness. Then, after a kiss that almost pried their lips apart, they rested, sensing a mutual consent, both a bit frightened. She lay her head on his shoulder as she had the evening on the swing. Her hand in his, he felt as if he had been sitting with her for an eternity, finally kissing her hair, inhaling its scent. And as he shifted his arm, luxuriously tingling with numbness from the pressure of her back, he looked up and bolted in a frozen deadly terror that impaled him like a stake driven through his heart.

Not a foot away was the looming, contorted face of a man. His father.

But it seemed the face of an enormity set loose from some inner circle of Dantean darkness.

The night burst with iridescent lightning, a ringing in his head like a world of bells gone mad. He lay on the ground, his face scalded with pain. Ellen's screams: high, thin, horrified, mounting with an hysteria that tore through the night and would not cease.

And then the clattering of a window, the deep bass voice silencing the cries. "*What is it?* What's happening down there?"

And Adam's father, in controlled, anachronistic phrasing, "Your daughter, sir, is a tramp."

"*What?*"

"This is Dr. Gregory. I say your daughter is a tramp."

What happened then he was not aware of; he stepped out of his body, leaving the flesh there on the ground, his spirit fleeing in wild panic. He heard the violent, contentless quarrel of two male voices, Ellen's crying, a sharp bass accusation: *Insane!* And then, like a crumpled manikin, being half-dragged back to his house, his father's voice: *Little animals. Filthy little animals!*

He knew why he had not been able to kiss her during the summer.

Why his face in the mirror reflected lovelessness.

Why he could not be a man.

Why he wished he were dead.

And all he could do was write her a letter from school—unanswered. And another—returned unopened.

At Easter he burned their initials from the trunk of the tree. And bowed before his father in fear, knowing that behind the set, mockingly benevolent face was an ambiguity capable of clarifying into a kind of murder.

"Yes," he said to the face, unable to look at it, "I've decided on medicine."

Then a hand placed so powerfully on his shoulder that years later, when he tried deliberately to fail his courses, its grip propelled him forward again, pulled him ahead.

And on the night before his return to school after Easter holidays he woke, grappling with the bedclothes, Prudence's hand stroking his cheek, calming him.

"You were having a nightmare. You were shouting."

"What?"

"Oh, a name."

He did not have to ask the name; he knew.

"Everything," she assured him, "is for the best."

"Yes," he said, hating her, hating his father, hating himself.

And when she left, he took a pillow in his arms, kissed it, cried into it, a scent of old feathers.

He heard a sharp step. Opening his eyes, he said, "Ellen?" Then shook his head, returning to the room, the sunlight, the young-old woman standing in the doorway.

"Do you wish a room?" she said; the smile was gone.

He stood. "No. I'm sorry. You see, I once lived here. In this house."

"Oh?"

"I'll go. I shouldn't have come up here without asking."

"No, you needn't go." She sat on the edge of the bed, full in the wash of sunlight; she was easily in her fifties, hair peppered with gray; and she sat there as if deliberately revealing herself in fulfillment of some harsh self-punitive design. She clasped her hands in her lap, her back straight, waiting.

"You won't think me foolish," he said, "if I wanted you to be someone I knew a long while ago?"

176

"Not at all, Dr. Gregory."

He almost reeled, then sat back in the chair, a wave of pure fear and awe.

She placed a wallet on the bed—his. "You left this on the table."

"I . . ." He stared.

"Thought we might have known each other? I'm sorry. It was a bit theatrical of me. So you once owned the Armourer?"

"Yes. Yes, many years ago. I had no idea it became an inn."

"Since 1950. We bought it from the Perriers. I suppose you sold it to them?"

"I don't know who bought it. It was arranged through my attorney and an agent. Before the war. I suppose I didn't care to know."

"And you returned."

"Yes."

"Curiosity?"

"Possibly. —May I ask you something?"

"Certainly."

"Have you lived in these parts for a long while?"

"Roughly. I've lived in Lee most of my life. We have—I have another inn near Lenox. My husband is not living; I'm afraid the 'we' came rather automatically."

"Then you wouldn't know anyone nearby?"

"Perhaps I might."

"You've never heard of my family?"

"No."

"Another family. Hale."

"I knew Hales."

"A daughter, Ellen." Then, with disbelief, "She would be close to sixty now. Perhaps sixty."

"I might have gone to school with Ellen Hale."

"But . . ."

"I'm no longer young, Dr. Gregory." She smiled—wan, but more genuine. "Clever hairdresser. Blessed, as they say, with a good figure. Actually it's because I've never had much appetite."

"Mrs. . . ."

"Weston. I'm sorry."

"Mrs. Weston, I very much want to know what became of Ellen."

"So would I. —There I go, being mysterious again. Her father went under in twenty-nine. I hesitate to attribute Ellen's change to that, so I really don't know why I mention it." He prepared himself for a lengthy story, but she said bluntly, "Ellen killed herself. Truth is, Doctor, I never knew why. No one did."

"How?"

"A word occurs to me. Strange, actually. I thought: gently. Pills. She went to sleep."

Guarding against his own emotion, he said, "You speak as if you were close to her."

"Oh, I was—though *she* couldn't have known. It's what I meant when I said I might have gone to school with her; I find that at my age I get some odd pleasure from creating enigma. My father owned the ice-cream parlor she and her friends went to."

"Of course. The Sweet Shoppe."

She winced.

"I remember," he said.

"I often helped at the counter."

"I remember a girl."

"It's all quite simple. If there was any girl in the world I wanted to be, it was Ellen. Her death affected me, well, past the bounds of reality, I suppose. I had wanted to be her, and she put fear into my aspirations when she died. And then I understood; at least, I think I did. No one loved her."

"No one?"

"Yet how could they not? I think that possibility frightened me even more. I would sit and brood and wonder: Why didn't anyone love her?"

"I don't know."

"Did you?"

"Yes." He smiled painfully. "Yes, very much, I think."

"You should not have let her go."

"Why do you put it that way? Isn't it possible that it was she who let *me* go?"

"No, because she was Ellen. Do you see?"

"Yes."

"We should never let each other go." She rose, extending the wallet; he took it and placed it in his breast pocket. "Now I *must* attend to things."

He followed her along the hall, down the stairs; she opened the door for him and took his hand.

"Tell me," he said, "though it's none of my business. Your inn is a failure, isn't it?"

She smiled. "I'm afraid it is."

He glanced at the walls, the rooms of empty chairs and tables, and, looking back at her, said, "The house has always been a failure, Mrs. Weston." He pressed her hand, released it. "I'm sorry for being a bother."

"Not at all, Doctor."

He left, shuffling back through the gravel to the car, not even turning his head.

⚜ 2

Driving through the center of Lenox he eased left around the monument and steered out along the road which passed the Tanglewood music festival, its buildings still bundled against the off-season. The reproachful quality of Mrs. Weston's remark suddenly struck him: *You should not have let her go.* He might have answered with a similar kind of conjectural truth: *I never have.* Perhaps she might have understood; she might have, but understanding was no guarantee against repudiation. The reproach (he was convinced of it) grew in his thoughts with cancerous intensity, the dead swollen cells of what once was blocking the flow of what could have been—a stasis, the stoppage of time.

And so she had killed herself; and her death, the knowledge of it, had rent the stasis like the cracking of an ice floe in the first spring thaw. He was sure that he could have answered: *I never let her go.* Because even though, pinned to easily validated reality, he had placed her chronological age at sixty, his inner image of her was of the golden face peering down at him, the touch of her fingers on the swing, her head on his shoulder in the darkness of her garden. Neither sixty nor dead, especially not dead. Now, suddenly denying her death, he could not grasp the vision of her face.

As he still cuckolded Arnold—Esther on the beach at Cape Cod, not Esther of the New York kitchen, graying, thickening at the waist; only the Esther he had kissed with his eyes. He examined his face in the rearview mirror, but its age did not complicate the paradox of his need to trap Ellen and Esther in their youth; instead, the reflection began to impose a fearful deadly logic on the puzzle, weakening its resistance, subverting its tantalizing enigma by a blow at the chains of his ignorance. He turned his attention quickly back to the road.

Well past the main entrance to Tanglewood he turned, with an unerring sense of place, through two gateposts made of small boulders set in concrete, and snaked along a tree-smothered drive. He parked in a clearing, left the car, and stood on a rise, gazing off toward a shallow valley pillowed by the low ridges of the Berkshires, mountains scaled down to a size he could comprehend. May green, a faint diaphanous shadow of blue gently tracing the tips and shaded clefts of trees until it vanished, blending into the deeper, blacker hollows of the branches, the darkness made almost liquid by the heavy warmth of a clear sun. Sluicing down from a tall slope in a peculiar unnatural grace was a long umber ski trail, a streak of earth color, a finger drawn along a canvas of textured greens and late-spring yellows, an afterthought, diffusing into a broad meadow where perhaps cornstalks would push through the skin of the summer soil. To the left of the trail end a too-brightly painted red barn and a silo with a mirror-sparkling aluminum skullcap catching and fragmenting the sun as if secretly signaling some spy. And then a man leaving the barn, a tiny animated dot of blue, pausing. He stopped; but unreal, he could see nothing; a moving part of the landscape, kept to his circumscribed area. Then he fused into the silo, and his movement, almost imperceptible, seemed to have activated the wind; the trees shook, the solid greens undulating in shadow; then the dry rustle of branches close by above the thickly graveled drive.

Feeling like a slouching, rootless beast Adam turned and walked on, after a short distance aware of the shuffling limp of a foot trailing through the gravel, cutting a wake. Aware, but he made no effort to control it; let it happen, like a man powerless to prevent the quiet determined pursuit of something unseen. Foot trailing, a *whoosh* in the gravel, he entered the old cemetery, almost pausing reflexively to orient himself, but he had no need of orientation, only a fleeting thought that Ellen might be there. But she wasn't; he felt that she wasn't, and so would not look; fruitless, like his search for the initials he had forgotten were seared away by his own hand.

The cemetery was unchanged: flat stones like teeth blackened by disuse, tilted awry as if the dead, weary of their flinty perpetuation were slowly, in the infinite time of timelessness, pulling their monuments after them. Packed around their bases were tangled shoots of dry uncut grass and weeds, like split stalks of straw brooms. Clumps of hidden earth knobbed up beneath his feet, narrow but deep furrows sucking at his ankles as if some eternal plowing took place there; a moment of intense anxiety as the lame foot sunk shin-deep in a valley of weeds. He jerked free, the foot suddenly alive, uncrippled.

He walked to the far end of the cemetery and stopped before a low wall, again made of small ochre stones wedged in concrete. Almost against it stood the small row of headstones: the older, leaning ones, his grandfather Josiah, his grandmother Elizabeth; to the right, the mother he had never seen; next to her, his father. He stared at his own name carved deep and immutable; stared with the same sense of unwillingness and denial that had tormented him when he had seen the cab driver's license, his name the same as Arnold's physician. Beneath his father's dates, the legend: *For of the Most High Cometh Healing.* Staring, his throat gone arid as if he had discovered some rare and terrifying archaeological enormity, he craned his neck forward, the strain forcing him to loosen the knot of his tie with a quick twitch of his fingers. The collar button popped, his thumb and forefinger absently kneading the tiny clump of threads.

Suddenly he felt dizzy, a watery dissolution of his knees. Mrs.

Weston's food had not been good, but only to the palate; and although he had eaten quite a bit, it seemed as if he had fasted for a long while, to the point of danger—an explosive torrent of sweat. He swabbed his face with a handkerchief, his fingers spastic, confounding themselves. Finally he sat amid the crusty, cracking stalks, husks of something once green, once pliant, and now deceptively straight and rigid; they crackled beneath his weight. He leaned back against a tree trunk and looked up past the headstones at the stone wall.

A darker place, another wall; not dark, he recalled, only dusk, the remnant of a broken fence at the side of a road; a bicycle trip so far away that they thought they might never return. He sitting below her, gazing up, always up, at her; she perched demurely on the fence, jack-knifed knees covered almost to the ankles by the skirt of the pale yellow dress hemmed in white lace, the filigreed edge hovering above tips of white shoes. Her face turned to him, contemplating him though with no particular expression, only a hint of expectation. The saddle of freckles on her nose, long pale hair, behind her a small bag with drawstrings.

"Adam? I wonder if I *do* want to get back."

"We can't stay out here."

"Why not?"

"Out in the *road?*"

She had looked at him then with a strange melancholy intensity. "I don't want to go back."

"You have to."

"Someday I won't have to do anything. —Adam? Swear if I tell you something you'll never tell it to anyone?"

"What is it?"

"First swear."

"Swear." He tapped his heart.

"I hate my mother and father."

"No you don't."

"Yes—I do. And they hate me, too. I always feel cold."

"Do you feel cold now?"

"No. I don't feel cold now."

"You know what I think? I think you're just angry at them, your parents."

"I'm never angry at them. I'm just afraid to go home."

"Why? —Ellen, you're getting me all mixed up."

She turned her face toward the sunset, a half disc of orange fire purpling the sky.

"Adam? I would like to walk into the sun. Then I wouldn't be so cold."

"You can't. Walk into the sun, I mean."

"I said I would *like* to."

She turned back to him; two fine trails of tears shone on her cheeks. Then quickly she laughed, a goose-fleshing mirthlessness.

"Look, Ellen, I guess we'd better go."

"Away from the sun."

He helped her from the wall and they bicycled home in silence, arriving just past full darkness; so they had not gone so far after all. Now he wondered if he had known that evening, known that one day she would walk "gently" into the sun, hiding somewhere in her darkness; knew it and denied it, masking his knowledge with a pretense of confusion. Because he knew it now, with a force that nauseated him, that snapped his head back against the tree, thumping, hearing but not feeling the impact. He closed his eyes and dreamed, wished, conjured her presence. She could only say what he wanted her to, yet also words he could not fully control, that existed of themselves, that were embodied only in her.

Adam.

I should never have let you go.

You never have. You said so.

I should never have left your garden—that night.

Ah, you did leave the garden. You left there at least.

But I couldn't help it.

No. You couldn't.

You never answered my letters.

Did you really send them?

Yes, of course, There were two.

Why didn't I answer?

You didn't love me.

But I did.

Then why?

I can't tell you.

Please.

Must you know everything?

Yes.

Are you so afraid?

Yes.

But my dear, you can't know everything.

I must.

Just to delude yourself? For you, knowledge is ignorance.

You're only a girl, Ellen, a child. Yet your voice sounds old, like mine, and I don't understand you.

Still mixed up? Adam, Adam. You really know more than you admit.

I don't understand.

Good-bye, Adam.

No. Don't leave.

Let me walk into the sun, Adam. Not like that other girl, the girl by the river in France.

You won't let me understand. I didn't stop that girl from dying. If you have to know, I wanted her to die.

Fiddlesticks!

You see? There, that proves you're only a child, that silly word.

You're the child. You let her jump to keep her alive.

No.

She was never real to you. Like me: I stopped being real for you and so I lived forever. Now, good-bye.

Don't go.

I must die, can't you see that?

But I don't understand it.

Must you still know?

Yes.

Then know what you know. Look there.

He opened his eyes, using her, the words he had given her, the hidden words he had placed in her mouth, and looked at his father's headstone. And in his mind's eye the face appeared: scowling, furrowed, crow's feet like scars, armored and unchanging. It was his own face, the face in the mirror, the face in the

184

portrait, the same face, yet he could feel the power in the other, the strength, the magnetic compulsion; in his own, nothing. It was unfair, a fraud; to look alike, to show the world an equation perfectly balanced, yet to possess nothing. Like a cheap plaster imitation, but almost as if the copy were indispensable, needed to validate the existence, the truth of the original. His destiny was to have grown his own face; and he had failed.

He could hear mumbling echoes from the face: *Do what I wish. Only I am right. Do to others before they do to you. Love is a game played in darkness.* And the assent of the copy, the fake, the imitation: *I believe you. With hate and death in my every thought and feeling. Death. Because I believe you, my life is death, my death is revenge.*

His hand clenched high in the Loyalist salute, a fist he could not crush down into the other insolent face, the face that had burst into all the gardens of his life, that shouted into broken bones the entwined fingers of his disastrous loves. His clenched fist, the weapon of the murderer he had wanted to be; and its bluntness, its impotence prevented him from crossing the last country; he could not get past a girl on a quay. And he must have known that as he had known so much that he had buried in the grave of his soul, that he had tried to blunt the fear of his own revolt by pressing it into the service of a greater cause. Searching for a core of reason to justify his private murder, and so had betrayed himself, the cause. Then the loosening of his fingers, the flat-palmed salute of real murderers; and he brought it down on the copy, the imitation: hard, brutal, immobilizing.

And then, emerging from another grave, the figure of Arnold Goldman swinging his cane like a scythe, and both scowling faces, the copy and the original, began to quiver. Adam cringed like a child preparing for a blow he was not sure of withstanding. And looking into Arnold's face with its individual, rare curves and crags and hollows, he saw perplexity, sorrow, hate, passion, anger—and yet love. There was space for love, the soft eyes.

His head pressed against the tree trunk, he screamed with rage, the long wailing of a maddened wounded animal. And again the cry, almost outside himself, heard as an acho, as if his own voice were disembodied; yet the rage of sound swelling, engulfing him relentlessly until it clawed at his throat and he could no longer disown it. His rage, his murder, the desire to kill, unleashed with a power that whirled him into an ocean of limitless fear, the terror of the earth splitting open, yawning beneath him, swallowing him. Gripping the brink, he screamed at Arnold: *I hate you. I hate you for everything you have. For your wife, your children, the way you speak. For intruding on my life and proving that I have nothing, am nothing. Proving it to me day by day, minute by minute, that I don't even exist. Nothing. Nothing.*

But he hadn't screamed; merely thought that he must scream because the hate was so intense; he could only feel it. Silently screaming.

You pretended to love me.

I pretended nothing.

You did. Because you gave everyone your love. Not only me.

You didn't look too closely, you can say that. But I did give it to you.

I don't want it.

You took it. I gave, you took.

And I gave you nothing. Admit it.

Am I complaining?

Nothing. Then how could you give?

It's my business. Think what you have to. You always have to know everything.

To delude myself? Say it. Say it!

How would I know. Look, I'm dead.

Arnold!

Maybe that's what you should know: I'm dead. I said genug, enough, and I died.

His head snapped forward from the tree; his body contracted with a blinding agony; the grip of a mailed fist on his heart, breath bled from his lungs. He began to tear at his throat, but the pain was suddenly gone as quickly as it had entered him.

"Arnold!" he shouted, startling himself. And again, "*Arnold!*" A sleeper awakened by a shout from the depths of his dream. "*I did love you.*"

186

But there was no one. Just himself, staring at his father's headstone, sitting sprawled against a tree, alone; the cry to Arnold like the remnant of a taste on his tongue.

They were all dead—except him.

His right eye flickered, a brief flutter of tics. Blinking, he shook his head as if struggling against some occult and terrifying bodily transformation. The eye clouded, burned, and his flesh painfully extruded a single tear; it hovered in the safety of his lid, then broke loose, almost scraping along his cheek like a bead of rust.

And then the tears welled; stretched face down in the cradle of his arms, he felt the jerking, tugging spasms of his body. Felt them and had no desire to stop, knowing finally all that he could know: that slowly, for most of the years of his life, he had been coming to this place to mourn.

TEN

❧ 1

After stopping the night in a motel near Lenox, Adam drove back to the city late Sunday morning and returned the car, getting home near two. Leaving the elevator, he passed Vasiliev's door and saw it half open. Impulsively, he looked inside, immediately seeing Ford standing dejected, limp in the center of the large room; if his head were not hung so low he might have been staring, fascinated, out the window. Finally he turned, started slightly, then said, "Oh. Hello, Dr. Gregory."

"Mr. Ford. I saw the door open and thought something might be wrong. He's very careful about locking his door."

"There *is* something wrong, all right. Mr. Vasiliev died."

Adam nodded. Somehow he was not surprised; he had expected

a minor cataclysm when he had seen the door open, usually secured by a battery of chain-and-bar locks.

Ford said, "Yes, sir. It was awful. The elevator came down to the basement and I opened the door, and there he was, all dressed up to go out, laying on the floor. It must have happened between here and there, just like that. Ain't hardly a thirty-second trip."

"Heart?"

"Most likely. Can't see anybody going so fast except for heart. Anyway, I don't know what to do. It don't seem he got any family and I'm supposed to get rid of his stuff so they can rent the apartment."

"No will? Or a letter?"

"Don't seem so. I looked in all his drawers, but I couldn't find anything. The landlord says it's all right just to get rid of it, but I don't know."

"I have no idea what happens in a thing like this. Maybe there are some envelopes or an address book, some name you can contact."

"There's nothing at all. Just a lot of funny stuff."

The funny stuff, Adam saw, were heaps of Russian newspapers and oddly assembled chemical apparatus—Florence flasks and retorts strung together with glass tubing, stands for alcohol burners, test tubes. But no chemicals, just the glass, grimy and gummy with grease.

"What did he use this for?"

"I don't know. Don't look like he done anything at all with it; looks like it just set around."

Scanning the room, Adam realized that he had expected to find a dark, smelly cubbyhole, a Dostoyevskian niche; but the only novelistic touch was an icon in a corner, a Virgin and child glowing like a miniature Byzantine mosaic, below it a dead candle stub in a blue glass. Except for the array of chemical apparatus, the room was extremely tidy, even the corded stacks of newspapers. Near a small chipped desk against a wall was a bookcase stuffed with Russian literature. Lying flat on top of the case was a huge Bible, so heavy that Adam could barely lift it; he leafed through several pages of bold Cyrillic script, examined a number of ornate reproductions and illuminations.

190

"He was a very religious man," Ford commented.

Adam opened a desk drawer, finding an old frayed Tarot deck; limp cards, the Hanging Man face up, almost transparent from incessant use, secured by several rubber bands. Beneath the cards lay a book dealing with Etruscan charms and potions; three books on occult Egyptology; several more in Russian, obviously with the same occult theme, their pages illustrated by eyes gazing from the darkness of cupped hands, strange radiating mandalas, one with three eyes superimposed in a triangle; a book on Chinese acupuncture techniques. A dried animal's paw. At the back of the drawer was a cigar box filled with reddish earth and strips of various metals. He glanced at the chemical apparatus and raised an eyebrow. Alchemy? Had Vasiliev sat in his room alone, dabbling in black magic and sorcery? Now he half-expected to find a doll, its heart impaled on a pin; but the last discovery in the drawer was a pair of old redolent black socks, toes and heels held together by multicolored threads.

Closing the drawer, he turned and said, "I don't know what to tell you, Mr. Ford. I can call a lawyer I know and ask his advice."

"I'd appreciate that."

"It's one of these things you never seem to think about until they happen."

"I know what you mean."

There was a more personal nuance in his words, as if he were suddenly preoccupied by possibilities of future mysteries, not knowing what form they might take but wondering how they should be dealt with. He jangled a ring of keys.

"I suppose you want to lock up," Adam said, moving toward the door.

"I wonder," Ford said, "if I could talk to you—just for a few minutes."

"All right. Would you like to come in for a cup of coffee?"

"Well, I thought I would ask you to come down. Somebody might want me, and. . . ." He trailed off.

Adam agreed and they took the elevator to the basement.

Seated in the kitchen, Ford said, "I only drink tea. I don't keep no coffee."

"Tea's fine."

There was a slightly ritualistic silence as Ford sizzled water on the teabags, then placed on the table a bowl of sugar, a dish with several slices of lemon, a container of milk, spoons. He sat opposite Adam, tentatively touching the surface of the tea with his upper lip, his eyes slitting under an assault of steam.

Then he said, "I don't know what to do, Doctor. I don't mean about Mr. Vasiliev; about something else, and I guess I need your help."

"Is someone ill?"

"No. I. . . ." He retreated into the tea for a moment, then, "Well, Walter was here Friday night and took Lucille away. I guess you know what he wants to do with her."

Adam nodded.

"Anyway, I'm afraid something happened. I mean, not just that he done it, but maybe something worse. He ain't brought her back, Doctor. Been two nights now."

"Why didn't you stop him?"

"I wasn't here. I was cleaning out the incinerator like I do on Fridays. I came back and she was gone. He must of snuck in like a thief; left me a note." He made no effort to show the note, although he tapped his shirt pocket.

Adam said, "How can I help you?"

"I thought, well, maybe you know where he took her."

"I don't. Do you mean, did I arrange it?"

Ford nodded.

"No, he did it on his own," Adam said.

"Well, least I'm glad of that."

"Why?"

"No offense, Doctor, but I would of got the law on you." He lowered his head, embarrassed, as if he had perpetrated some treachery, at least something incredibly impertinent. "I'm going to call the law on Walter if he don't bring her back soon. Maybe I'll do it anyway."

"Your own son?"

"Don't make no difference. I wanted to do it yesterday, but I thought just what you said: He's my son. I mixed myself up and before I got myself straight again I figured he already done it to Lucille anyway."

"Mr. Ford, if you call the police now it will only be to punish him, not to stop an abortion."

"I know that. Somebody's got to punish him. I'm too old to do it with my own hands."

"He could get in serious trouble."

"He brought it on himself."

"I don't think you're that hard, Mr. Ford."

"No, I ain't. I never was hard, never hard enough. All I want is my girl back. And I wanted that child, I don't care who done it to her. A child is something good, don't matter it came from somebody's evil. Walter had no leave to do what he done. He left his home was his business. But not this. —Doctor, if I was a young man I'd beat him bad. I'd whip him till he near died, till he got down on his knees and prayed to God."

"Why do you want the baby so badly?"

Ford looked up from the tea, straight into Adam's eyes, his own eyes scarlet shot and teary. "Dr. Gregory, what else do I have? What else?"

Adam nodded, and this time *he* retreated into the tea.

Ford said, "I guess I never complained much, and maybe I'm wrong to do it now; but a man's wife leaves him, his son don't want no part of him, his girl got something awful wrong with her. Maybe that baby would of been something different, maybe something good. I don't know, but just maybe." He folded his hands, then steepled the fingers. "Doctor, I don't want to end up like Mr. Vasiliev. I don't want some janitor not knowing what to do with my stuff. I don't want to have nobody. That man had *nobody*." He shook his head. "I don't want that at all."

Adam nodded, and after a time said, "Did you try to call him? Walter?"

"Every hour. He ain't there or he don't answer the phone— More tea?"

"Maybe some hot water; I let it get too strong."

As Ford rose, the door opened.

Walter stood on the threshold, his face defiant yet vaguely abashed, disenchanted. He wore a dark gray suit; across his left shoulder was a paisley tie blown back by the wind. He stared at his father, then said dully, "Surprise."

He swung the door wide and brought Lucille in front of him, his hands on her shoulders. She was grinning shyly, a red lollipop clutched in a white-gloved hand. Ford was struck frozen; in tune with him, Adam could almost feel his eyes bug. Lucille was dressed like a fashion model, if it was at all stylish for models to be obese: deep blue leather shoes and matching bag, white patterned stockings, an opulent pale blue suit that looked like cashmere, a tiny blue hat. The Peter Pan collar of the jacket was decorated by a plain dull gold pin. Still grinning, she licked at the lollipop.

Walter said, "If nothing else, she might as well look halfway like a woman."

Ford began to cry; then looking at Adam, he tried to stifle the tears, failed, and almost ran into the bedroom.

"Lucille," Walter said, "you go say hello to your daddy. Give him one of your lollipops." When she had left he said, "He told you all the action?"

"Yes. He was going to call the police."

"Well, well—the *police*."

"You're a pair of fakes."

"Do tell."

"So hard. Underneath as soft as a ripe cheese."

"Disappointed?"

"Have a cup of tea."

"Tea? The drinking kind? Sure, why not?" He sat, inundated a teabag, then said, "So let me tell you all about it, now you're part of the family. Friday night—a lovely night, Doctor, stars and spring smells from New Jersey, like that—I sneaked her out of here and took her to this woman. This woman really rots. And I took one look at her Goddamn awful face and I saw a skull and crossbones in each eye. A pair of iodine bottles. And I said to myself: She's going to kill Luce. No I don't know why I thought that, because this woman is a real pro, but that's the way it was. So I said: Grim Reapress, I'm sorry to have wasted your time; forgive me for troubling you. Of course, what I really said was I didn't have enough money, that I misheard my friend's—*quotation*. Now I don't know what would have happened if that lady had started to bargain or offered me a charge account. Because in the room was this big thing that looked almost like a man, like somebody had tried to abort him fifty times and missed each shot, and I had the feeling that they could just as well work me over with the tools they would use on Luce. So I sweated. But all the nice lady was was just pissed. Said she wasn't running no charity, and if I wanted a job done I'd best get the hell back with the whole three hundred. Yes ma'am, I said; yes ma'am, I sho'ly do just that. Luce thought she was pretty."

Adam was grinning.

Walter said, "My, my."

"Idiot."

"Mm, yeah. Anyway, I haven't got to the really wild part yet. Saturday morning I took her to Saks, just like in thirty-year-old movies where the rich guy takes the poor girl to a classy shop, and said: 'Outfit this here girl from inside to outside.' I swear they didn't know what to do. They looked at her, at me, at her again, and then some really competent-looking middle-aged chick takes over, and I said: 'Lady, there ain't going to be any sit-in here. Just you outfit my little sister.' Well, they did; and we got alterations at a tailor shop, and you saw it; and I must admit it sure is something. What, I'm not sure of; but it *is* something."

"Your tea's getting cold."

"After the tailor I took her for lunch at—hold your breath—La Fonda del Sol, and then to Radio City. Today I took her to the zoo—she broke her balloon, damn clumsy kid—and after to the museum. She sure must like pictures because she laughed up a storm. And you know something? I got a lot of kicks." He extracted the teabag from his cup. "I sure did."

"Did you really see death in that woman's eyes?"

"You don't believe me."

"Did you?"

"No. I cooked it all up. I never even saw the woman."

"What are you talking about?"

"That scene from *Dracula*. What's true is Saks and the zoo and the lunch—all the *good* things. The rest I made up. I think."

"Talk straight."

"Why? What good does it do? Anyway, maybe the pregnancy wasn't straight."

"Meaning?"

"So I was all set to take her to the land of Mordor, and there she was, bleeding all over my nineteen ninety-five cotton foam-back rug. That sound like the normal course of a pregnancy?"

"I don't believe you."

"No? Okay. We went after all. She screamed, moaned, thrashed around like a caged squirrel, and twenty minutes later, *plop*. In any case, what I'm trying to tell you is that there is no baby. *Now*, there is no baby. If there ever was is beside the point, and maybe always was."

"All right, tell me exactly what happened."

"No. It's your turn to trip all over yourself; no fun to be off balance, is it? Suffer, Daddy. You want to find out, you go right into the bedroom and give her a checkup. I quit." He blew at the steam curling from his cup. "My guts have been twisted by two old men who haven't got the Goddamndest idea of what's real in this world. Now I don't mind getting screwed up by something I can see or feel—something. But, baby, I draw the line at this. It's your show. Here's the script: I did and did not take my sister to an abortionist; she did and did not have an abortion; she was and was not pregnant. Take your pick, the alternatives that suit you naturally."

"Are you trying to say that your father invented the whole thing?"

"Invented? Hell, no. Let's say she wasn't pregnant. Let's say he just wanted to believe something that was all a mistake—for one, your cockeyed resident's skill. Now if we say she *was* pregnant, it adds up to the same thing anyway, doesn't it? And when he sees there's no baby, he'll just *know* I did it—assuming I did. Or he might just overlook her present natural monthly cycle; that is, if it's cycling. How in hell do I know what he wants or wanted, or needs? But I know one thing for sure, for a dead fact. You wouldn't give me a straight answer on this thing because in some weird way you wanted that baby too. You weren't feeling for my father; you *were* my father. Man, *that's* integration. I'd tell the old man progress is really here, if he could handle the idea."

196

"He told me he has nothing. Are you glad that he hasn't?"

"Come on, Adam. He'll just dream something else if he needs it bad enough. You will, too. Look, both of you, go croak on your loneliness. I have no pity on either of you. You have nobody, go suck somebody dry. But not Walter. No more." He drank half the tea, screwed up his nose, then eased his chair away from the table. Finally he stood. "I *did* get kicks buying her that outfit. First thing I ever gave to a woman in my life." He took a key from his pocket and placed it in front of Adam. "Your key—to the *atelier*."

"You're quitting?"

"God, what a deduction! I just want out—of this whole fairyland, Disneyland building."

"What are you going to do?"

"First I'm going to climb a big building and yell. Then try to believe it all happened—and I don't just mean Luce. Then, do something all by myself; something I won't screw up."

"Such as?"

"I'm going to parade down Fifth Avenue. Marching four abreast, right in front of me, are the Reverends Adam Clayton Powell and Martin Luther King, and Roy Wilkins and an effigy of Lumumba. And here comes Walter Ford, blowing "The Star Spangled Banner" on a kazoo. —No, Adam, I just want a little life." He nodded toward the bedroom. "Say so long. I'd do it myself, but by this time he's probably got her back in sackcloth and sneakers, and I don't feel like seeing it. Also, thanks for the work. That's straight."

He left; and after a few minutes Ford, looking dazed, entered the kitchen and said, "Dr. Gregory, she—Luce . . ."

"Yes," he said, and waved his hand. He could see Lucille emerging from the bedroom and decided that he did not want to see the sneakers either. He rose and went home.

❧ 2

"Sit," Esther said. "Please." Slightly confused, she indicated two chairs at once. Then she removed her apron, hung it on the handle of the refrigerator door and sat at the table opposite him. "Can I make you some coffee?"

"No," Adam said. "As a matter of fact, I came to return this." He placed Bernard Goldman's journal on the table, pushing it toward her with his thumb. "I should have phoned before I came."

"You don't have to call to come here. Also, you didn't have to bring this back."

"Well, not only that. I wanted to say hello. How are you?"

"All right. Good—considering."

He set his lips.

"It's all sunk in," she said. "I mean Arnold. I didn't think I could live with it, and then I said to myself: 'Funny, but you can.' I wasn't sure; but I *was* sure." She shook her head. "I'm a different person. My mother, I can remember her when my father went. She wouldn't believe it. She didn't cry, maybe she wasn't even sad. He was lying on the bed already gone, and she said, 'He's sleeping; beware you don't make noise.' She told the doctor, even the rabbi, there were things even they didn't understand. She never believed it. With me, I knew. I knew he was dying and I knew it when he died. But for a minute I wished I could be like my mother. Now I'm glad I'm not."

"Glad?"

"Ah, she didn't believe in so many things after that. Everything was what she wanted it to be. A herring could be a whale in her eyes. I would rather not have such things happen to me."

She began to speak of David, and Adam watched her, thinking with faint amusement that if once she could not talk to a gentile, she was making up for lost time. His eyes drifted to the journal and he realized how flimsy, how preposterous it was to have served as an excuse to bring him here. All day he had meant to come purely to see her, yet he had needed some justification, regardless of how weak. Perhaps because he had not come as a sympathetic friend. Then as what? He refused to follow the thought, turning his attention back to her, the hair laced with gray, deepening wrinkles, skin leathering from too much sun. Her talk of David wove securely through time, from his childhood to his current plans for graduate school; listening to her words, disconnected by his thoughts, he felt almost as he had when he stood gazing at the mountains the day before: He didn't belong here, and particularly for the reasons he had really come. He did not want to discuss David or even Arnold; he wanted to speak of her, of himself; and then he allowed himself to follow the thought, which was less unsettling than he had expected. He wanted to recapture those moments on the beach, to resume, as if the past twenty years had been merely a meaningless gap, empty time, a forced interruption during which life itself had stopped, as if she had been waiting for him.

She was saying, "It's going to cost a lot, but Arnold was smart that way. Very often his head in the clouds, but a businessman? Always."

Her talk excluded him, yet she could not know that, not really; could not possibly know that he had come to her house, the journal tucked under his arm, the first time he had ever failed to phone, to claim what Arnold possessed, to take not only his limp, the pain in his heart, but his wife as well. He looked hard at her, gauging, seeking some hint that she might have sensed his purpose and so was talking around him, protecting herself with words, with the unassailable facts of her world, preventing some approach. And then he was awed by the depth of his presumption; his complacent belief that the memory of that day on the beach must necessarily be as mystically significant for her as it had remained for him. Perhaps she had forgotten it as he had once forgotten Ellen, or at least had turned her whole being away from it.

What could he accuse her of wanting to prevent? A sexual assault? He almost laughed aloud, staring down at the backs of his hands, stretched with dusty skin, a nest of liver spots, fingernails brittle and fluted. And her—certainly no longer young, but within her a measure of joy and comfort that aging could not deny.

He slitted his eyes, fuzzing, softening her face, immunizing it

199

from the glaring kitchen light. *Abracadabra*—she on the perpetual beach, he eternally young. She would not change from the tricks of his vision; there was no sex now as there had been then; and he found himself wishing that by some miracle he could softly sneak into her thoughts, hear himself spoken of with the same concern as David, the same respect and affection as Arnold. But, he admitted, he was in fact nothing to her, and he wondered if that day, that immemorial day, had not really pushed her closer to Arnold instead of weakening her.

So he had come to her only to pull her into his old age, to sit with her at the kitchen tables of dotage and gum memories like milk-sodden bread. He had been trying to pull her after him for an eternity; she was no different from his other women, his Ellens. Sex? He nearly laughed again. Because it struck him that he had lived a whole life like the few senile years of an old man he had once seen at the clinic, over seventy and morbidly addled, who had complained to him of some bizarre resurgence of sexual desire, convinced that his feelings signified the beginning stages of death. He had listened impassively, grand in his competence and omnipotence; but now he understood the old man's tragedy, his own misery—that neither could direct his desire, sprung from God knew what amalgam of guilt, fear, and confusion, toward such a simple thing as a woman. For apparently women were not simple; not for the old man, not for the man who had always been old. Somewhere, hidden from the world in his soul, the strange old man must have possessed his own Esther, his own Ellen, and so possessed nothing; and the feelings which belonged only to them had suddenly burst from their secret place and had overwhelmed him.

He started; she had stopped speaking and was looking at him curiously.

He said, "What will you do now?"

"So, I still feel capable and not *so* old. I don't think I am ready to give up yet." She smiled. "I was thinking that after David goes away to take a smaller apartment."

"Alone?"

"There's plenty to do. I enjoy plays, so I'll go to plays. One of my friends is going to Russia in August. I don't know how it will look so soon after Arnold, but I'm going with her."

He understood so little about her, the real things in her life, what she was beyond the narrow bounds of his perception of her. For all he knew, she was fluent in Sanskrit or Coptic, or anyway in Russian, since she said, "The reason I can get on this special flight with such short notice is that they need another interpreter. So they can get me on the plane, no trouble." She paused, then, "You should take a vacation also, a good rest. Do you have plans?"

"No."

"You work too hard, I think."

I will go to Paris and sit like a Buddha on the Pont des Arts and draw in crayon on the pavement the heart, lungs, liver, and everything else I'm not certain I own, and watch on my left and right the girls walking along the quays of the Seine.

"No, I just work. It passes the time—like sitting on a stool and whittling. When I get the block of wood down to a little toothpick I'll take my vacation."

Perhaps I will sit alone in a home for aged physicians, alone with the wheezes whistling through the lesions in my lungs, with my flatulent heartbeats, with my staggering heaps of last month's magazines.

It was self-pity, but it felt good. Nevertheless, it was private to him as her world was private to her.

He rose and said, "Thank you, and David, too—for the journal."

"You can keep it."

"No. Reading it was enough."

"No coffee? Are you sure?"

"Yes. It's getting late and I barged in."

"You're always welcome here."

"I believe you." He pressed her hand, looked at her, and thought: *No, you never wore a soft yellow dress, never held my head in your lap.* "Esther Goldman," he said, "have a magnificent trip."

On the street he walked without purpose toward Columbus

Avenue, the neighborhood off Central Park West immediately whirling through an almost primitive metamorphosis. Clusters of Puerto Rican children hovered around the glow of streetlamps like moths around flame; to his left the stoop of a pocked brownstone was filled, like bleachers at a ballpark, with chattering men and women, their fists curled around beer cans, watching a television set that had been placed on the sidewalk, its long extension cord snaking down from a first-floor window. All set free from a long May of cold nights.

Farther on, watched by another filled stoop, was a violent quarrel between an adolescent girl and a middle-aged man; while she stared defiantly, he slid the belt from his trousers, wrapped the buckle end around his hand, then, with dazzling speed, lashed her once across each bare arm. She screamed; the belt cracked across her right leg, and, as she bent, the man seized her hair and flung her to the sidewalk.

Adam sidestepped, walking close to the gutter, almost tripping over a small boy urinating on a cat. Then through a growling midway of blaring television sets and transistor radios; somewhere a cadenced drumming; always shouting; curtainless windows glowing cerise, chartreuse, iridescent blues and greens. He shook his head, remembering: *Viva la quince brigada. . .*

Perhaps Walter was right, that all around him were people trapped peculiarly in the present, that one day they would enter a false tomorrow, new dreams primed for breaking. He looked at the street bulging with the filth of garbage, animal dirt, glass, bent cans, demolished automobile parts. Turning, he saw the man who had struck the girl beating his breast and shouting, tearing at his face with his hands. Revolt? Evolution?

Viva la quince brigada. . .

Not in his lifetime.

And then he realized that what he truly felt was disgust, waves of it; he could not longer look at it. He wanted to vomit.

He crossed the street and walked quickly back toward Central Park, deliberately, almost spitefully, entering it at 96th Street, adjusting his eyes to the bluish glare of the lamps lining the path. He walked on into dimness, thinking that if he believed the newspapers he was headed for mugging, murder, and—wasn't anything possible?—rape of one sort or another. He sneered. Why should he believe the newspapers? Hadn't he just seen the forward movement of the anti-poverty program? The newspapers loved the anti-poverty program.

He walked on, then finally sat on a bench; here the night was truly cool, almost chill, but he sat resolutely in the weak light of a nearby lamp, listening to the wind in the trees, feeling, inviting the twinges of fear that did not drive him out of the park but which instead mildly excited him.

And when they came, he watched intently, rooted to the bench in amazement, tempted to look behind him; perhaps he might find someone else to support the strange evidence of his eyes. There were at least fifteen of them, small boys no older than ten or eleven, their faces pale and weirdly Oriental in the dusky light. They stood looking, staring, then began to circle him, their eyes trained on his, circling until they formed a moving wheel; and he saw that each carried something resembling blunt sticks or rods; and as the wheel drew tighter around him, he realized that what they carried were tightly rolled newspapers.

A whisper, close to his ear: "*Maricón.*"

He closed his eyes; perhaps if he sat still, inert, they would go away, vanish. But even when he wished them away they would not go.

Again, even closer: "*Mira, maricón. Mira.*"

He had to speak; he opened his eyes and said, his voice soaring an octave: "What do you want? Money?"

"*Dinero, dinero, di-ne-ro.*" They chanted, then laughed.

A light tap on his left shoulder, a stinging blow across his right shin. Then, blinded by rage and pain, he sprung from the bench and flailed out with his hands and feet, feeling them swarm against him like biting insects, dragging him down. He felt the impact of his hand on a head, and then they were gone; he could hear their bare or sneakered feet plopping away. A light pounded into his eyes, then dropped a bit to his chest.

"Are you nuts?" a voice said. Blinking, he could see, not far away, the spotlight of a police car scanning the trees. "What are you hanging around here for, Pop?"

"Just taking a walk."

203

"Identification." Adam held out his wallet; in a moment it was returned. "Okay, Doctor, do your walking some place else from now on. You might be educated as hell, but you act like a jerk." And when Adam didn't answer, "Are you all right?"

"I think so."

"You want a lift to the street?"

"No."

"Okay. So please leave."

"Who were they?"

"I don't know. Just be careful; next time you might not walk out of here."

Adam retraced his path to 96th Street, emerging again on Central Park West, and then felt the full force of his fear, his helplessness. Shuddering, he gripped the wire mesh of a trash can and vomited; then, after breathing deeply for several minutes, he hailed a cab.

When he had settled in the seat and given his address, he said, "Fine night."

His comment unleashed a torrent from the driver: the weather, baseball, the perils of hacking uptown, a hernia operation. But he was grateful for the voice, the words, the fragments of someone else's real world.

ELEVEN

⚜ 1

It was almost eleven o'clock on Monday morning when Adam was caught short by a sudden memory. He left the drawing board and went quickly to the laboratory, automatically slipping into his white coat. A special lecture was due Wednesday, and he had let its preparation slide by for more than three weeks. And then he wondered why he had come; he had given the same lecture for ten years, its immutability reflected by the small stack of yellow legal-size pages, the browning edges working inward like a slowly spreading stain. There was no need to prepare, but he found him-self weary of the repetition. Lighting a cigarette, he tried to sketch out a new approach—not only to engage the students but also to engage himself.

The thought of students caused him to remember a "failing" dream he had had the night before. But it had been different from the others, and he had waked from it with no anxiety. He was an intern this time, and for some dreamlike reason was also enrolled in a statistics course. For a year he had been working hard with patients; and after he had seen the last one, on the last day of his internship, he realized that he would fail the statistics course. No panic—he was aware that he had consciously sacrificed it to work with his patients, knowing somehow that he could not have done both well. He was saddened by the failure, but had thought: There's always summer school.

When he woke, he was glad that he had finally left a dream stage of grade and prep school; he had made college. And especially glad that he had not bolted up in a cold sweat; perhaps, he thought, all the anxiety was linked to the hopeless failure, that it had been dispelled by the realization that he might make up the statistics course in the summer.

Satisfied with his interpretation, he uncovered a body, took several fresh sheets of paper, and began to think.

He had gotten through two new pages of notes and was barely aware of the door opening; hearing it, he held the sound in abeyance until he finished the development of a point. Then he turned.

"Right down to the wire, Miss Ramsey? The term's almost over."

"I didn't come to work—just to get some things. I'm sorry. I didn't know you'd be here."

"That's all right. I won't bite you."

Ignoring him, she unfolded a laundered lab coat and hung it behind the door, then set a huge volume on the bookshelf.

"I thought you came to *get* some things," he said.

"Did I say that?"

"Distinctly. You must have getting on your mind."

"That's quite possible. But I don't care to discuss it."

He placed his pencil on the yellow pages and leaned back in his chair. "I didn't ask you to discuss anything."

"Then maybe *I* want to. Like the 'getting.' As a matter of fact, I wouldn't be surprised. I've been feeling a little like a Freudian freak."

"Sticking with Freud, Miss Ramsey, you must have had a real old-time trauma. You've dropped your scatterbrained, incompetent act."

She flushed with anger and jerked her head toward him. "Drop the abuse, Doctor. Do you people always have to treat students like *things?*"

"No."

"Then why do you do it?"

"Some precedent that everyone feels comfortable with."

"But you can't say why."

"Not off hand."

"Then your answer to my question is: 'I don't know.' Why not settle for that?"

"What's wrong, Miss Ramsey?"

"Wrong? Something *must* be wrong, mustn't it? Would that preserve your impregnability and wisdom if it were true? Do people who won't respond like programmed machines scare you? Look, Doctor, I'm just being direct. I'm not crazy or irrational just because I'm not playing the 'yes-sir' game. So don't waste your time on it."

"I didn't ask you if something were wrong only to stop your directness. I asked you because you're hell bent on sucking me into some cheap rebellion. You don't even give me a chance to respond."

"Cheap?" She laughed almost hysterically. "It's literally worth thousands."

"Get to the point."

"I brought the things back because tomorrow morning I'm informing whoever I'm supposed to inform that I'm leaving school. Not a leave of absence, just a fast retreat out of here. 'Quitting' is the word you'll invariably think of, so I may as well say it first. I am definitely *quitting.*"

"Everybody is quitting," he said flatly, "or leaving."

"I don't know about everybody, but *I've* had it."

"You're in excellent standing."

"Bully. I've still had it."

"Is it the work here? You seem angry enough at me."

"No. I've decided you can get used to all kinds of dead things."

He winced, impelled to retaliate, convinced that she could mean only him; yet her tone had been a bit too reflective. He said, "Then it's highly personal and I have no right to inquire."

After a long silence she said, "Since I'm being direct, let me say I didn't expect that."

"What?"

"What you said. I thought you'd barge right in on me. Defender of the profession—all that."

"I'm tired of barging. Besides which, if you knew me you'd realize that ordinarily I wouldn't give a damn if you had left ten minutes ago. As it is, I don't feel like treating you as a thing."

"You don't sound patronizing."

"I'm not."

"Have you had a trauma too?"

"Maybe. Why?"

"I'm afraid I couldn't stand the change. Can I say something *really* direct?"

"Asking permission? Weakening?"

"Yes, damn you. Don't change now; you're so beautifully symbolic of everything I'd like to tear to pieces."

"Tear."

"So you can land on me? So you can tear me back? Better, more viciously, more thoroughly?"

"Miss Ramsey, I don't know *what* I'll do back. Maybe I'll even be hurt."

She seemed less surprised than suspicious, and he couldn't blame her; he was slightly suspicious of himself. He could not remember the last time he had shared his possible vulnerability with anyone; in a way, not even with Arnold, not truly.

Tentatively, she asked, "Why did you say 'cheap' rebellion?"

"Maybe it's a poor word. But because somehow I don't think you know where your real target is. Or if you do know, you can't or won't aim at it. And then you suddenly want to quit when all you have to do is wait a week, finish the term, and have a whole

208

summer to think it over. So maybe 'self-destructive' is a better word than 'cheap.' "

"That sounds worse."

"It's what you're doing, isn't it?"

She stared at him for a moment, then sat on a stool. "May I have a cigarette?"

He offered her the package; she removed a cigarette and he struck a match for her.

Inhaling, she said, "Another question. What did you mean about a scatterbrained, incompetent *act?*"

"The way you've always behaved with me—like a child fifty fathoms out of her depth. The word just popped up when I saw all that anger beneath the silliness. There was a time when I wanted to turn in a negative report on you, but when I checked your record I was a bit staggered."

"Yes?"

"Among the notes in your folder was a recommendation written by a professor who couldn't have said a word of it if he thought you were the slightest bit silly—never mind inept. He sees any complaint short of terminal cancer as the height of flightiness and self-indulgence."

"Landau?"

"Yes."

"Didn't you just do something terribly unprofessional?"

"Probably."

"You're a strange man."

"All things being equal—and they never are—you may be right."

"And confusing."

"No more than you. Let me tell you a parable. I once published a paper and it was criticized as follows: 'Dr. Gregory's study may well be important; unfortunately, it doesn't communicate.' "

She smoked in silence for a time, then stubbed out the cigarette and said, "It wasn't an act; I mean obviously I had very little to gain from an act like that. I was scared, and when I'm scared I'm six years old. I don't like being scared, so I tell myself it's better to feel fear than nothing at all."

"Was that a swipe at me?"

"No."

"I have to beware. Everything seems very personal lately." He smiled, absently tapping the shoulder of the corpse with his forefinger.

"Must you do that?"

"What?"

"Touch it like it wasn't there!"

He drew back his hand, then looked at the body: the parts connected suddenly, an entire once-human thing, the sheathed head presiding eerily over the torso and legs. He covered it with the plastic sheet, his lips turned down at the corners.

"I see what you mean."

"It would be awful if *you* became afraid of the things."

He shrugged, but thought that she could not possibly realize the profundity of what she had said; he needed to work, whittling the block down to the sliver.

"I'm sorry I attacked you," she said. "It *was* a cheap rebellion. Really."

"Self-destructive. Just finish out the term; don't need it to be so final. You might want to come back and there'll be no way to do it."

"I have no one else to hurt but me."

"You must have broken your favorite doll once."

"Twice. I really did a job the second time."

"When I was ten I had a model ship—a full-sailed schooner with intricate woodwork, tiny ladders, all of that. I smashed it in a tantrum. It wasn't the kind of thing you could break twice." His head was lowered, and when he finally looked up he saw that she was crying. "Whatever you've got," he said, "it's in an acute phase of exacerbation." He handed her a tissue.

"I guess."

"Still breaking the favorite doll."

"Maybe I'm acting now."

"I doubt it. Just don't let it ruin your talent. Somehow that's easy, too easy." Then, "You're in love, aren't you? And the whole thing fell apart."

"It's not just this one time. In fact, I don't know what this time was all about. I can't connect—ever. Not with anyone."

He rose and went to the window, strangely unable to face her directly.

"Look," he finally said, "I've never talked like this to anyone, and it's frankly unsettling me. Maybe I can talk because I'm impressed suddenly with a rather hideous, unpalatable thought. Miss Ramsey, I have absolutely nothing in this world to lose. Nothing at all. A man should have something to lose." He paused, then, "On the other hand, you have everything to lose, and you're a bit too young to have only a past." He turned, his hands braced behind him on the sill. "I don't know what I'm going to do in the future. All I know is that I've lived one life rooted into the ground and the other in a daydream. *I* connected in the daydream, and I still connect there; and for that reason I don't want to give it up. Because the alternative seems to be very puzzling; it doesn't seem to have for me what it has for other people.

"But I believe—I hope I believe—in one thing: If I can connect without the daydream, there's not much I won't do to have it happen, if I can see it, recognize it. Sounds bizarre, I suppose, coming from an old man. What do I have in mind? A nice old lady, a young girl, simply a friendship? Perhaps all I can ever hope for is a good loyal dog."

"A dog?"

"Why not? Maybe a good dog is hard to find."

"I have a daydream too."

"What you do with it is your business. I find I want to give you advice, but I'm going to resist, because it can only come from the cheapest kind of retrospective logic. People who have lived never need to give advice; they've been too busy living to have figured life out, or wanted to figure it out. To them it seems natural. If I advised anyone about their daydreams I'd just add a touch of shame to something I'm already disgusted about." He pointed to the body. "My friend. All of them, my friends, colleagues, countrymen, even the subjects of my art. And I'm afraid of these dead things as much as you are. Except that your fear has the decency to be straight fear. I'm an expert in only one thing—this place.

Stick with it; you're a lousy anatomist but I think you can make it. I humbly bow to Landau."

He came to her, looked at her eyes, and said, "Dry. Good. Now an old man, on the ragged side of sixty, suddenly has the great desire to buy lunch for an attractive young woman—in an Italian restaurant on Broadway. May I?"

She looked at him steadily.

"And for another reason. In case you decide to stay, I don't want you to feel that you have to become a thing again. I hope you can be direct with me—anger aside."

He removed his lab coat, began to hang it behind the door, then turned and draped it over the shoulders of a skeleton which hung from the ceiling. Washing his hands, he saw her smiling and said, "Miss Ramsey, I'm going to tell you the story of my life. I hope it doesn't propel you into a psychiatric residency."

On the street, a quiet breeze from the Hudson River at their backs, he looked up at the sky, the racing clouds filigreed with yellow and turquoise. He remembered the images he had seen in them as a child: fluffy balls of ice cream, creatures from fairy tales. Now they seemed full with arabesques of Arnold, Esther, Walter, even Vasiliev—who for all he knew might have tried, in the locked vaults of his sorcery, to arrest their motion, quench the light of the sun. The sun into which Ellen Hale had walked. And he also saw, beyond the clouds, the clear blue infiniteness of his fear, and then just the blue.

He took her arm, clutching softly at their contact, and said, "The story of my life. On February 3, 1906, upside-down, my feet dangling by a rubber-gloved fist, I first saw the light of day. I did not know what to make of it."

She began to laugh. He quickly swept her across the street.

About the Author

Paul Olsen, who has just completed his Doctorate in Clinical Psychology at Columbia University, is the author of a number of short stories which appeared in such publications as the *Virginia Quarterly*, the *Texas Quarterly*, *The Southern Review*, *Cosmopolitan*, and in an anthology called *Beyond the Angry Black*. He is the author of two earlier novels, *The Virgin of San Gil* and *Country of Old Men*, both published by Holt, Rinehart and Winston and has traveled extensively in Europe. He is now at work on a fourth novel set in Spain.